PRAISE FOR TH

Here are some of the over 100,000 five star reviews left for the Dead Cold Mystery series.

"Rex Stout and Michael Connelly have spawned a protege."

AMAZON REVIEW

"So begins one damned fine read."

AMAZON REVIEW

"Mystery that's more brain than brawn."

AMAZON REVIEW

"I read so many of this genre...and ever so often I strike gold!"

AMAZON REVIEW

"This book is filled with action, intrigue, espionage, and everything else lovers of a good thriller want."

AMAZON REVIEW

IN HOT BLOOD

A DEAD COLD MYSTERY

BLAKE BANNER

RIGHTHOUSE

Copyright © 2024 by Right House

All rights reserved.

The characters and events portrayed in this ebook are fictitious. Any similarity to real persons, living or dead, is coincidental and not intended by the author.

No part of this book may be reproduced in any form or by any electronic or mechanical means, including information storage and retrieval systems, without written permission from the author, except for the use of brief quotations in a book review.

ISBN-13: 978-1-63696-025-8

ISBN-10: 1-63696-025-1

Cover design by: Damonza

Printed in the United States of America

www.righthouse.com

www.instagram.com/righthousebooks

www.facebook.com/righthousebooks

twitter.com/righthousebooks

DEAD COLD MYSTERY SERIES
An Ace and a Pair (Book 1)
Two Bare Arms (Book 2)
Garden of the Damned (Book 3)
Let Us Prey (Book 4)
The Sins of the Father (Book 5)
Strange and Sinister Path (Book 6)
The Heart to Kill (Book 7)
Unnatural Murder (Book 8)
Fire from Heaven (Book 9)
To Kill Upon A Kiss (Book 10)
Murder Most Scottish (Book 11)
The Butcher of Whitechapel (Book 12)
Little Dead Riding Hood (Book 13)
Trick or Treat (Book 14)
Blood Into Wine (Book 15)
Jack In The Box (Book 16)
The Fall Moon (Book 17)
Blood In Babylon (Book 18)
Death In Dexter (Book 19)
Mustang Sally (Book 20)
A Christmas Killing (Book 21)
Mommy's Little Killer (Book 22)
Bleed Out (Book 23)

Dead and Buried (Book 24)
In Hot Blood (Book 25)
Fallen Angels (Book 26)
Knife Edge (Book 27)
Along Came A Spider (Book 28)
Cold Blood (Book 29)
Curtain Call (Book 30)

ONE

IT HAD BEEN RAINING FOR TWENTY-FOUR HOURS SOLID. It wasn't cold, though. It was muggy. Sometimes the rain eased to a drizzle, but pretty soon it picked up again, swelled to a downpour, and then became torrential, drumming on roofs and cars and lashing wildly against windows. Sometimes it's nice to lie in bed and listen to the rain, especially if you're in good company; but not so much when it sounds like the world is coming to an end outside.

Dehan was asleep. She had that knack of being able to sleep wherever and whenever she wanted to, but lately she had been arriving home exhausted from her volunteer work, and she sparked out as soon as her head hit the pillow. All I could do was look at the reflected ripples and raindrops in the smoky, orange light on the ceiling and occasionally check the time.

Three o'clock in the morning. F. Scott Fitzgerald's words went through my mind: *In the real dark night of the soul, it's always three in the morning.*

I rose and went to look out the window. The road was flooded: a river turned copper by the streetlamps. The trees, jagged stencils against the water, bowed ponderously in the wind.

Twenty years earlier I would have smoked a cigarette at a time like this. I would have pulled a beer from the fridge, cracked it, and sat with the window open and my feet on the sill, smoking, drinking, and thinking.

Dehan stirred, and I turned to look at her. Long, brown limbs tangled in the white sheet, an ocean of black hair. My wife. For an instant I almost spoke, almost went to her to wake her, but the words died on my lips, and I turned back to the window.

When I grew tired of watching the spray, and the luminous interference patterns of the drops falling on the liquid copper river, I returned to the bed and lay staring at the ceiling again.

Four in the morning. Dehan was still asleep.

At five thirty I got up and went into the bathroom to shower. The bright light and the alternating hot and cold water cleared my head some. I stepped out of the shower, toweled myself dry, and went back to the dark bedroom with the orange streetlight reflected on the ceiling. Dehan was sitting up, on the edge of the bed, with her head in her hands. She looked up at me and smiled, sleepy.

"You're up early."

"I couldn't sleep."

She stood, put a hand on my shoulder, and kissed me on the cheek.

"How come?"

She didn't wait for an answer. She went into the bathroom and started brushing her teeth. I dressed and went down to make coffee.

She joined me about fifteen minutes later. Her expression was serious. She stood staring at me a moment. I had my ass against the sink, I was sipping coffee, and I had a piece of toast in my hand.

She said, "Are you having breakfast standing up?"

I shrugged. "We seem to have got into that habit."

A small contraction of her brows. "That's only while I'm working on the project, Stone."

I didn't answer, and she moved into the kitchen and started making pancakes. After a moment she stopped and turned to face me.

"It's six in the morning, Stone. We have time to sit down and have breakfast together."

I nodded, said, "Sure," and took the butter to the table. She watched me.

"You didn't tell me why you couldn't sleep."

"You were brushing your teeth and you wouldn't have heard me."

"Okay, what's going on?"

I didn't look at her when I answered.

"I wish I knew."

"What's that supposed to mean?"

"It means I don't know what's going on, but I wish I did."

"That's not helpful."

"Nope." Now I looked at her. "But it's the best I can do."

"You want to talk about it?"

My answer came out more bitter than I had intended. "Are you sure you have the time?"

She spread her hands in a gesture of helplessness and I went to get the maple syrup and a couple of plates. She was shaking her head.

"I don't believe it. You're mad because I'm involved in the project?"

"I'm not mad."

"You're sure acting like you're mad."

"I'm not mad," I repeated more deliberately, and then my mouth started talking on its own. "I just miss you. I miss having a wife. Instead of a wife I have a partner at work."

She sighed and sagged. "The kids really need this, Stone. It's a really important project..."

I nodded. "Sure. I guess it must be. It occupies all your free time, and lately that includes your days off. I see you at work and while you're asleep. When was the last time we had dinner

IN HOT BLOOD | 3

together, at this table?" She didn't say anything, so I answered my own question. "Four weeks ago yesterday, a takeout pizza." I arched both my eyebrows. "I have a number of things I could ask that question about. When was the last time we—fill in the blank."

"I know, I know. There has been so much to do. It's hard to get volunteers, and Tony can't do it all by himself."

I was aware of a cold fire in my belly. I fought to control it.

"How long," I said quietly and deliberately, "is this going to continue?"

"Stone . . . !"

"I am not asking you to stop. If it means this much to you, then obviously you have to continue. I just want to know when, if ever, I am going to get my wife back."

"Of course you are! It's just . . ." She spread her hands again. "Another few weeks."

"Yeah, that's what you said three months ago. In fact, what you said was that you were volunteering for a month. Then it was a couple of weeks more, and then we just stopped communicating. I saw you at work, you stopped coming home for dinner because you were eating pizza with 'Sergeant Tony Sanchez and the guys' at the youth center, and when you got home you were too tired for anything except sleep."

"Stone, be fair . . ."

"Does he know you're married?"

"Of course he does."

"Is he?"

"Stone, stop it!"

"Is he married?"

"Yes!"

"Where do you eat all these pizzas?"

Her cheeks colored with anger. "At the club!"

"Yeah? Maybe I should surprise you with a visit one of these nights."

Her voice started to rise. "I would be very pleased if you did!"

"Really? Well, you know what, Dehan. I'd be pleased if you came home at night occasionally. You are a grown-up woman, and you are free to do exactly as you please in life, with me or with Tony. But you need to get your head out of that club just long enough to remember that you have a husband, you are married, and this..." I made a back-and-forth motion between us with my finger. "This is not how marriages work."

She frowned hard at me. "What the hell are you saying, Stone?"

I took a deep breath. "If you are developing feelings for Tony..." I paused because the name was like poison on my tongue. "Then you need to address that before things go any further."

Her jaw sagged. "You think..." She shook her head. "You can't possibly think..."

"Why? Why not?"

"But..."

"He's a good-looking guy, he has a likeable, engaging personality. He's a good, noble person, and he is passionate about his project and about helping the kids, just like you. Hell! He's your age! You probably have a lot more in common with him than you have with me. You certainly prefer spending your free time with him rather than with me."

She was shaking her head. "Stone, no..."

"Really?" I went to the dresser and opened a drawer. From it I took out a long, glossy envelope with a picture of a tropical beach on it. I carried it to the kitchen. "That cabin on the beach, on Espiritu Santo, in Vanuatu, is where we should have spent last night. The first of seven nights. It was your birthday present to me last November. Do you remember that? While we were supposed to be traveling, we were working. While we were supposed to be checking in, you were at the club, with Tony. And while we were supposed to be having oysters and champagne, you were eating pizza... with Tony. So now tell me, Dehan, that you don't prefer to spend your free time with Tony rather than with me."

She had gone pale, and there were tears in her eyes. "Stone, why didn't you remind me?"

"I can't lie to you, Dehan. I didn't remind you because I was so sick and tired of the damned project, and especially Tony, that I wanted to see if you would remember. You didn't."

"Stone, I am so sorry."

"I don't want you to be sorry, Dehan. I want you to be clear. If our relationship has run its course, then acknowledge it and tell me. We are both grown-ups, we both know how these situations play out. How long before the two of you are left alone having pizza one night . . . ?"

"No, Stone! I swear! Sure, I admire Tony for what he does, but I *do not* have those feelings for him! This is *not* about him! This is about the kids, Stone. You *have* to understand that!"

"I don't have to understand anything that you don't communicate to me, Dehan. And lately the only thing you communicate to me is that you have zero interest in spending time with me."

She drew breath to answer, but the doorbell rang. I glanced at my watch. Six thirty. I looked at Dehan and was aware of a growing anger in my belly.

"Is this Tony? Had you arranged for him to pick you up and forgot to tell me?"

She was still frowning and shook her head. "*No!*"

I went and pulled open the door. It was Mo. I scowled at him. "Mo? What the hell are you doing here? Do you know what time it is?"

"Yeah, Stone, I know what time it is. Is Carmen here?"

The anger I had been repressing suddenly flared up. The heat in my belly surged to my head. "Of course she's here! Where the hell do you think she'd be at six thirty in the morning?"

Dehan appeared at my side. "Good morning, Mo. What's going on?"

He eyed her a moment, then looked at me resentfully. "Take it easy, Stone. You gonna invite me in or what?"

I sighed and stood aside. "Yeah, sure. Come on in. You want some coffee?"

Dehan added, "I'm making pancakes. You want some breakfast?"

He hesitated, licked his lips, then said, "Just some coffee, white, three sugars."

She poured it for him, and he sat at the table, half-set for breakfast. He spoke to his cup.

"Look, sit down, will ya?"

We sat, and I scowled at him. "What the hell is it, Mo? Has something happened? You need help?"

He closed his eyes and shook his head.

"No, I don't need help. I had the late shift tonight. Couple of hours ago I was called to a homicide on Eastchester Bay."

I frowned. "Why? That's not in the Forty-Third."

"It's complicated. The crime scene was in the Forty-Fifth, so the boys from the Forty-Fifth were there. Jim Blakemore was lead. Victim was a cop, from the Forty-Fifth." He looked straight at Dehan. "Sergeant Tony Sanchez."

I watched her. She went pale and put her hands to her mouth. "Tony?" There were tears in her eyes. "What happened? Why did they call you?"

"He'd been shot, practically point-blank."

"What about his wife? Is she okay?"

His voice was wooden, and his face was hard. "She found him."

Dehan frowned. "Found him? Where? When we left the club he said he was going straight home."

"That's where he was found, at home."

"She wasn't there with him? Where was she?"

"Out with friends. She has an alibi, Carmen. You said you were at a club? You guys were pretty close, right?"

Dehan's frown deepened. So did mine. She said, "We weren't close, Mo. We were working on the same project at the *youth* club."

"Sure, so what time did you guys leave the club?"

She glanced at me, and I could see the first stirrings of fear in her eyes. "I don't know exactly. Nine thirty? I got home at what, ten?"

"Ten fifteen."

Mo's eyes darted from Dehan to me and back again. "So did you go straight home from the club? Or did you go on somewhere else?"

I snarled, "Take it easy, Mo. What are you driving at?"

I felt Dehan's hand on my arm. "We talked for ten minutes or so about what needed to be done today, and then I came straight home."

"And he told you he was going home, to his wife?"

"Of course. He didn't say, 'Okay, Carmen, now I'm going home to my wife . . .' but that was what I understood."

"What *did* he say?"

"Uh . . ." She closed her eyes to think, then shrugged her shoulders. "'Okay, I'm dead beat, I'm for home.' To which I replied, 'Yeah, me too.' He got in his car and I got in mine. I came home."

"Was there anybody else at the club?"

"No, everybody had left by then."

He held her eye, and I saw her breathing quicken and her cheeks color. He said, "What time did the last person leave the club before you left?"

Her eyes swiveled and met mine. She was fighting the tears. "About nine o'clock, maybe a little before that."

"So you were alone with Tony for maybe forty-five minutes."

"Half an hour or forty-five minutes, yes."

"What did you do during that time, Carmen?"

"Tony was in the office, doing the accounts, and I was cleaning up the club."

I put my hand on Dehan's arm and leaned forward.

"Okay, that's enough, Mo. Dehan isn't answering another

goddamn question until you tell us what the hell is going on here."

He stared at me like he was trying to work out what was wrong with me.

"What's going on? What's going on, John, is that as a courtesy, the Forty-Fifth has requested that a detective from the Forty-Third come and have a talk with Detective Carmen Dehan, about a murder. But not just any murder, the murder of a cop. Because the last person to see that cop alive, at nine thirty last night, was Carmen. And it so happens that for maybe forty-five minutes, they were alone together. So I am real interested to know what happened during those forty-five minutes."

"Cut the crap, Mo! Does Dehan need a lawyer?"

"I don't know! Does she?" He turned to Dehan. "Do you?"

"*Of course not!*" She scowled at Mo and then at me, trying to read my face. I don't know what she read there. I had no idea what I was feeling except rage. Dehan was speaking again. "Mo, this is ridiculous! You know me!"

He shook his head. "Uh-uh, sister. Nobody knows nobody. And you can be thankful they didn't send a couple of patrol cars to take you in!"

"I did not kill Tony!"

"Really?"

She leaned forward, her expression close to panic. "Of course not, Mo! I came straight home! Stone will tell you!"

"Yeah, but Stone wasn't with you at the club. From what I hear, you haven't seen a lot of Stone for the last three months. But you *have* been seeing an awful lot of Sergeant Sanchez, every night."

"At the club, Mo! With people everywhere!"

"Not last night."

"Come on, Mo! I saw him at the club. He went home and I went home. I did not kill Tony!"

"Well, if that's true, if you didn't shoot him, explain to me why the hell your prints are all over his gun, the gun that killed him."

"*What?*"

He shook his head. "I really hate to do this, but Carmen Stone, I am placing you under arrest for the murder of Sergeant Anthony Sanchez..."

TWO

THE CHIEF, INSPECTOR JOHN NEWMAN, LOOKED queasy. He kept shaking his head and avoiding my eye from behind his desk.

"John," he kept saying, "you know how much I value you and Carmen. Not just as damned fine cops, but as friends. But I can't discuss this with you. You have a conflict of interests. You're compromised, John. You must see that. I have to hand her over to the Forty-Fifth."

"Sir, this is Dehan we are talking about. The idea that she would kill a fellow officer is not crazy, it's outlandish."

"I know! I know!" He raised his eyebrows high, hunched his shoulders, and gave his head quick little shakes. "But the law doesn't give a good goddamn about what we think, or what we know for that matter. The law is a process, John, you know that! And it is the same process for you, for me, and for Carmen. That's the rule of law."

"Sir, I am not asking you not to investigate her association with Sanchez—"

"The Forty-Fifth will investigate her association with Sanchez, John."

"Obviously they have to do that. And obviously I am not asking to be part of the investigation. Clearly that is out of the question. All I am asking is that you hold off on arresting her until you have more substantial evidence. Her fingerprints could have got on that gun any number of ways. She's interested in arms. She might have picked it up to look at it. Bottom line, sir, if you don't arrest her you don't have to hand her over to the Forty-Fifth."

He sighed and leaned his elbows on the table. "John, if I don't arrest her, the Forty-Fifth will. What would you do if she was not your wife and your partner? If you didn't know her? She was the last person to see him alive, they were alone for almost an hour, she had been spending increasing amounts of time with him for the last three months . . . And now he shows up dead, shot with his own revolver, at point-blank range, and her prints are all over the gun."

I sagged back in my chair. "There is one very obvious point, sir."

"Tell me."

"You have often said yourself that Dehan is an excellent cop. She is smart, and she is cool-headed."

"That's true, John. I have said it, and I maintain it."

"If she had shot Sergeant Sanchez, her prints would not be on the gun."

He smiled. It was a very sad expression. It said my argument smacked of desperation.

"People can act in very bizarre ways when they are . . . confused, or panicking. The arrest is proper and correct, John. We have made it clear to the DA that we do not oppose bail and that we do not believe she is a flight risk. What Detective Blakemore will have to say about that, we will have to wait and see. The most you can hope for is a modest bail. I am very sorry."

I nodded. I knew he was right, and there was damn all I could do about it.

"Can I at least have a copy of the case file?"

"That would be very irregular, John."

"Goddamn it, sir! This is my wife! One of the best detectives at the precinct! We owe her that much! Mo has made up his mind that Dehan is guilty, when you and I both know she isn't!"

He sat in silence for a good fifteen seconds before he leaned forward and flipped a switch on his desk.

"Bring me a copy of the Sergeant Anthony Sanchez case file." Then he sat back and laced his fingers over his belly.

"Sanchez was found shot to death in his bed, by his wife, at twelve thirty last night. She's a Realtor and an entrepreneur, Astrid Meyer, and she had been out with colleagues celebrating a big deal they had pulled off. Exactly what happened is not very clear right now, but the doors onto the backyard were open, and it seems the killer fled that way."

"Sir, Dehan left him at the club . . ."

"That's her story, John, but so far it is uncorroborated. She says they were alone, at the club, for about forty-five minutes or an hour before she went home. That's enough time for her to get from the club to Sanchez's house, kill him, and get back to Morris Park by ten fifteen. It is feasible, Stone, that when the last member of the club had left, Carmen and Sergeant Sanchez went back to his house."

"That's insane!" A wave of nausea washed over me. "Dehan would not do that!"

He gazed at me with very sad eyes. "Nobody would do it, John. And yet, it happens all the time. We humans have very little control over what we do. You know that. When passion strikes . . ."

"She has too much integrity . . ." I said it, and in my head I was hearing our argument that morning. "And, even if she had fallen for him, why would she kill him?"

"We don't know that she did, John. But we have to investigate the possibility, and we need to know exactly what time they left the club. We have men on that even as we speak."

There was a tap on the door, and a uniform leaned in and

handed the inspector a slim manila file, then left again. The inspector dropped the file in front of me.

"You may have mistakenly got the impression that I had given you permission to take this file. If you did, I didn't notice you take it. Obviously it is impossible for you to investigate this case, as you cannot be objective about it, neither will you be able to work on another case while Carmen is being investigated. So, I advise you to take a couple of weeks' paid leave until this is all over."

"Thank you, sir."

I went to stand. "John?"

"Yes, sir?"

"Under no circumstances are you to undertake a private investigation of this case."

"I won't, sir."

The phone rang. He grabbed it, and I stood.

"Yes, Inspector Newman here . . ." He raised a hand, telling me to wait. "Yes, ma'am, Carmen Stone." He listened for a while. "They both have a superb record, ma'am, outstanding. Ethnicity?" He frowned. "Part Mexican and part Jewish, is that relevant, ma'am?" He nodded and rolled his eyes. "Yes, of course, I see that. The victim was a white male, ma'am . . . indeed . . . a police officer . . . Thank you, ma'am, I will tell her husband. Good day to you too."

He put down the phone. "The DA. John, bail is set at twenty-five thousand dollars. Can you post that now?"

I nodded. "Thank you, sir."

"You know that normally in a case like this you would have to wait for the hearing, and bail would be much higher."

"I know that, sir."

"The DA knows Carmen, or at least thinks she does, and is willing to . . ." He drew breath, searching for words that would not imply something untoward. I said, "I understand, sir. I'll go and get her."

"Yes, go and get her, John. And, John?"

I paused with my hand on the door. "Yes, sir?"

"You'd better find out what the hell happened. Fix this."

I nodded and left.

Downstairs I sorted out her bail. Then I went to our desks in the detectives' room and collected our personal effects. Mo's desk was just across from ours, but he wouldn't look at me. I didn't say anything to him either. I collected our stuff and went to wait outside on the steps, watching the incessant rain and listening to it patter.

Fifteen minutes later she came out and stood staring at me a moment. Then she hunched her shoulders, walked down the steps, and crossed the road to where my ancient, burgundy Jag was parked. I followed her, unlocked the car, and we climbed in and slammed the doors. She sat a moment wiping the rain from her face with a paper towel.

We drove in silence, heading slowly back toward home. For a while the only sound was the incessant squeak and thud of the wipers. When we had turned off Story and onto White Plains I said, "I think you need to explain a few things to me."

"Like what?"

"Well, we could start with, what the hell is going on?"

"I don't know."

"Followed by, what the *hell* has been going on for the last three months?"

She sighed and closed her eyes. When she spoke, she articulated very precisely and very carefully.

"Nothing has been going on. I saw the flier on the board at the station asking for volunteers for a youth club to help kids get on the straight and narrow. I called and got involved. I got too involved. But I got too involved with the *kids*, not with Tony! Tony was a nice guy, but I had absolutely no feelings for him, Stone. What I cared about, and what I was involved with, was the jeet kune do classes I was teaching the kids. Nothing more. I don't know how you can think . . ."

I cut her dead. "Don't. We can't do that. You're a prime suspect in a homicide investigation, and your prints are all over the murder weapon. We need to stay cool and focused, and I need to know the truth."

"I'm telling you the truth, Stone!"

"All of it!"

"Yes, all of it!"

"I need to hear you say it. I need you to look me in the eye and I need to hear you say it."

She stared at me. The windshield wipers squeaked on the glass, steady and rhythmic. Outside the downpour hissed. I stopped at a red light and turned to face her.

"Did you at any time have an affair with Tony Sanchez—and by that I include a secret cuddle and a kiss!"

She shouted the answer at me, balling her fists: "*No!*"

"Was the relationship between you, on either side, his or yours, ever anything more than professional?"

"No, never!"

"Did you go to his house yesterday, or last night?"

"No, absolutely not."

A honk behind me told me the lights had changed. I put the old Mark II in gear and moved off. She was watching me, waiting for the next question.

"Did you kill him?"

"No, Stone. I did not kill Tony Sanchez."

"How did your prints get on his gun?"

This time she took longer to reply. I glanced at her. She was staring out at the rain. Finally she said, "I don't know."

"That's not good enough. We can't have secrets, Dehan. If you're done with me and you want to move on . . ."

She turned and almost screamed at me. "*I am not done with you and I do not want to move on! Stop saying that!*"

I let her finish, then went on. "Even if you were, you can start keeping secrets after, but you are looking at spending the rest of your life in prison, Dehan. You cannot afford to keep secrets from me. Not now."

Her voice was quiet. "Not now, not ever."

"Then why the long, thoughtful pause when I asked about the prints?"

"Because I am trying to work out how they got there."

Neither of us talked again until we turned onto Morris Park Avenue. The clouds were so dense overhead that the streetlamps were on and the cars had their headlamps on even though it was midmorning. The traffic was slow moving, and the water looked an inch deep on the blacktop. Dehan finally asked me, "Do you believe me?"

"Of course I do. I just needed to hear you say it." I hesitated. "It's the first thing I've heard you say in three months that wasn't either work related or, 'I'm beat, I'm going to bed.'"

She sighed. "You made your point, Stone. I'm sorry."

I gave my head a brief shake. "I don't want your apology. I want you to understand that bad things happen to relationships when the communication breaks down."

She didn't answer for a while, then put her hand on my arm and said, "Yes."

"So, somebody is trying to frame you."

She made a face like brain-ache. "But, who? I'm sitting here going through all the people at the club one by one, trying to work out how the hell they got my prints onto that gun, and why in the name of all that is holy they would want to frame me!"

I grunted. "Wrong question, Little Grasshopper."

"Yeah? So what is the right question?"

"Who wanted Tony dead—aside from me, of course."

She flashed a look at me. "Stone! Don't even joke about that!"

"Who says I'm joking?" I said sourly. "In any case, setting me aside, focus on the question. Who wanted Tony dead?"

"Okay." She nodded. "That makes sense. Framing me could be opportunism. So who would want him dead?"

I turned into Haight Avenue and pulled up outside our house. The lights were still on from that morning, when Dehan had been led away. The limpid glow from the living-room window made wet highlights on the sidewalk. I turned to face Dehan.

"It's three months, Dehan, and whatever you say, you got to know him pretty well in that time. You must have heard him make phone calls, you must have seen him talk to people, he must have made a hundred comments—a thousand!—that at the time meant nothing to you, and you disregarded them. Now you have to make your mind go back over those three months again, every minute of them, with a fine-tooth comb. You have to sift through every word that he said. What other relationships did he have? How did he get on with his wife?"

The rain drummed on the roof of the car. The windshield filled with droplets, and the lonely, quiet street vanished into an abstract of fractured light. Somewhere outside the dark cocoon of the cab I could hear the slap and patter of water overflowing from a gutter. Dehan's voice came quiet in the shadows.

"Stone, I'll try, but whether you believe me or not, we never talked about personal stuff. We talked about the club." She reached out and took hold of my hand. "If I was unfaithful to you, it was with the kids who wanted a better shot at life, the ones who wanted to escape from the gangs, learn to fight the good fight."

I nodded, understanding perhaps better than she did right then what she was telling me.

"Okay, let's go inside and get out of this rain. We have a lot of work to do, Dehan. We are fighting for our lives, and failure just isn't an option."

We sat a moment longer in the gloom, looking at each other. Then, very quietly, she said, "Okay."

We got out of the car, locked it, and ran, hunched into our shoulders, across the sidewalk and up the stairs to the front door. I turned the key in the latch, she pushed, and I went in behind her and slammed the door closed behind us. Then we were standing, dripping wet, just a few inches away from each other. Her hair clung in wet strands to her cheeks and brow. Her eyes, huge and dark, searched my face. Her hands went up to my face, and her fingers stroked my cheeks.

"Stone," she whispered the word, "there has never been anyone but you. There never will be. I am so sorry I made you go through this."

I drew breath to answer, but what happened next made all words unnecessary.

THREE

We showered, and while she made an early lunch, I made a fire. We didn't need a fire; it wasn't cold. It was muggy. But there was an unspoken agreement that we needed the comfort of the fire.

Neither of us was very hungry, so she made mini DIY pizzas with bread rolls, tomato, cheese, herbs, and salami and we cracked a couple of beers. After that we sat at the table, where it was still half-set for breakfast, and ate in silence. When Dehan had put the last piece of toast, cheese, and tomato in her mouth, and was licking her fingers, she said:

"Astrid Sanchez, though professionally she goes by her maiden name, Astrid Meyer. She inherited a realty business from her father, whose great-grandfather emigrated from Germany as a child with his parents. They all worked real hard and became prosperous Realtors, family business. Mom died when Astrid was a kid, Dad kept things together, strong, authoritarian, German patriarch type. He wasn't thrilled that his daughter was going to marry a Latino, but at least he was a cop. Then he—Dad—died of cancer so the issue became academic."

I waited till she'd finished, then asked, "He told you all this? I thought you only discussed the club."

She grinned. "I never realized you were so jealous, Stone. This is a new side to your character."

"You never gave me reason to be before. I'm at home eating alone out of a can, and going over cold-case files, while this guy is telling you his life story."

"No, that's not what happened, and he didn't tell me all that. You asked me to piece things together. That's what I did. Remember, I wasn't the only volunteer there. There were also a couple of guys from the Forty-Fifth. I guess they were pals because they talked about everything, and I couldn't help overhearing. Sometimes I think they forgot I was there. Anyway, that's what I pieced together."

"She ever visit the club?"

She nodded. "Yeah. She told me once she liked to think of her family as philanthropists. I know she often discussed the tax breaks of putting money into the club with Tony. She came to visit several times."

"You didn't like her."

She spread her hands and raised her shoulders. It was an oddly Italian gesture. "Like?" she said. "She wasn't important enough to *dis*like, Stone. I wasn't interested. I didn't care. I had a dojo, I had a gym, I had thirty kids from age five to age fifteen, and they all wanted to learn Bruce Lee's secrets of self-control, and how to overcome limitations. Ask me their names. I know every single one of them. Ask me about their home lives, about their parents, about their brothers and what gangs they're in. I know every detail. But Astrid Meyer? She wasn't why I was there, Stone. And neither, for that matter, was Tony."

I smiled. "Okay, I believe you, Dehan, you don't have to keep proving it to me."

"Good." She paused a moment. "And I'm sorry you had to eat alone going over cold-case files. I should have been aware of that."

I smiled. "Yesterday's rain," I said, and in response the wind lashed the kitchen window, and the trees in the backyard nodded and bowed.

She stared a moment, out at the darkening afternoon, then down at her empty plate.

"Anyhow, Tony was this kind of angel, devoting all his time to good works, helping the kids, preserving the environment of the bay, you name it, he was involved. And his wife, who made stacks of money, was always there supporting him financially—or at least talking about it—and, I guess, to some extent, taking the credit. They have—had—a big house on the bay, Bayshore Drive. Her father bought two houses and knocked them into one, right next to the Huntington Woods."

"You ever been?"

"No, Stone, I have never been."

"So what about other women, Dehan? Were there any girls or women who were interested in this angel, whom he seemed close to, or who wanted to get close to him?"

She sighed and sagged.

"It is so hard to answer that, Stone. I have this huge motivation to say yes, because if there was, maybe I escape spending the next thirty years in prison. But am I being honest and objective? I don't know!"

"So, that's what we have cops for, and lawyers and courts, to test the evidence. If there is a possibility that one or more women were interested in him, or if there is a chance he was having an affair, we need to look into it, even if only to discard it, however uncomfortable that may be for you."

"It's not uncomfortable." She lifted her hands, palm up, then dropped them on the table again. "It wasn't just boys who went to the club. Girls went too. Tony was fun, likeable, and I guess he was good-looking, so a lot of girls used to hang around him. And he was a good guy, so I guess they felt safe with him. You know? For a girl growing up in the rough parts of the Bronx, feeling safe with a guy can be a big deal."

I waited, and after a moment I asked, "So?"

"So, does that mean he was having an affair with one of them? I don't think so, but maybe he was."

"The opportunities were there?"

She nodded. "Yeah, the opportunities were there."

"That's important."

"I know."

"You can't protect this guy, Dehan."

"I'm not protecting him." I didn't answer, and after a moment she had to fill the silence. "He was a good guy, Stone. Okay? I didn't feel anything romantic or sexual for him, but I liked him. He was a rare, honorable human being in a cruel, selfish world. And if he is dead, then his memory should not be sullied, because his memory can continue to help those kids."

"Okay, I understand, but we need to get past that point."

"What do you mean?"

"I mean you are fighting for your life. The clock is ticking, and you are already running out of time. You cannot afford to worry about protecting Tony's memory. Because the price for protecting his memory could be thirty years in jail. Get past it, and start thinking about what women—we need their names and addresses—what women he might have been sleeping with."

"Jesus, Stone!"

"Three months was quite enough. I don't want to lose you for another thirty years. Let's get real, Dehan!"

"Look, Stone, he was just an idealistic guy who wanted to do something for the kids in the Bronx. He worked hard, and in the evenings he would go home, sometimes with his wife, sometimes alone."

"How do you know he went home?"

She shrugged. "I don't, but people talk. Especially if an upright person who is trying to set an example starts to stray. People talk. But nobody ever talked or gossiped about him. And like I said, he always left alone if he didn't leave with his wife."

I nodded. "Okay, Dehan, we're going to get an attorney and we're going to get you off these charges. We'll get them dropped or we'll get the case thrown out."

"How?"

"Because we'll discover the truth." I gave it a moment, then said, "This is the last time I am going to raise this subject. But I have to say this, for both our sakes. You don't have to tell me everything—at least, not yet—but when you meet with your attorney..."

"*My* attorney? Not *our* attorney?"

I nodded. "That's my point. You don't have to tell me everything, but you will have to tell *him* everything, in detail, warts and all. Do you understand? Because if you lie to protect me or my feelings, or somebody else you care about, whatever lies you tell will come back to haunt you down the line."

She looked weary, and there were deep shadows under her eyes. She stared at the tabletop for a long time, then raised her eyes to meet mine.

"Enough, Stone. Enough already. I am telling you everything, and I am going to tell *our* attorney everything, A, because you are my husband and I love you and I have no secrets from you! And B, because I am smart and I know how this works. Enough already! I think I have earned your trust by now!"

My cell rang. I picked it up and answered, "Stone..."

There was a brief silence. Then Joe, from the lab, said, "John, I am not calling you. This call never happened. I'm in a phone booth, and I have to make this quick."

"What is it, Joe?"

"I've been putting in my own time on the Sergeant Sanchez case. The whole house was dusted for prints, and I have analyzed the results personally."

My heart was pounding and my belly was hot. I controlled my voice and said, "What did you find?"

"Carmen was there, John."

"That's got to be a mistake."

"How many times do you think I checked it? Her prints are on the banisters to the upper floor, on the doorjamb and the frame, they are on the windowsill and on the foot of the bed and the bedhead. There is no mistake, John. Carmen's prints are all over that room. The room where he was killed."

I was quiet for a long moment, then said, "Okay, thanks, Joe."

I hung up and sat staring at the phone. Dehan was watching me and finally said, "You'd better tell me what that was about, Stone."

"Your prints."

"What about them?"

"They are at Sergeant Sanchez's house."

"*What?*"

"They are on the banisters going up to the bedrooms. They are on the doorframe and the doorjamb, and they are all over the bed, the foot of the bed and the head."

She stood suddenly and shouted across the table at me.

"*For Christ's sake, Stone!*"

She strode across the room toward the bay window, one hand on her hip, the other running fingers through her hair. She turned toward me and shouted again, her face beginning to collapse into tears.

"*I did not kill Tony! I was never at Tony's house! I did not have an affair with Tony! I wouldn't!*"

I stood and went to her, and put my arms around her and kissed the top of her head.

"I trust you because I know you are good and loyal and faithful. But above all, Dehan, you're the best cop I have ever known."

She raised her damp face to look up into mine.

"Thanks," she said with a damp voice, "but what's that got to do with anything?"

I pointed to her leather jacket hanging on the back of her chair.

"Go reach in your right pocket. Pull out what's inside." She did as I said and stood a moment staring at the blue latex gloves in her hand. I went on. "As soon as he said your prints were on the banister, I knew. Then when he said the doorframe and the jamb, and the bed

". . . I knew it couldn't be you. You would never make such a stupid, elementary mistake, especially knowing that you always carry gloves and evidence bags. If you'd done it, they'd never have caught you."

I sighed and rested my ass against the back of the sofa.

"But, Dehan, unless you were there on some earlier occasion and you don't remember . . ."

"Don't be ridiculous."

"Then we are up against a very skilled operator who understands forensics and is very determined to put you in the frame."

She stared at me for a long moment, and her face was very pale.

"Who the hell would want to do this to me?"

"Not you." I shook my head. "*Him*. Get this clear in your head. You are a convenient scapegoat. *He* is the intended victim. You need to think, kiddo. If the killer was aware enough of you to select you as a scapegoat, you are aware enough of him to know who he is."

She nodded slowly. " . . . Okay . . ."

"Now, I am going to phone Saul Cohen . . ."

Her face flushed. "We can't afford Saul Cohen, Stone! Besides, the guy is a rat! He's on the payroll of every Mafia in New York!"

I nodded as I dialed. "And you know why? Because he's the best. I'll sell the Jag, I'll mortgage the house. I'll do whatever we need to do, Dehan. We have to beat this rap . . ."

A female voice that sounded like it had spent the morning being rubbed by a whetstone sliced in, "Cohen and Cohen Attorneys, how can I help you?"

"Yeah, I need to talk to Saul, Saul Cohen, tell him . . ."

"Have you an appointment?"

"I don't need one. Tell him it's Detective John Stone . . ."

"Detective Stone, perhaps I wasn't clear. Mr. Cohen is extremely busy. He is not able to simply drop what he is doing and . . ."

"Let me explain what is going to happen, sister," I growled into the phone. "First, when Saul finds out you failed to put me through he is going to be *very* upset with you. After that he is going to spend the next ten years apologizing to me for not having made you aware of me, and you are going to spend the next ten years doing everything and anything he tells you, trying to make up for the very *big* mistake you are about to make. Now, quit wasting my time and put me through to Saul!"

After five minutes, Saul Cohen's deep, smooth rumble oozed down the line.

"John, I am not quite sure what's going on. I was about to tell Maggie to tell you to go to hell, but the message was so totally not you, that curiosity got the better of me."

I put the cell on speaker and laid it on the table.

"My wife, Carmen Dehan . . ."

"I know of her, the cold cases you both run, damn fine cop. What about her? Don't tell me you're getting divorced! I don't do divorces, Stone."

"Shut up, Saul. She's being framed for the murder of a cop."

"Ho! Ho, ho, ho! Is it Christmas? Was I a good boy? *Man!* So what? You want me to represent her? Tell me you want me to represent her!"

"Yeah, that's what I want. Will you do it?"

"*Do it?* Are you crazy? Have you any idea how much this is going to hurt the NYPD? I am going to drag them kicking and screaming through the mire, and then I am going to feed them their own . . ."

"Saul! How much is this going to cost?"

"Seriously?"

"Quit being a pain in the ass, Saul. How much?"

"I want the exclusive rights to write and publish the book."

"We'll talk."

"You're not wrong. We'll talk. And if you give me a hard time you can run your own defense." He laughed. "The NYPD goes after one of its own! The blameless, virtuous cold-case couple, Stone and Dehan, turn to the loveably wicked Saul Cohen, savior of evil Mafiosi from Maine to San Diego, darling of the Mafia, brother to the Devil himself, and he and Stone battle courageously together, brothers-in-arms, to save the virtuous Carmen. Man, I cannot *wait* to get my hands on this case. Where are you?"

"The Bronx . . ."

"Where did the crime take place?"

"Eastchester Bay."

"Eastchester Bay? I have heard mutterings. They're trying to keep a lid on it. So that was your wife, Carmen? I'm at my house on Oyster Bay right now. Hold on, I'm going to get back to you. I'll call you on this number in five minutes."

He hung up, and we sat staring at each other across the table. After a moment Dehan said, "Even if he gets me off, Stone, this will be the end of my career as a cop. The cop who used Saul Cohen to humiliate the NYPD and the Forty-Third."

"We're fighting for our lives."

"I'm not saying we're wrong. I'm saying it will cost us our careers."

I shrugged. "So we'll open a firm of private investigators. I'll be Nero Wolfe and you can be Archie Goodwin. We'll have to move to Manhattan and buy a brownstone."

"Stone, I am serious."

"So am I."

I was about to say something about crossing bridges when we came to them and the phone rang.

"Yeah, Stone."

"It's Saul. I'm booking a suite at the Bay View on Country Club Road. You know it? I'll set up an operations room there. We'll have breakfast tomorrow at nine. Bring *everything*. You're a good cop, so is she. You know what I need. Conference at nine sharp."

He had hung up again before I had a chance to thank him.

And I really wanted to thank him.

FOUR

THE BAY VIEW HOTEL WAS A QUARTER OF A MILE south of the Pelham Bay Youth Club, where Sergeant Sanchez had set up his project to give the more marginalized kids in the Bronx a safe haven and a healthy environment where they could not only learn sports, useful skills, and self-discipline, but also make contact with other kids from different backgrounds, and form relationships and friendships that might last into adulthood, and maybe forge a path out of crime and violence and gangs and into a new, worthwhile life.

A quarter of a mile in the other direction, to the north and east, was the Sanchez-Meyer house. We ignored both, badly as I wanted to go and take a look, and we plowed through the steady rain and arrived at the ancient hotel at ten minutes before nine.

It was a bizarre building, dating back to the turn of the nineteenth century, that blended Spanish, French Colonial, and Edwardian in a way that must have been grotesque when it was built but, with the passage of time, had acquired the legitimacy of age. It was the kind of building you stopped to look at, even if only to scratch your head and frown, and wonder why they had done it.

It was constructed around a central patio with a cherub fountain in the middle. A Romanesque mosaic decorated the floor, and twelve marble columns supported galleried landings on the second and third floors, where the rooms were.

In the short sprint from the car we got sufficiently wet to enter brushing off our sleeves and our hair. The guy on reception had strange blond hair, acne, a film of sweat, and a burgundy jacket. He watched us with a mixture of curiosity and alarm while he picked his fingernails and cringed.

Dehan leaned on the counter with her hands and said, "We're here to see Mr. Saul Cohen for breakfast..."

He dithered a moment, unsure what to do with this information, then asked, "Should I let him know you're here?"

Dehan nodded and grinned malevolently. "That sounds like a good idea, because otherwise he won't know."

He nodded and reached for the phone. I said, "Where's breakfast?"

"Eh?"

"We're meeting him for breakfast. Where is breakfast eaten?"

We followed his directions through the colonnade, through an arch, and into an old-fashioned dining room where the tables had white linen cloths and the napkins were also made of white linen. It was empty, and a single waiter in a white jacket greeted us with ill-concealed surprise. He showed us to a table under an ancient ceiling fan, and we ordered coffee and croissants.

Dehan leaned back in her seat, watched me a moment, and sighed.

"What am I going to tell him? What are we going to tell him? That I was the last person to see him alive, that my prints are on the weapon, all over the banisters and in the bedroom where he was found dead? And that, by the way, for the past three months I forgot I was married and spent every spare minute of the day at Tony's youth club?"

I nodded. "That is exactly what we are going to tell him."

"What can he do, Stone? It's a slam dunk..."

"Not him, Dehan, us. We have faced tougher cases than this

one, but we weren't the ones facing jail, so we could afford to stay cool and think things through. This is the same thing, but this time we, and in particular you, are in the hot seat. But if ever there was a time when we needed to keep a cool head and think..."

"This is it."

"We have two fundamental questions: one..."

"Who killed Tony?"

"And two..."

"How did my prints get on the gun and the woodwork in the house?"

"Exactly. Now, we know that you did not handle the gun, and we know that you were never at the house, so that leaves only one possibility."

"Yeah, I was thinking about this all night. And there were just two things that came to mind. They are far-fetched, Stone, but I am out of explanations."

"Okay, so what is it?"

The waiter arrived with the coffee in a silver pot, hot milk in a jug, two types of sugar, and a basket full of hot croissants. He wished us "bon appétit" and left.

"This must have been a month ago, first week of June, maybe. It must have been the Wednesday because I had the seven-year-olds, with Zipper..."

"Zipper?"

"Yeah, he's six and a half, he's got crazy hair and he's really fast." I laughed quietly, and she went on. "So this guy came in. Tony wasn't there. He was on duty that night. This guy gave me the creeps. He was flash, he had a sharp suit, long hair slicked back. One of those guys you just know he's nasty. But his teeth, Stone, black and broken and crooked. And he was always smiling, showing those damned teeth! And his breath was disgusting. He was black, must've been six three or four, very tall.

"Anyway, he comes in while I was doing the class, and I could see him talking to Jones, the janitor-cum-factotum guy who takes care of things there. And I could see Jones looking at me and telling this guy something. You know the kind of thing? Like, 'Yeah, she's a cop and she's real good at martial arts . . .' that kind of thing."

"So this tall guy was interested in you?"

"At first I thought it was just the typical thing of guys thinking with their dicks. Now I'm not so sure."

She ripped off a piece of croissant, dunked it in her coffee, and stuffed it in her mouth. She spoke around it.

"Sho, whem I finusht de clash . . ." She swallowed. "When I finished the class, this guy sashays up to me."

"The tall guy who'd been talking to Jones."

"Yeah. He says his name is Tombs. At the time I thought it was because of his teeth, which were like old gravestones. He really freaked me out, Stone. He was so tall and thin and he just looked slimy. Anyway, so he tells me he's recruiting for a job. The pay is superb and am I interested. To be honest, Stone, I thought it was BS. I thought he was trying to impress me." She shrugged. "But I thought I'd play him along and see what he had. So I asked him, what's the job? So he says, he can't tell me. His boss would have to tell me, and that kind of convinced me that it was a crock, and I told him I wasn't interested."

She paused and ripped another piece off a croissant. I asked, "How did he react to that?"

"He told me how much it paid."

"How much?"

"Ten grand for a day's work."

"So it was a hit."

"I don't know. Looks like it now, doesn't it?"

"That kind of fee? It was a hit."

"Yeah, but at the time I thought it was just some sad asshole trying to impress me. It's not the first time some jerk has used a line like that on me."

"What did you do?"

She grinned. "I asked him if it was a hit. He said again he couldn't tell me. He worked for some very powerful people, and I should discuss it with them." She shrugged, opened her hands like she was showing me a book. "I had two options. Consider it a lead and pursue it, or tell him to take a hike. Honestly, I thought it was a waste of time. So I slammed him against the wall, made him spread 'em, frisked him, opened and searched his attaché case, and kicked him out of the club. I figured it would be a useful lesson for the kids."

"How'd he take that?"

"He gave me that dangerous look and told me I'd be crawling back to him soon. Then he left, and I never saw him again."

I sighed and swirled my coffee around in the cup.

"It's not a lot."

"No, at most it says that this guy was looking for someone to make a hit. What's weird is that Jones had probably told him I was a cop. He doesn't know me from Adam. All he knows is that I'm a cop volunteering at a club designed to help kids get out of crime and gangs. So, how does that make me a good candidate as a hit man?"

I sucked my teeth and thought about the fact that that was, indeed, weird.

"Anything else?"

"Yeah . . ." She glanced over at the entrance to the dining room. "I could do that again. Where is this guy?"

She signaled the waiter and made a circular motion meaning, "I want to do all of this again." He nodded and went away.

"Then there was a game we played."

"A game? What kind of game? Who played it?"

"It was a Friday, I think. Not many kids had showed up. In fact the last class had not showed up. So we were hanging around and I suggested we should go home. I was tired and I hadn't seen much of my man for a while." She gave me a rueful smile which I acknowledged. "But someone, and I just can't remember who, suggested a game with balloons. Somebody had brought along a whole box full of those plastic bags full of balloons. So they started blowing them up . . ."

"You didn't participate?"

"Not at that stage, no. I started collecting the mat and the gloves and stuff. I really did intend to go home. Then they started playing that game—it's not really a game as such—I whack the balloon at you, you whack it back at me, the balloon is unpredictable, so you never really know where it's going to go. Somebody batted it at me, I hit it back, but I was telling them I was going home.

"I took the stuff into the locker, and when I came out Shanna was sword fighting with Tony, but they were using those big sausage balloons. It was funny and everybody was laughing." She paused, looking up at the ceiling, to her left. "I'm trying to remember the exact sequence of events. I was crossing the floor. It's a big space. They were over here"—she waved her left hand—"on my left, and here on my right there was a trestle table partially covered with balloons. There was a lot of other stuff, paint, brushes, glue, all the stuff you'd be using with small kids doing crafts, right?"

I nodded. "So what happened."

"They were all running around like kids, chasing each other, letting off steam. Then suddenly Shanna lunges at me with one of those big sausage balloons and shouts, 'On guard!' I was going to tell her some other time, but she was laughing and pointing at another one of those balloons that was lying on the table. So I thought, simple, I lay about her, make her run away, and leave, right?"

"Lay about her?"

"You should know that one, Stone. It's old-fashioned, literary English. Like you. It means attack."

"I know what it means, Dehan. Just carry on."

"So I grabbed the balloon with both hands, meaning to go for her, but it was covered in glue."

I raised my eyebrows and sat forward. "Glue?"

"White or transparent. The balloon was white so I couldn't see it. I swore. Shanna came running over. Someone popped the balloon, I forget who, but they were saying something about making a lampshade. I wasn't really paying attention. I was tired, I had glue on my hands, and I just wanted to go home."

"But it wasn't glue," I said, "it was silicone."

She smiled. "You think?"

"Dehan, you have to think real hard. Because whoever put that silicone on the balloon is our killer."

"I know." She sat and shook her head for a while. "But I just can't be sure."

"Who is Shanna? You said she was play fighting with Tony before she pointed out the balloon to you. Were they close?"

"She's a shrink. She was there to supervise and oversee, and write regular reports on the kids. She also helps out with creative stuff. She's a good artist."

"So what about her relationship with Tony?"

She started a shrug but held it for a few seconds while she thought. "I mean, yeah! Maybe. There was definitely chemistry between them. How serious it was I wouldn't like to say. They definitely liked each other, they talked a lot, and you got the vibe that they were on the same wavelength. They were both pretty childish sometimes, in their sense of humor, that kind of thing. But I never saw anything go down between them, they never left together, never saw them kiss . . . nada."

I grunted softly. "Okay, so who collected up the pieces of the burst balloon?"

"Yeah." She nodded. "That's the one, Stone. That's the million-dollar question. But I don't know because I was headed for the bathroom to wash off the glue."

"Who burst it, Dehan?"

She stared at every corner of the dining room before she answered. And then she drew breath and bit her lip, shaking her head.

"I don't want to say it, Stone, because I may be wrong."

"Who burst it, Dehan? Who was the guy, or the girl, who

would be making string lampshades out of balloons with the kids?"

"Oh man, it doesn't make any sense, Stone."

"Who?"

She opened her hands wide, then let them flop in her lap. "Jones, the janitor factotum."

"The same one who was talking to Tombs."

"Yeah, that one."

"We need to talk to him *real* bad."

"He wouldn't, Stone. He is a real nice guy. He just would not do that!"

"I know, Dehan, but people change when they have a gun to their head. If they have gambling debts, if they owe money to loan sharks, if you threaten their kids . . ."

She sighed a deep sigh and sagged a little lower.

"I guess."

A commotion made us turn, and Saul Cohen entered the room looking like a Spanish galleon in full sail. He had three waiters with him, and he was talking to them and all waiter-kind simultaneously. The universe was his waiter, and he had merely to say what he wanted, they would serve him.

"Bacon, good Danish bacon, don't count the rashers! Bring extra on another plate, I am sure I'll want more, eggs, four, sunny-side up, trim the whites, whole grain toast with creamery butter, two on the plate, under the eggs, and the others in a basket under paper—not a napkin, it does not serve the purpose! And mushrooms, garlic, onions. And aside from that I want blueberry jam, a pot of coffee, hot milk, and brown sugar. That will do!"

He advanced on us as the waiters fled for the kitchen, beaming and showing perfect teeth. "John, such a pleasure to see you again. It has been too long. And the ravishing Carmen. My darling, you should be a supermodel! Sit, sit, sit, and tell me all about your problem. Then we shall discuss my fee, or, alternatively, my remuneration!"

He laughed noisily and sat heavily in his chair. Dehan drew breath and started to talk.

FIVE

COHEN WAS A BIG, BOMBASTIC, WELL-DRESSED MAN anywhere between forty-five and sixty-five. He had black hair, huge hairless hands, and a big gold ring that said he was married and meant you to know it. He also had big, round eyes that shifted around your face and read you while you talked, with the same kind of concentration other people use to do algebra.

A steady stream of waiters had started to flow to and from the kitchen, bringing hot rolls, more coffee, more bacon, and more of everything that Cohen required. Meanwhile he had a look at Dehan, then sized me up and said:

"Let *me* talk. I want you to understand something. If it were not for the potential I see in this case to build my reputation, to stick it to the NYPD—*and* to make a killing on a book and a TV movie—I would not touch this case with sterilized latex gloves."

He sat back, broke open a roll, and started spreading thick wads of butter on it.

"I read the file on the way over. You don't stand a chance in hell. I hope you understand that." He glanced at Dehan and gave a sickly smile. "I don't know if you did it or not, Carmen, and to be perfectly frank, I don't care. All the clients I represent did what they were accused of doing, and much more besides. That's my niche market. It's why you called me, and it is why I am a very rich man."

He stuck the bread in his mouth and chewed with exaggerated pleasure.

"But I am not a magician; almost! But not quite. So unless you've got something really special up your sleeve, my advice to you, on the evidence as it stands, is plead guilty. I want you to understand that, right from the start, because I don't want you tearing me to pieces later in the press. I'm telling you straight, from the start, as it stands, even I cannot win this case. This case cannot be won."

He started scraping rashers of bacon onto his plate, followed by mushrooms and a couple of eggs. Then he spilled coffee into his cup, took a sip, and said, "Shoot."

Dehan answered, and the look on her face said she was going to take all three hundred pounds of him and kick him into the Eastchester Bay, but her voice was even and steady.

"First of all, Cohen, you'd better understand that if Stone had not pressured me, I would not have let you near this case if you were the last attorney on Earth and I was wrapped in sterilized plastic. And second, you had better get something into your twisted little brain, pal. Not everyone on this Earth is a corrupted, scheming criminal like you and your clients. I am *not* guilty. I did not kill Tony Sanchez, and I am *not* going to plead guilty, because I did *not* do it!"

He held up one of his big hairless hands.

"You have to go on the stand!" He looked at me. "She has to go on the stand. The jury will fall in love with her. I am going to let the insults pass because I know how stressful it can be to face a heavy sentence. But, John, Carmen, I have to be honest. To me your guilt or innocence is a matter of complete indifference. It might make you feel better if you think I believe in your innocence, but the fact is that kind of clouded, emotional attitude is just a hindrance to clear thinking. You need to believe in your innocence, John needs to believe in your innocence. I don't. I need to know how I am going to flip the court."

In a few rapid movements, like he was making up for wasted time, he stuffed his face so full of food I thought he was going to choke. Then he sat ruminating, looking from Dehan to me and back again. Eventually he swallowed and said:

"I need facts. What we deal with in court is *facts*. And right now it is a *fact* that you, Carmen, were at the scene of the murder, and it is a fact that you held the murder weapon. The jury will extrapolate from that that you killed Sergeant Sanchez. If we want a different outcome, then we need to change the facts. And by the way . . ." He winced at her like he felt queasy. "Unless you want to be sent away for the rest of your life, you'd better stop calling him 'Tony.'"

Dehan sagged back in her chair. I hid the expression on my face that said I liked what I was hearing. I could see why he was the best. At the very least he was a realist and not some naïve idealist. I nodded.

"We understand that. Now I want you to listen to me. You're going to get the prosecution's file, and between the three of us and your team, we are going to go over it with a fine-tooth comb looking for inconsistencies—because there have to be inconsistencies."

"There do? Why?"

"You're not listening, Saul. There have to be inconsistencies because Dehan was *not* at the scene, and she did *not* hold the gun. And she did *not* shoot Sergeant Sanchez."

"So, what? You want to plead that she was framed? That is a notoriously dangerous defense."

"But it happens to be true."

"Now who's not listening? I told you, truth has nothing to do with this."

"Listen to me, Saul. There are inconsistencies, and I am going to find them. I'm going to take everybody in this case to pieces, from Detective Blakemore and Astrid Meyer to the janitor at the youth club, and I am going to find out who did kill him. I am going to get enough facts for you to create, at the very least, a reasonable doubt. The plea is *not* guilty. Period."

He spread his hands and shrugged. "You pay the piper, you call the tune. Have you got any evidence of a frame? Anything at all?"

I turned to Dehan and sat back while she told her story for the second time. Cohen remained absolutely silent and seemed to read her while she spoke, like he was reading a document, his eyes darting here and there, as though he was double-checking her statements and facts against the tells on her face and in her gestures. When she'd finished, Cohen slumped back in his chair, made a temple out of his fingers, and studied it with an expression of deep disappointment, like he'd been hoping for a solid gold Hindu temple to ultimate truth, and he'd got a Calvinist sermon on the work ethic instead. After a moment he bellowed at the waiter and made a stirring motion with his finger, which meant "bring more coffee."

"I need much, much more to work with. So far you have given me a mysterious man with bad teeth called Tombs, and a perfectly innocent balloon covered in glue."

Dehan leaned forward. "But if it was silicone, it could have been used to reproduce my prints!"

"Could've, would've, should've! Nothing but words and speculation that the prosecutor will laugh at, and have the jury laughing with him. Bring me molds! Bring me the silicone used! Bring me an expert who can explain it to the jury!"

"I'll do better," I said. "I'm going to find Tombs and make him talk. And I am going to take Jones and grill him till he tells what the story was with the silicone."

"That would be something. But be careful, I don't want any illegally obtained evidence. Now, what about the weapon? My office has already requested the prosecution file, and we are going to be all over that like VD. But tell me about the weapon, a .38, right? Who found that, and where?"

Dehan sighed. "As far as I know, it was found at the scene of the crime. It was his weapon, ballistics are a match, and my prints are on it. I have never touched his weapon. So the only way that could have happened is if my prints were lifted and transferred onto the gun."

He grunted. "Speculation." Then he gestured at me with his right hand. "This is your department. You say you can get evidence, get it. Get it legally, and please don't get the NYPD telling you not to interfere with the police investigation. Now, the big question: as far as I can see, everything hinges on this one question. Who wants this man dead? Who benefits from his death?"

Dehan shook her head. "There are candidates, for sure. Statistically, his wife. But then he was a cop who was working hard to clean up the gangs. It is very possible he pissed off a gang. Tombs, the guy who came around to offer me a job, could well have been a gang member."

I sighed. The waiter brought more coffee, and when he'd gone, I sipped mine, black and hot, with no sugar.

"It's not a lot to go on," I said. "But I need to get talking to people and turn it into something more. We'll see what his wife can tell us. She might be able to give us more background on who Sanchez had pissed off, what enemies he might have had."

He turned a sigh into a long grunt as he wiped his mouth with the white linen napkin.

"All right, it won't be easy, but we'll give it our best shot. It will be worth it just to poke the NYPD in the eye. Present company excluded, of course.

"Here is my reading of the situation, and what needs to be done. I will get the full prosecution file tomorrow, or I shall want to know why. My team and I will go over it with a microscope. Based on what you have given me so far, I shall inform you, John, of every weakness I find. You, meanwhile, will endeavor to pick what I give you apart.

"I want to know nothing of your methods. I know you both

to be scrupulously honest, by-the-book detectives, but I will say this. Remember that illegally obtained evidence is *not* admissible in court, however probative it may be. If you obtain evidence illegally, cover your damn tracks!"

He placed his palms on the table, thought for a moment, and went on. "Things that come to mind: find the man who offered Carmen a job, find out who his employer is. Meanwhile, let us analyze the murder itself. One of our strong points may be that Carmen has a very small window of opportunity in which to have shot Sergeant Sanchez. So, at what time was the 911 call made, where was Carmen at that time? What was she doing? And, above all, let's take a magnifying glass to Sergeant Sanchez's life. He pissed somebody off mightily. So who did he piss off enough to want him dead? Who benefited from his death?

"And his wife: How often did she go out alone to celebrate deals? With whom did she go? Did she go with that person often? What is this woman's story?" He shrugged, made a slightly bewildered face. "If she had stayed home with her husband, would he have ended up murdered in the prime of his life? I need . . ." He paused and eyed us both. "I need a lot of doubts to cast before the jury. That means a lot of shit to throw at the people who were close to Sanchez. It won't be pretty. You'd better be prepared to be tough." He paused a moment and regarded each of us from under his brows. "Neither of you is going to be very popular with the NYPD after this. You need to know this."

Dehan sighed and twisted her mouth into a wry smile. "Nothing new there, then."

I echoed her sigh. "We'll cross that bridge when we get to it. For now our objective is clear, and as far as I can see there is only one way to achieve it. So that is what we do."

We talked a little more, and then members of Cohen's team began to arrive in ones and twos, wiping water from their hair and their sleeves, and Dehan and I took our leave.

The rain had eased during the morning to a steady, heavy drizzle. We still ducked into our shoulders to cross the road, but we didn't need to run. As I was opening the car door, my cell rang. I tossed Dehan the keys and lifted the phone to my ear.

"Yeah, Stone."

"Detective, I was wondering if you were free to talk this morning."

I frowned. "Who to and what about?"

There was a pause. Then, "My name is Astrid Meyer, I don't know if that means anything to you."

"Yeah, it means something to me. My wife is under arrest for your husband's murder. What do you want to talk to me about?"

"I'd prefer to discuss that in person. Where are you? I can send a car."

"Hold on." I muted it and looked at Dehan, who was leaning on the roof watching me, with trickles of rain running down her face. I said, "Astrid Meyer. She wants to send a car!" I raised an eyebrow. "And talk to me."

Her raised eyebrow echoed mine. "Go, it could be useful. I'll go home and see if I can dig anything up online. My access will be suspended, but yours ain't." She winked, and it looked somehow vulnerable and brave. "I know your passwords. Come straight home, okay?"

I nodded. "Of course." I put the phone back to my ear. "Mrs. Meyer. That would be fine. I'm at the Bay View Hotel."

"Here at the Eastchester Bay? Well, that's just down the road. My driver will be there in five minutes."

I thanked her and hung up. Dehan and I stood a few long moments looking at each other, with our hair and our faces getting steadily wetter. I was aware of a feeling of wild panic in my belly, and I could see that same feeling reflected in her eyes. Finally I said, "Hang in there. It's going to be okay. Stay cool. I'll be back for lunch."

She nodded. "I'll make moussaka. You need something hearty with this weather."

I nodded. "Sounds good. Now get going, you'll catch cold . . ."

She climbed in the car, and as she took off I could see her wiping her eyes on her wet sleeve.

Five minutes later a dark blue Audi 4 crawled around the corner and stopped in front of me. A guy who might have been black West Indian, with thick curly hair and a big moustache, climbed out and came around to open the door for me.

"You Detective John Stone?"

"I am."

"Stuart, at your service, sir."

I smiled and made to climb in the car. "Thank you, Stuart. Much appreciated." I climbed in the back, and he closed the door with a heavy clunk. I watched him climb in the front and caught his eye in the mirror. Once we were under way he said, simply:

"Not everybody gets her, but Astrid Meyer is a good woman."

SIX

For a moment I felt like asking him what was good about her, but decided that was unreasonable and instead asked, "How's that?" in a more or less pleasant tone of voice, which didn't really reflect the way I felt.

"Her daddy was in the marines. Colonel Wilfred Meyer. My daddy was in the marines too. Sergeant. When Miss Astrid, that's Mrs. Meyer—I never did like Sanchez as a name, never seemed to suit her, for my taste . . . Anyhow, old age makes me digress if you know what I mean. When Miss Astrid's daddy retired from the army, my daddy retired with him. Used to be like that in them days. People took care of each other. He took him in, and he took care of things around the house, drove the car, fixed whatever needed fixing."

I was going to say something about the feudal system being underrated, but he wasn't listening and just kept on rolling along.

"In them days," he said, "they had a chambermaid and a cook. My daddy liked that cook . . ." He paused to laugh ponderously. "And I guess she liked him too because . . ." Now he laughed high in the upper register. He reminded me of a parrot screaming. "Man! I guess she liked him too," he repeated, subsiding. "Because that cook was my mammy. We was happy in that house. I grew up happy. And when time came, I took over from my daddy. I have my place in the world. See what I mean? And that place was given to my daddy and me by Miss Astrid's daddy."

I was saved from having to answer because we had arrived at the end of Bay Shore Avenue, where it turns into Watt Avenue, and were entering through a large gate onto a crescent driveway outside a mock Georgian mansion with white Greco-Roman columns supporting a Roman Ionic pediment. The walls were white, and the windows had blue wooden shutters that gave it a Colonial rather than classical look. Either way, the house didn't look more than seventy or eighty years old.

He pulled up at the bottom of four broad, shallow steps, climbed out, and came round to open the door for me. He snapped open an umbrella and held it for me all the way up to the front door, where I was met by a cute maid in a French maid's outfit, who took my coat and led me across a three-dimensional checkerboard floor that made you feel you were either going to trip and stumble or get badly seasick, to a white door with a brass knob. She knocked, leaned in, and said, "Detective Stone is here, ma'am."

There was a muttered reply, then she stepped back and held the door open for me. I passed through.

I'm not sure what I had expected, but it was not what I found. Astrid Sanchez née Meyer was an attractive forty-something-year-old, which made her at least ten years older than her deceased husband. Her hair was platinum blond, and her eyes were a very bright, deep blue. Her skin was that kind of milky white which allows you to see the blue veins at the elbows and the wrists, amongst other places.

She was sitting at a large oak desk, and the wall behind her was taken up by a vast, floor-to-ceiling bookcase, which was also painted with a brilliant white gloss.

Directly opposite me, on her left, there were two tall, narrow windows, and on my right the room opened out into an L shape with burgundy rugs and animal skins cast here and there. The walls were lined with books on every conceivable subject, some venerable old hardbacks, others more disreputable, thumbed paperbacks. There was a Georgian marble fireplace and in front of it an eclectic nest of comfortable, old battered armchairs and a sofa.

She didn't stand up when I came in. She leaned back in her chair and studied me. Her face was more than expressionless; it was humorless.

"Detective John Stone, of the Forty-Third. You have a reputation in police circles. Anthony"—she pronounced it with a soft lisp instead of a hard *t*—"was very excited when he heard that your wife was volunteering for his project. He was childlike. He got excited by things."

I didn't know how to answer that, so I said, "I was very sorry to hear about Sergeant Sanchez's death."

"Don't you mean murder?"

"Yes, murder."

"By your wife."

"That is far from proven, Mrs. Sanchez, and personally I don't believe it."

"Meyer," she corrected me. I didn't say anything, and after a moment she said, "I don't like Sanchez. It is a Spanish name. Nothing to be proud of there. I assume you have been instructed not to conduct an investigation on your wife's behalf."

"Mrs. Meyer, why did you ask me to come here?"

"I want to ask you some questions."

"Really? I'd like to ask you some questions too, so maybe we can trade. But for starters, if you're not going to ask me to sit down, I'm going to leave, and you can have this conversation with one of my colleagues downtown."

Something like a smile snaked through her lips, but not of humor, rather of pleasure. She gestured carelessly at the chair opposite her own across the desk. I sat.

"You have employed Saul Cohen to defend your wife."

"Have I?"

"He has set up his war room at the Bay View." I didn't answer. She narrowed her eyes. "This little corner here is not like the rest of the Bronx, you know. This is still like the old villages—things work differently. My father knew that. He was respected, as am I. I had hoped that Anthony would one day command the same kind of respect."

"What's your point, Mrs. Meyer?"

She gazed out the window and blinked a few times before replying.

"I'm not sure I am making a point, Detective. I just feel perhaps you should know that not a lot happens here in the Bay without my knowing about it."

"Okay, so now I know that."

"What do you think, Detective Stone?" she said, still gazing out of the window. "Were they having an affair?"

"No."

"You would say that. You would want to believe that..."

"Then why ask me?"

She swiveled eyes that were suddenly very hard and looked at me.

"Have you anything more than a mere desperate hope that your wife was not sweating, groping, and grunting with my husband on a regular basis at that youth club, in the locker rooms or the bathrooms?"

"Yeah, I have something more than a mere desperate hope."

She seemed not to hear me. "I used to go there to check up. I would turn up at leaving time, without warning."

"Did you ever catch them at it?"

"No, and I never saw you there."

"That's because I trust my wife."

"Fool..."

"Was that all you wanted to ask me?"

"And why did she kill my baby? And why are you trying to

protect her when she has betrayed you, having sex with another man."

"She didn't. She didn't do any of those things."

"How can you say that? Her prints are everywhere in my house..."

I cut her short. "Not everywhere. They are on the banisters, on the doorframe, on the doorjamb and the bedstead and the head of the bed. Nowhere else."

"Except the murder weapon, of course. Are you a completely naïve fool, Detective? What about your pride? Think what this woman has done to you."

I leaned forward with my elbows on my knees. "There are a couple of things I would really like you to think about, Mrs. Meyer. I am convinced, by what evidence there is, that Detective Dehan is being framed for your husband's murder. Now, maybe I am wrong, but if I am right, and they succeed, it will mean that your husband's killer will get off scot-free."

"Don't you feel remorse for your wife's actions? Don't you feel even partly responsible for what she has done? If you had kept proper control over your wife..."

I barked a laugh. "Excuse me? Proper control?"

She thrust a hand across the desk, palm up, indicating me. "Well look at you! How old are you? How old is she? She must be almost twenty years younger than you! Obviously, meeting a younger, handsome man, she is going to want to stray. You should have been on top of that..."

"Mrs. Meyer, I am going to ignore those comments. I am telling you, categorically, that I have good reason to believe that your husband was killed by somebody other than Detective Dehan. Are you not even a little curious?"

"Curious? You come here, to my house, and try to *protect* that *slut*, telling me lies about how she is not guilty! What am I going to do with my life now, Detective? Who is going to help me and protect me, now that Anthony is gone?"

"I can't answer those questions, Mrs. Meyer, but I can tell you that sending an innocent woman to prison for thirty years is not an answer and will not bring him back."

Her face flushed, and she rose from the desk. "You're a fool! My father would have known how to deal with you and that *whore* of a wife of yours! Thirty years? Thirty years is too good! She should *hang*! Or go to the chair! Murdering a policeman, and my beautiful boy! You come here trying to protect that murdering bitch! What possible reason could you have to believe she is innocent when her prints are all over the weapon and my house? What *possible reason?*"

Her face flushed red, and tears spilled down from her eyes, streaking her cheeks. I felt for her, but I stood my ground.

"What reason? Putting it bluntly, Mrs. Meyer, if Dehan had done it, her prints would not be all over your house, or on the weapon. She is an exceptionally good, experienced pro who habitually carries latex evidence gloves in her pocket. She had latex gloves in her pocket on the night that Sergeant Sanchez was killed. If she had come to your house, she would not have been so stupid as to grip the banisters or put her hands on the door and the bed, especially having latex gloves in her pocket. Carmen Dehan is being framed, Mrs. Meyer, and your husband's killer is going to get away."

She stared at me, with her face twisting into a grotesque pink-and-white knot of pain and grief.

"Get out of here," she said, "before I call Detective Blakemore and have you thrown in jail for complicity to commit murder!"

I sighed and stood. "This is what you brought me here for? For nothing?"

"I thought you would understand what your wife is, how she played you and my husband. How she manipulated you. But you are just a blind fool."

"Fine, thanks for your time." I paused at the door and turned back, pointing my finger at her like a gun. "But remember,

Carmen Dehan is one of the best detectives at the Forty-Third, and possibly in New York. She would not commit such a basic mistake. And that means somebody is framing her. So if Dehan goes down, your husband's killer will be free. He probably lives right near you, maybe even visits with you and has coffee with you. Think about it."

Her eyes were hard and cold, wet and crazy. She spat the words at me. "Get *out*!"

I stepped out into the crazy, 3-D hall and crossed to collect my coat from the stand by the door. Nobody came to see me out.

I closed the door behind me and stood a moment looking at the rain. It had stopped being heavy drizzle and had become a steady downpour. I pulled up my collar, thrust my hands in my pockets, and started to walk back south, hoping to see a cab. They say that if you just raise your hand in New York a bunch of yellow cabs will screech to a halt. But like Astrid Meyer had said, this little corner of the Bronx was not like New York. It felt more like some remote part of New England. No hand-raising here, and no yellow cabs.

Then, there was Uber. But when Dehan had first tried to make me use it, she had said something about downloading an app, and that was pretty much where that conversation had ended. She had downloaded the app onto her phone, muttering something about dinosaurs. Now I was walking home in the rain.

I headed back toward the hotel, figuring I'd call for a normal cab from there (an unter cab?), and started thinking about what my next move would be. To some extent, logic dictated I should talk to the janitor who put the glue on the balloon. But my gut told me I'd get more out of a conversation with Detective Blakemore.

Yet another part of my brain told me, judging by the things Meyer had said about "this corner of the Bronx," Detective Blakemore might prove less helpful than I thought.

I pulled my cell from my pocket and called the 45th. When they answered, I told them who I was and asked to be put through to Blakemore. By the time he answered, I had almost reached the hotel. His voice was deep, hard.

"Stone? This is Blakemore."

"Yeah, I was wondering if we could meet to discuss the Sergeant Sanchez case."

"You fishing, or you got some evidence to give?"

"I'm not fishing, Blakemore. Your prime suspect is my wife, obviously I have an interest in the case, but equally maybe I can offer you an insight..."

"An insight? I'm not contemplating my fucking navel, Stone!" His voice grew dim, and I heard him say, "Hey, Stone, from the Forty-Third, yeah, the cop killer's husband. He says he wants to offer me an insight!" There was a lot of laughter. After a moment his voice came back. "Yeah, you know, one thing I don't need is insight, Stone..."

A sudden surge of anger made me flare up.

"Cut the bullshit, Blakemore. You've got fuck all to teach me about good police work! I have the best arrest record at the Forty-Third, and we do real police work over there, so quit riding me. I have a couple of points I need to discuss with you. You don't want to talk to me, I'll make damn sure I tell Cohen so he can make an issue of that at trial!"

"Okay, okay, okay... What's it about?"

"I hope to convince you that there is no way Detective Dehan could have killed Sergeant Sanchez."

"Is this insight you're going to offer me based on something more than just the fact that she's your cute wife?"

"Yeah, Blakemore. It's based on reasoning and deduction. I know you probably don't do a lot of that, helping cats down from trees for sweet old ladies, but I am confident that even you will be able to understand it. If you have a partner, maybe you can work it out together."

"That's funny."

"Yeah, I know, deep down funny, where it's not like funny

anymore. Now if you're done being an asshole, when can we meet?"

"Tomorrow, ten a.m., at the Forty-Fifth."

I hung up and went into the hotel, soaked from head to foot, and told the reception clerk to call me a cab. Then I called Dehan to tell her I was on my way home, and to start fixing me a large Bushmills.

SEVEN

The 45th Precinct was on the corner of Barkley Avenue and Revere. It was a traditional, New York police station: a big, three-story cube, with the ground floor faced in concrete and the upper stories in redbrick, and two big green lamps outside the main entrance. It was an image that should have inspired confidence and trust, but today it didn't. Today it gave me a bad, sinking feeling of menace.

I climbed out of the Jag. The blacktop was slick and shiny from the incessant rain, and though it was already ten minutes before ten, the cars all had their headlamps on, reflected in broken spills across the road.

I crossed and climbed the four granite steps to the big, black arch of the door and went inside. I showed the desk sergeant my badge and told her I was there to see Detective Blakemore. She gave me a look that said it would be offensive to the scum of the earth to call me scum, and picked up an internal phone.

"Detective Stone here to see you, from the Forty-Third. Yeah, that one . . ." She hung up and pointed. "Through that door, up the stairs, detectives' room, fourth desk on the right." She curled her lip. "He might not be there. So you might have to wait."

I leaned on her counter. "I haven't got time to wait, sister, so if he wants to talk to me, he'd better be there, or he can come and see me at the Forty-Third."

I pushed through the door, climbed the stairs, and found his desk. He was sitting at it watching me as I arrived. He was big, muscular, and had a face that looked like it was used to smiling at violence. He gestured to a chair opposite his own. I sat. He jerked his head at the tall window beside his desk.

"This rain, huh? Is it ever going to stop? They say it's caused by El Niño, down off the coast of Chile. Can you believe that?"

"Yeah, that's real disturbing. I'm here to talk about Detective Dehan."

He smiled. "Oh, I can talk about the weather all day, Stone. But I cannot talk *to you* about Detective Dehan or the Sergeant Sanchez case. Now, you . . ." He pointed at me, in case I didn't know who I was. "*You* can talk about Detective Dehan till the cows come home. Be my guest. I am like the guy on the radio, right? I am listening!"

"Detective Dehan did not kill Sergeant Sanchez."

"Okay, so I have a background of a growing and deepening relationship between the victim and the accused, I have her prints at his house and on his bed, and I have her prints on the murder weapon. Tell me why I should believe that she didn't kill him?" He wagged a finger at me. "And answer me something else. You went to see Mrs. Meyer, the deceased's widow, right?"

"That's two questions."

"Correct me if I'm wrong, Stone, but as I understood it, our captain asked your inspector to make sure you did not interfere in this case. Now, going to see witnesses, especially the deceased's widow, for me counts as interfering in the investigation. You want to tell me what the hell you thought you were doing there?"

"Not especially, Detective Blakemore. I already told you I came to discuss Detective Dehan. But if you really want to know, Mrs. Meyer called me and asked me to go and see her. She even sent a car . . ."

"What did she want?"

"She wanted to know if I thought Detective Dehan and Sergeant Sanchez were having an affair. Now..."

He smiled like a man who is about to kick another man when he's down. "What did you tell her?"

"I told her I was sure they were not. Now, can we talk about Detective Dehan?"

He leaned back in his chair and smiled down at his thumbs. It was more of a sneer than anything else.

"You know? I'm sorry for you, Stone. I heard you're a good cop with a great track record. I heard you're one of the good guys, with integrity. I also heard nobody can stand you, but hey, nobody's perfect, right? It's gotta be tough, getting to your age, with a beautiful, young wife, and have her fall for a younger guy, and screw him behind your back. I guess age, you know, he could probably do things for her you forgot how to do twenty years ago, right?"

I didn't answer straightaway. When I did, I spoke very quietly.

"I'm going to suggest something to you, Detective Blakemore. I suggest you leave your badge and your gun in your drawer, and I'll leave mine in my car, and we go over to Huntington Woods, by the crime scene, and then you repeat what you just said to me about my wife."

"Is that a threat, Stone?"

"It's a suggestion. Now, how about you quit acting like a fourteen-year-old asshole and you listen to what I have to say? *All of this comes out at trial.*"

He didn't answer. He just watched me, and there was something in his eyes that was dangerous. I went on.

"You're aware of the cold-case unit's track record?" He gave a minute nod. "Then you are aware of Detective Dehan's track record and her reputation as a cop." Before he could answer, I kept going. "So you should know that both Detective Dehan and I *always*, on and off duty, carry evidence bags and crime scene gloves in our jackets. The morning after Sergeant Sanchez's murder, I checked Detective Dehan's pockets, at about six fifteen, and she had the gloves and the evidence bags in her jacket. Now, I have to ask you, do you think it is credible that an experienced, first-class detective, who is *that* aware of forensics, is going to enter a house where she intends to kill a cop, take hold of the banisters, lean her hands all over the doorframe and the jamb, and then take a hold of the bedstead and the bedhead? And, having done that, then take hold of the revolver, shoot the victim, and leave, leaving the weapon at the scene. And last of all, make no effort to remove her prints? All the while with evidence bags and gloves in her jacket pocket! Does that sound credible to you?"

He sighed and looked at the window in disgust, then looked back at me with hooded eyes.

"Whether it's credible or not, it's what you've got."

"She's being framed, Blakemore, and you know it."

"Aw, c'mon, Stone! Give your ego a rest for a while, will ya? I heard all about you. You think you're the bee's fuckin' knees. Smarter than everybody else, always looking for the cute angle that shows how fucking brilliant you are. A wife with legs all the way to nirvana and the best fuckin' brain on the force. Well I got news for you, pal. Reality just came knocking on your fuckin' door. Your beautiful wife just screwed a younger guy, and then she shot him. And there is proof—forensic proof. This time you go down. Welcome to the big, bad world."

"You make a lot of noise, Blakemore, but there wasn't a single piece of logical reasoning in what you just said. There is cause for at least a reasonable doubt . . ."

He cut me short, talking so loud he was practically shouting. "You're wasting your time, Stone! What's worse, you're wasting my time! Now, unless . . ." He leaned forward and leered at me. "Unless you have a semen sample, or some sample of bodily fluid for the forensic team, I suggest you get the hell out of my face and let me do my job."

"That's just the problem," I snarled. "You're not doing your damned job!"

He leaned forward, shouting, "What can you tell me, Stone?

If she wasn't there, do you know where she was? Can you tell me how her prints got into Tony's bedroom? Can you tell me how they got on the murder weapon? Can you do anything besides whine and complain?"

"Maybe."

He shook his head. "Uh-uh, there is no maybe. Either you can or you can't. And you can't. And if you can't explain those three things, *then you are wasting my time!*"

"Detective Dehan did not kill Sergeant Anthony Sanchez."

"Can you prove it?"

"Not yet, but you could if you would listen to me."

He narrowed his eyes at me. "What do you mean, not yet?"

"I plan to find out who killed him." I smiled and gave my head a little shake. "Detective Dehan is one of the most skilled detectives you are ever likely to meet. I know because I have worked with her for almost three years, and I know she didn't kill Sergeant Sanchez precisely *because* her prints were at the scene."

"That's bullshit. That is typical of you, bullshit."

I shrugged. "Suit yourself, Blakemore, but I am going to expose you and your supposed investigation for what it is, a sham and a frame-up." I stood and pointed down at him. "And you'll be lucky if all you get at the end of this is a reprimand."

He stood, and he looked ugly.

"Stay out of my way, Stone, and stay out of my investigation, or I'll give you more trouble than you know how to handle."

"Save it for the little old ladies whose kittens you rescue." I smiled like he actually amused me. "You just made a big mistake. You're going to pay the price, and I am going to bring you the check."

I went down the stairs and out into the rain. I looked up at the sky. It was midmorning but it looked like early evening. A gust of wind whipped small raindrops into my face. El Niño was causing trouble, I thought. We'd see how much trouble I could cause back.

I was turning the key in my car door when my cell rang in my pocket. I wiped the drizzle from my eyes and thumbed the screen. Astrid Meyer. I raised an eyebrow and answered.

"Yeah, John Stone here."

There was silence—almost. I could hear breathing. It wasn't quite heavy, but heavy enough to hear.

"Mrs. Meyer, how can I help you?"

There was still no reply, so I pulled open the door, climbed in, and put the phone on the dash, on speaker, while I dried my hair with a handkerchief.

"I don't know what it is you're aiming to accomplish, Mrs. Meyer." I slammed the car door and went on. "I am here and alone if you want to speak to me."

"I . . ." I waited. There was only the sound of the breathing.

"I'm listening, Mrs. Meyer. I can hear you."

"I . . . I was perhaps rude when you came to see me." I didn't answer, so she went on. "After all, I sent for you. It was wrong of me to turn you away. Perhaps . . ."

"Yes, Mrs. Meyer, perhaps what?"

"You could, if it's not inconvenient I mean, perhaps you would care to . . . I could send a car."

"Are you asking me to go and see you again?"

"If, if that's not too much . . ."

"Last time I went to see you I had to walk all the way back to the Bay View in the rain just to get a cab."

"Yes, I should apologize for that . . ."

"Don't worry about it, Mrs. Meyer, but I'll use my own car. Why the change of heart?"

She muttered something and the line went dead. I called Dehan, told her I'd be delayed and where I was going, and then drove slowly through the hissing wet streets back to the big mock Georgian manor on the corner of Bay Shore Avenue. I rolled in through the drive and killed the engine at the foot of the steps. As I climbed out, Stuart opened the door of the house and stepped out with his umbrella.

"Seems this rain ain't never gonna end."

"Yeah, it's all the fault of El Niño," I said.

"Is that so? Miss Astrid is waiting for you in her study. She ain't feeling great."

I stepped into the checkerboard hall. He closed the umbrella and took my coat.

I gave him a look and said, "I came to see her yesterday, remember?"

"Yes, Detective, I do remember..."

"She kicked me out."

He gave an amused chuckle. "I know that too."

"Yeah, I had to walk in the rain all the way to the Bay View."

"I am sorry about that, Detective."

"Never mind. Any idea why the change of heart?"

"I have some idea, but I think it's best she tell you herself. What I *can* tell you is that, even though she can be difficult, she is a good person. She can be tough, but she's fair an' just also."

"Yeah, I'm sure."

He made a gesture that I should follow, like he was the maître d' in a restaurant. Then he led me back across the floor to the study door, tapped, and opened it. "Miss Astrid, Detective Stone to see you."

He stood back, and I stepped into the study for the second time in as many days.

She was not behind her desk this time. She was seated by the fireplace in an armchair, with a silver tray of coffee in front of her on a low coffee table. She was wearing heavy black glasses. She stood but did not look at me, and I heard the door softly close behind me. I approached and saw that there was two of everything on the tray. She gestured to the chair and the sofa.

"Please, wherever you are most comfortable. Will you have some coffee?"

"Thanks."

"Detective, I hope you will accept my apology for the way I behaved yesterday. I was, and still am, half out of my mind with grief over Tony... But that is no excuse for my behavior."

"It's understandable. Please don't worry about it." I sat, and she sat too. I said, "What did you want to see me about?"

She poured me coffee—black, no sugar—and handed me the cup. Then she fixed herself a cup, and I thought I detected the whiff of booze on her breath. I sipped the strong, black brew and decided I had run out of patience.

"Mrs. Meyer, forgive me for being blunt, but, why the change of heart? Yesterday you were practically accusing me of abetting my wife in your husband's murder . . ."

"Please try to understand that I am not entirely in control of my emotions. I am in shock, trying to process the fact that Tony is gone. And he is never coming back. Never. So I don't always see things too clearly at the moment."

"That's understandable."

"Please, don't patronize me." She closed her eyes and sat like that for a while. Finally she went on. "Once my anger, and my pain, had died down, I decided to have you looked up. What my man was able to find, in the little time he had, was that you have a reputation for integrity. You have an exceptional track record, both on your cold cases and before that in homicide. You remind me, a little bit, of Tony. He was more outgoing, concerned with society as a whole. You are a loner, more concerned with the individual. But you are an honest man. A man of integrity, as my father would have said."

She paused and, holding her cup in two shaking hands, she gulped her coffee, then set down the cup with care.

"I am a rational woman, Detective Stone." She smiled and removed her glasses to squint at me. Her eyes were puffy, and she had deep blue bags under them. It was evidence of hard crying you couldn't fake. "That rarest of things. My father raised me, you know. A good German with a profound understanding of the fundamental differences between Germans and the rest of the world, and German men and women. The German man is the epitome of discipline, order, organization, and power. The German woman is the mother of the German man. Powerful emotions focus"—she closed her right fist, and I knew she had seen her father do that same thing a thousand times—"the German man's mind. Powerful emotions make of a woman, any woman, an irrational liability. So my father taught me to control my emotions and focus my mind. Still, estrogen can make that difficult sometimes."

I was frowning, trying to find my way through this tsunami of madness. I tried to reach for the chronology and asked, "Forgive me, but I understood it was your great-grandfather who moved to the States..."

"And you think that because of this my father was not German but American. But you see, I can be born in a stable, but that does not make me an ass. This disgusting obscenity you call your melting pot, it creates social discord, confusion of identity, lack of patriotism, social psychosis. My father was not an American, and I am not an American. Nobody is an American. But I, and my father, we are Germans."

I was frowning harder than I had been when she'd started talking. I said, "But, Tony..."

"Tony, also, was German."

EIGHT

We sat in silence. She was staring sullenly into her cup. I was staring at her, wondering if she had completely taken leave of her mind. Finally I said, "Antonio Sanchez . . . Antonio Sanchez was German?"

"A lot of Germans settled in Mexico, Argentina, and Brazil. Some kept their names. There are many—Muller, Schmidt, Becker, Schneider, Wagner . . . Others, an exceptional minority, had reason to lose their German names and adopt local names. Tony was from one of those exceptional families, in Mexico. But you never saw him?" I shook my head. "He had golden hair, blue eyes, a fine, German jaw. He was beautiful."

She quietly slipped her black glasses back on. Outside a gutter was spilling, spattering water. I said, "I see. I am a little at a loss . . ."

"Because a man, a good man, will see with clarity, even when he is wracked with powerful emotions. He remains calm and focused. If my father had received you yesterday, he would have calmly listened to what you had come to say."

"I see," I said again.

"But when you had gone, I investigated and I discovered you are a good man. You are of good, old blood. Not like . . ." She trailed off, then resumed. "And your track record and your reputation... Nobody likes you, but everybody respects you."

"Is this a roundabout way of telling me you are prepared to listen to what I have to say?"

"Yes, this is a long-winded way of letting you know who I am, and why I am prepared to listen to what you have to say about your wife."

I shook my head. "Not my wife, Detective Carmen Dehan."

"A Jewess."

I sat for a while, watching her, wondering whether to answer her, and if so, how. Wind and rain rattled at the window, urgent and impatient. I sighed softly.

"Detective Dehan is an exceptional policewoman. Her skills in the martial arts are exceptional, and I have been with her and seen her under fire and under threat of imminent death on multiple occasions. I have never once seen her lose her cool. She is, both in investigation and under fire, coolheaded, efficient, fast, and thorough."

"I get the idea, Detective."

"It is now about three years since we started working as partners, and I have never once seen her falter or act in a stupid, careless way."

"Admirable." Her tone was dry, bored. She didn't like hearing other women praised. I drove my point home.

"By the very fact of who she is, it is impossible—*impossible*—for Detective Dehan to have murdered your husband. Detective Dehan had latex gloves in her pocket the night Sergeant Sanchez was killed. We always carry them with us. It's a habit. If she had come to your house intending to kill him, she would not have touched the banisters. She would not have touched the door. She would not have touched anything until she had pulled on the gloves. She is too much of a professional."

She nodded slowly. "I understand what you are saying. It is not proof, but it is very compelling reasoning."

"I can guarantee to you that it is an impossibility for Detective

Dehan to have carried out such a sloppy, unprofessional crime. And that means that somebody else did. And *that* is something that should be worrying you."

She was quiet for a while, then nodded. "Okay, assuming I accept your argument, what do you want from me?"

"I need to know what happened that night. I need to know why you went out without him, where you went, what time you got back, exactly what you found . . ."

She made an odd "Pfff!" sound. "I hadn't been out with Tony for months. He was obsessed with his damned social club. So we had pulled off a property deal, and we went out. When I say 'we,' I mean the office, to celebrate. We had dinner, a couple of drinks—"

"Where?"

"At the yacht club here on the marina. And at half past eleven, maybe a quarter to twelve, I called Stuart and told him to come and collect me."

"Stuart lives in this house?"

"Well, not *in* the house. He has a small cottage which is close to the house. When I go out, he knows he has to wait up for me to call him."

"So you got back just before twelve?"

"Yes, eleven thirty, eleven forty-five."

I sighed. "I need to see the crime scene."

Her face went from pale to deathly. "It hasn't been touched. The police have been over it, taken things . . . I haven't . . ."

"Just tell me where it is. I'll find it."

She hesitated, stretched a hand out toward the door, and looked like she might pass out. "Up the stairs. The master bedroom is down at the back of the house. It still has the police tape . . ."

I nodded. "There was something about shots being fired in the house."

"I think I disturbed the killer. I always carry a gun. We

exchanged a couple of shots, and she went out through the French windows in the drawing room."

I offered a thin smile. "I'll need you to show me, and walk me through what happened."

"Of course. I just can't face going upstairs, imagining what he must have felt..."

I left her crying softly behind her black glasses and once more crossed the checkerboard hall. In the distance I heard a rumble come in, deep and menacing off the Atlantic. The staircase was a polished granite carpeted in plain burgundy, and I climbed it to a gallery that looked down over the entrance hall, under a gabled ceiling supported by vast oak beams. Two passages fed off the gallery into each wing of the house. I followed the one that led to the master bedroom, pulling on my gloves. At the end of the passage an arched window filtered damp light onto the hardwood floor.

The master bedroom was the last door on the right. A strip of yellow police tape hung limply across it. I pulled it down and opened the door.

What I saw, and smelt, stopped me dead in my tracks and made me turn away, fighting the urge to retch. The room was large, spacious. Wet, gray light lay on the walls, with the trickling shadows of rain droplets moving toward the floor. The light came from a plate glass door that led out onto a small terrace. Another door, half-open on the right, led to an en suite bathroom. This floor was also polished hardwood, and one wall was taken up by a built-in wardrobe. At its mirrored doors I saw myself, a menacing silhouette framed in the door. Directly in front of me, about fifteen or sixteen feet away, was a heavy oak four-poster bed.

At first I thought that the duvet and the sheets were russet or orange. But when the stench of putrefaction hit me I realized with a lurch in my belly that they had been saturated with blood; blood that was drying and putrefying as it dried. I closed the door behind me and stood absorbing the scene.

There was a lot of blood. So much that it had spilled off the bed and onto the floor. I could see where the surfaces had been dusted, and here and there, there were prints: Astrid's, Tony's, and Dehan's. I fought down an irrational surge of anger and moved to the bed.

The midsection of the mattress and bedding had been drenched. And about three feet from the bedhead the mattress had been punctured. I squinted at it and scratched my head. On closer inspection I decided it had been made by a number of closely grouped bullets. Though the area had then been damaged further, I figured, when it had been ripped to extract the slugs.

I pulled the duvet back over the sheet. The same holes were there. Four of them, closely grouped. Whoever killed him was a good shot, and unemotional. His hands had not been shaking. He'd had control over his weapon, and of his emotions. But I noted with a sick feeling in my belly that he had not shot him in the head, to execute him and finish him off, though he was clearly capable of it. He had deliberately shot him in the belly. One of the slowest, most painful deaths imaginable.

If it wasn't a punishment killing, there had been vengeance or hatred in the motive.

I thought about it for a moment, then pulled my phone from my pocket and called Joe at the lab. He sounded nervous, uncomfortable.

"Stone, what can I do for you?"

"You and Frank were called to the crime scene where Sergeant Anthony Sanchez was found?"

"Frank was. I was on another case. I sent a team. Why? You're not supposed to be involved in this case, John."

"That's okay, because I just called you to talk about Dehan's next birthday celebration."

"Yeah?"

"Yeah, May, the weather will be good. I was thinking maybe a barbeque. But, while I have you on the line, there is something I want to run by you . . ."

We talked for five minutes, and after that I went back downstairs to find Astrid Meyer where I had left her. She looked embarrassed and kept her eyes on the coffee tray.

"I haven't been able to . . ." she said. "I can't go near it."

"I know, it's hard to face." After a moment I added, "You want me to take care of it?"

She glanced at me and frowned, then shook her head. "No. No, thank you. One of these days I am going to have to face it. I'll tell Stuart. He'll deal with it."

I nodded and said, "I need to see where you exchanged fire."

She stood, like her body weighed a quarter of a ton, and headed for the door on unsteady feet. "It's through here."

I followed her across the polished marble entrance hall and through a tall set of doors. The room was long and broad, running from a large bow window at the front of the house, where wet trees bowed and bobbed in the downpour, to tall French doors at the back, where water was pooling in the sodden lawn. Beyond the fence, not far away, I could see the dense foliage of Huntington Woods.

Set into the far wall, there was a large Georgian fireplace. Surrounding it, at a distance, were modern armchairs and a sofa. There were good Impressionist prints on the walls and an eclectic selection of good, though not fantastic, antique furniture.

It took me longer than I had expected to find the bullet holes. One had embedded itself in the wall, about seven feet off the ground, halfway down the room. Another had narrowly missed what looked like an original Varvara over the credenza.

"Those two were mine," she said.

"Talk me through it."

"It was about twelve midnight. I'd just come back from dinner. As you know, Tony had been at the club, with . . . It had been some time since we'd been out together, as I had told you. When I got home I came into the living room." She gestured at a tray of decanters on the credenza. "I intended to have a nightcap before bed. I stepped in and switched on the light. She was there."

She pointed down toward the Varvara.

"How was the intruder dressed?"

She stared at me a moment in surprise. "Um . . . She was wearing dark pants, jeans perhaps, a dark roll-neck sweater or a sweatshirt, I am not sure. It was all so sudden. She had a ski mask over her face. She was armed with a revolver, and she fired at me. That's the shot, there in the wall."

She pointed. The bullet hole was above and to the left of the door, about three inches from another painting. I pointed at it.

"Is that an original Picasso?"

"My great-grandfather acquired it, before Picasso became mega famous. I can't imagine what it is worth now." She looked back at the sideboard, where her husband's killer had stood. "I was slow to react. To be honest I was stunned. My mind was reeling. She fired again before I could draw my weapon. The second shot is over here . . ."

She walked toward the bow window and pointed to a hole in the wall, some seven feet from the floor.

She turned back to me. "So, I managed to react. I pulled my gun and let off three wild shots, all of which missed her. She tore open the door and made off across the lawn, into the woods. I didn't bother to give chase or call the police. My only thought was Tony. So I ran frantically up the stairs and . . ." The blood drained from her face. "I found him in that unspeakable . . ." She trailed off.

"I am sorry, Astrid. I have to ask you this. Did you check that he was actually dead?"

Her eyes went wide with horror. "Of course! Immediately! What are you implying? It was my first thought. But he was quite obviously dead. So I called Blakemore."

I thrust my hands deep in my pockets and went to stand by the door, trying to visualize the scene. The killer, whoever it was, had stood six feet from the fireplace, between the armchair and the French doors. He, or she, had been about thirty feet or a little less from Astrid. He had fired once and missed. He, or she, had fired one more time before turning and running. Meanwhile

Astrid had pulled her own weapon and fired three times, missing the killer and a number of valuable items in the room. I shrugged, with my hands still in my pockets, and said:

"I'm afraid this just confirms to me what I said before: that it is impossible that Dehan committed this crime. At thirty feet, the moment you stepped through the door, she would have plugged you between the eyes with a single shot." I gestured at the walls. "This is the wild shooting of a panicking amateur."

She nodded. "I understand."

"Who were Tony's enemies, Astrid?"

Her eyes went wide. She looked startled, as though the thought had scared her. She spread her hands wide. "But that's the thing. He had no enemies. Everybody liked and respected him. He was loved by his colleagues, and as you know, there is no serious crime in this corner of the Bronx. It's a peaceful neighborhood. I have tried and tried, and the only person I could think of who had become close with him was your wife."

"He was younger than you?"

"Yes, considerably." She crossed the room to the fireplace and lowered herself ponderously into one of the large armchairs. "I'm forty-two. He was thirty-two, and had the body and the energy of a twenty-year-old. He was rarely at home. He was either at work or at the youth club."

"Do you know who he mixed with there?"

"To begin with I trusted him implicitly. We had agreed, if we ever felt the need to stray, we would tell each other before doing anything. But when Dehan showed up, I began to suspect. He liked her, who wouldn't? He talked about her too much. She was always there, with us, wherever we went!"

I couldn't suppress a smile. I said, with a twist of irony, "Tell me about it."

"Now you tell me that there was no such affair. And I am beginning to believe you. So, what am I left with? Was he involved in some criminal activity . . . ?"

"Astrid, he was a cop. It was his job to be involved in criminal activity. The question is, who did he piss off so much they decided to kill him? Did he ever speak to you about the gangs? About anyone who came to the club to threaten him?"

"No, but he didn't talk about his work much, only the club."

"Did he ever mention the name Tombs?"

She shook her head. "No."

"How about Shanna? What can you tell me about her?"

She stared at the wall with no expression on her face. "Shanna?" She shrugged. "She's the psychologist. She kept an eye on the kids. She kept an eye on the activities and gave advice." Now she turned to look at me. "There was nothing special about Shanna."

"I'm asking you what kind of relationship they had."

"Have you seen her?"

"No."

"Well, you should see her and try and imagine her taking a gun and shooting somebody. She's beautiful. Not like your wife is beautiful: feline and primal. Shanna is like an angel, a black angel. Soft. So delicate." She shook her head emphatically. "Impossible."

I leaned my forearms on the back of the chair and looked down into her face.

"It's that simple for you, and maybe it was that simple for her. But if some other guy was in love with her, maybe it wasn't that simple for him."

"What are you talking about?" She sighed and rubbed her face and her eyes with her palms. Then she looked at me, with her skin flushed. "Are we overcomplicating this? Blakemore believes that your Detective Dehan fell in love with Tony, that Tony turned her down, and she killed him. Sane people become crazy when they are in love."

"Maybe his theory is right, but his suspect is wrong. Or maybe it was more complicated than that. I heard that your husband and Shanna were pretty close friends. What if there was somebody else interested in Shanna, who thought that Tony and Shanna were more than just old friends?"

She shrugged and made a face eloquent of a lack of enthusiasm.

"It's possible, I suppose."

I looked at my watch. "Stuart lives on the property, right? What about your maid?"

"Stuart has a cottage at the back of the house. Sally lives in town."

"Stuart didn't hear anything?"

She shook her head. "No, obviously Blakemore asked him." She sat awhile, looking at the floor between her feet. The dull, gray light cast gloom instead of shadows. "Blakemore is wrong, isn't he?" She looked up at me. "He has decided she's guilty and he is going after her, regardless."

"Yes."

"But that's not what I want. What I want is for my husband's killer to be caught, and punished. Do you think you can do that?" She closed her eyes and sighed before I could answer. "I know you are not allowed, but it's your life, your wife's life . . ."

I nodded. "Yes. If you'll help me."

"I'll talk to Blakemore and ask him to cooperate. I'll see if I can get access to the file, have him share what information they have . . ."

I smiled. "It's not that easy."

She seemed not to hear me. ". . . I carry some weight in this town . . ."

"This town, as you call it, is the Bronx, the city of New York . . ."

"This little corner is a haven. The Meyers have had influence here for a long time. We own a lot of what you see and lease or let it." She smiled grimly. "We own the yacht club *and* the police station house! Blakemore will toe the line." She sat forward suddenly and stared hard at me with her icy blue eyes. "I'll get you *anything* you need. Just find my husband's killer. Find her, and bring her to me!"

NINE

Stuart opened the door for me, and I stepped out under the shelter of the Georgian porch. He reached for an umbrella to see me to the car. I shook my head and smiled. "This way I don't have to wash my hair this week."

He returned the smile. "That's one way of looking at it."

"Stuart, the night of the murder . . ."

"Night before last."

"You didn't hear anything? Four shots were fired in the bedroom. Another five were fired in the dining room. I'm surprised you didn't hear anything at all."

He pulled down the corners of his mouth and looked out at the green hedge, spattered with rainwater. A chill crawled up my back and I realized the temperature was dropping.

"It ain't so strange as you might think, 'tective. All the doors and windows in the big house are triple-glazed. My cottage is thirty yards yonder"—he pointed back into the house—"across the yard, and my doors and windows are also triple-glazed. So if you have the windows open, you can hear most everything. But if they're closed, man, you can't hear nothin'." He gave his head a ponderous shake. "I sure as hell wish I had heard something, Detective Stone. Sergeant Sanchez was a good man, and I was mighty fond of him. But all I heard that night was the wail of a banshee."

"A banshee?"

"Yeah, a terrible howl. Made my blood run cold. Must have been about eleven o'clock. I think it was an omen of what was to come. Came from the woods over yonder."

I thought about it. Time and location were wrong. "What time did you go home to your cottage?"

"Sergeant Sanchez said he was gonna go straight from the station to the youth club, and Miss Astrid said she was goin' to dine out. So I went to my cottage about eight."

I stood awhile looking at the gray puddles in the gravel, with their ever expanding concentric circles making complex interference patterns. I looked up at the sky and sighed. It showed no sign of relenting. Finally I glanced at Stuart again.

"A banshee?"

"That's what it sounded like, Detective, howling into the night from among the trees. I know it was an omen for the sergeant's passin'. Ain't no other explanation far as I can see. There is more to this world, Detective Stone, than we can ever see with our worldly eyes."

I nodded for a while, slow, with my mind lost in that dark, rainy night where the banshee howled. Then I thanked him and made my way down the sodden granite steps to my car.

I drove back home and found Dehan in the gym she'd set up in the prefab shed we'd had installed in the backyard. She was kicking seven bells out of a sack she had hanging from the ceiling, and between volleys of kicks she was laying into it with volleys of four and six punches. She didn't notice me arrive, so I leaned on the jamb for a bit and watched her. How had Astrid described her? Beautiful, feline, and primal. I smiled. She was all that, but she was also an angel, a soft, delicate, feminine angel.

"You bored?"

She stopped and turned. "Where have you been?"

"I went to speak to Blakemore."

"How'd it go?"

"Not great. He is not very receptive. But..."

"You didn't call. I thought you'd call and fill me in."

I nodded and blinked a couple of times. "I called to say I was going to be delayed..."

She wiped her face with a towel, sat on a stool, and offered me a smile that wasn't really a smile.

"But you didn't call to tell me what happened."

"No, that's true." I watched the bag swinging slowly, losing momentum. "You want me to tell you why, or do you want to get mad at me and vent your frustration on me?"

She didn't seem to think that was funny. She just watched me.

"I called to tell you I would be delayed because, as I told you at the time, Astrid Meyer called me again."

Her face contracted into a frown. "*Astrid?*"

I responded with a small, slightly confused frown of my own. "Yeah, Sergeant Sanchez's widow. I told you."

We both stared at each other in silence for a moment till she asked, "What did she want?"

My frown deepened and I pushed off the doorframe. "Am I missing something here, Dehan? Is there something I need to know?"

"What the hell are you talking about?"

"Okay, shall we start with the cool, hostile reception? I just spent the morning trying to save you from thirty years behind bars, I get home, and for some reason I feel like an underperforming employee. Once we've dealt with that, we could examine your reaction to the name Astrid Meyer, which if you, as a cop, had observed it, you would have found odd, to say the least."

She heaved a big sigh that was more about self-control than it was about self-awareness. Then she told the floor, "I am sorry about the reception. I am *very* stressed and *very* frustrated that I am stuck at home with nothing to do while I rely on other people to save my ass."

"I understand that. It doesn't mean you can't be nice to me."

I'd hoped for a smile, but I didn't get one.

"As to your problem with jealousy, there's nothing I can do about that, Stone. That's something you have to deal with yourself."

I saw the regret flicker in her eyes the moment she'd said it. But the anger had already risen inside me, and I didn't know how to deal with it wisely.

We both stared at the floor a moment. Then I gave a single nod.

"There has been a misunderstanding here, Dehan. At least one. Let me clear one up for you, and then maybe you can clear up the rest for me. I have not got a problem with jealousy. I am not jealous of anybody, living or dead. What I am is very worried that I am going to lose the woman I love, either to prison, or to somebody else. I understand how stressful your situation is. I wonder if you can put yourself in my shoes, and understand how I feel?"

I went to leave but stopped.

"If you and I, back when we were close, had seen that reaction, the one you had to Astrid Meyer's name, we would both have understood instinctively that it meant something. Maybe now I'm just the pain in the ass who is making a crap job of trying to save you from thirty years behind bars. But I am also the only one, because everybody else is ready to hang you out to dry. So, forget I am your husband, if you haven't already, and think of me as a crap investigator instead. Because I need to know what that reaction meant. Not because I have a problem with jealousy, but because your life might depend on it."

I sighed, feeling suddenly weary and depressed. "When you're ready to talk to me in a civil manner, let me know. I'm going to make a sandwich for lunch."

She muttered something at the floor. I said, "What?"

She took a deep breath and said, "I made moussaka. It's in the oven, keeping warm."

"You made moussaka?"

"Yeah, I went to Vintners, the wine specialist, and I got you a bottle of Marqués de Riscal." She sighed and shrugged. "Well, I didn't get it for *you*, I got it for us. But you probably don't want it now."

"Dehan." She looked at me and looked away again. "That's kind of the whole point I am trying to make, Dehan. I *do* want it. I want the moussaka, I want the wine, I want you to remember the holidays we are supposed to spend together. I *do* want my wife back."

She didn't answer for a while, then said, "That's what I was trying to do. When you didn't call, and then you did call to say you'd be late . . ."

"You got mad."

"I guess."

"Lucky I'm a bit more patient than you, huh?"

She sighed and gave her head a sideways twitch. "I don't know, Stone. Maybe if you'd got all butch and macho on me two and a half months ago none of this would have happened."

I grunted. "Maybe you're right at that. Something to be said for the old ways, huh?"

She didn't smile, just nodded and looked back at the floor. After a moment I said, "There's an elephant in the room, Dehan."

"I know."

"I'm not going to ignore it. You need to explain."

She spread her hands in a gesture of helplessness. "You're not going to believe me."

I frowned. "If you tell me it's true, I'll believe you. But it's not enough to tell me bits of the truth, Dehan. I need to understand everything that happened, and everything that you felt, and feel."

"Don't start on that again, Stone!"

"Then stop making me feel that you're hiding something!"

Another sigh; she closed her eyes and seemed to count to ten.

"I don't like Astrid. She is a domineering, manipulative, arrogant . . ."

"Anti-Semite."

"Probably. And Tony—I'm sorry, I just feel really awkward saying this now because I'm scared you'll misunderstand. But Tony was a good guy. I liked him. Not in that way, but I liked him a lot as a pal, and I never understood why the hell he was with her. What he saw in her. It wasn't something I lay awake at night worrying about either. It was just like, she'd turn up, you'd look at her and think, 'What the hell does he see in her?,' and you'd forget about it."

"Okay."

"But it was mutual, she really didn't like me. Now all this has happened I realize a lot of people must have thought there was something going on with me and Tony, and I feel really bad about that. I swear to you it never even crossed my mind. You-are-my-man, Stone! There can never be anybody else. But *she* didn't know that, did she?"

"No, and apparently neither did half of the NYPD. But to add salt to the wound, she *is* an anti-Semite."

"Oh, well, that kind of makes sense. So anyway, my reaction was sort of, 'What the hell did *she* want,' rather than anything to do with Sanchez or the club."

"Well, prepare yourself for a surprise, kiddo. She called to ask me to explain to her why I believed you were innocent." She arched an eyebrow. "She said she had had 'her people' look into me, she had found I had integrity and was a good man, and an outstanding cop . . ."

"Is this still her or are you free-form improvising here?"

"This is her, sourpuss. And when I explained why I thought it was impossible, she was convinced. I got to have a look at the crime scene too."

She gave a small snort. "Be careful, Stone. I wouldn't trust that woman as far as I could kick her. And that is a long way, believe me."

I nodded. "Preaching to the choir, kid. Let's go eat some moussaka and let that wine breathe."

Over a long, slow lunch I filled her in on the events of the morning. Nothing very concrete emerged from the conversation, but at shortly before four, while we were loading the dishwasher and making coffee, my phone pinged. It was a voice message from Astrid Meyer. I played it for Dehan as she pulled a couple of cups from the cupboard.

"Detective Stone, this is Astrid Meyer speaking. I have spoken to Blakemore. I have recommended he listen to what you have to say. I stressed to him, I do not want swift justice at the expense of true justice. I want whoever killed Tony caught and . . ." There was a pause, with slightly labored breathing. The message stopped and a second one started. "He is not happy. I think, personally, that he feels threatened by you. But after I made things clear for him, he is willing to cooperate. I really want you to find my Tony's killer, Detective Stone. It is very important to me."

Dehan put down the coffeepot, squinted her eyes, and gestured at me with both hands. "See? You see what I mean? Why? What is that at the end? 'I really want you to find my Tony's killer.' What is that? Why does she have to sound weird? 'It is very important to me.' Well, it's your damned husband! Of course it's important!"

I burst out laughing.

"She's weird, Stone."

"Weird or not, it's good news. If she believes in your innocence, and Blakemore dances to her tune, that bodes well for you."

But even as I was saying it I was hearing the hollow ring to the words. Dehan poured the coffee and handed me a cup.

"I can't think of a single reason why that woman would want to help me."

I took the coffee and sipped it.

"Well, maybe she doesn't want to help you, Dehan. Maybe she really did love her husband, and she wants the real killer caught."

She made a doubtful gesture with her head.

"Yeah, maybe."

When I'd finished my coffee, I called Blakemore.

"You're on a mission, huh, Stone? You're determined to make my life a misery."

"This may come as a surprise to you, Blakemore, but this case is not about you. It's about Sergeant Sanchez and Detective Dehan. What I am determined to do is to make sure that Detective Dehan does not go down for a murder she didn't commit."

"Oh, well I guess that makes you one hell of a special guy, Stone."

"You got a call from Mrs. Meyer?"

He made sure I heard the sigh. "Yeah, I got a call from Mrs. Meyer. She asked me, as a special favor to her, to listen to what you have to say, and cooperate with you."

"Well, it sure is heartening to see that law enforcement in the Forty-Fifth is impartial and evenhanded, Detective."

"Kiss my ass."

"I'll let somebody else do that, Blakemore. I'll bet you have a lot of candidates. I'll be there in half an hour."

I had a shower, changed my clothes, and drove back to the 45th. The rain had eased to a spitting drizzle and there was a heavy, claustrophobic stillness in the air, like a storm was building out at sea.

Blakemore was expecting me, and the surly desk sergeant told me to go on up. I found his desk, and he jerked his chin at an empty chair. He leaned back and sighed as I sat and picked up a file which he tossed across the desk to me.

"I don't know how you did it, Stone, but you sold the old lady on your cock-and-bull story."

I ignored the jibe, opened the file, and started leafing through it. I spoke as I scanned the pages.

"If Dehan had done the job, you'd have two homicides and no suspects. It's as simple as that. If you'd taken the trouble to look at her track record and her qualifications, you'd have come to that conclusion yourself."

I paused, reading. The revolver had been recovered in the yard by the fence at the back of the house. I laughed out loud.

His face and his voice were sour. "What's so funny?"

"Tell me something," I said, without looking up. "The slugs you recovered from the mattress, and the slugs you pulled from the wall in the drawing room, were they from the same weapon?"

"Yeah, ballistics showed they were all a match, all from the same gun."

"So here's something you should be having trouble with, Blakemore."

"What?"

"Here's your killer. Somehow, we don't know how, he gets into the house, he climbs the stairs, and goes to where Sanchez is sleeping, and, in the dark, he puts four beautifully grouped rounds into Sanchez's belly. At this point he . . ."

"Or she."

"Yeah, or she, is cool enough to make four perfect shots into Sanchez's belly, in the dark. Now, having killed his victim, he goes downstairs to the living room to make his escape through the French windows. But right at that moment Astrid Meyer walks in. But this time—" I leaned forward, counting out the facts on my fingers. "With the light on, facing an unarmed woman, at thirty feet, he shoots high and wide, twice, like a panicking amateur, and he runs. Does that sound to you like a highly trained officer, three times state pistol shooting champion, third dan in tae kwon do, master of jeet kune do, with more arrests under her belt than any female officer her age, and more than most men twice her age?"

I leaned forward and pointed my finger at him like a gun.

"I have seen Dehan kill a man on more than one occasion, and believe me, she keeps her cool." His face told me he didn't know what to make of that comment, so I told him. "Your killer panicked. Dehan doesn't panic."

"Yeah, tell your attorney to base his defense on that, Stone."

I stopped leafing and squinted at him. "Cut the crap, Blakemore. We're not in court and this is not a competition. This is a murder investigation. I'm a detective trying to communicate with a fellow detective, and I am pointing out to you a powerful line of reasoning. You have the shooting of a pro upstairs, and the shooting of a panicking amateur downstairs. And you should be asking yourself why!"

He sighed and spread his hands like he really didn't care. "What can I say? When she got downstairs she panicked because she knew Astrid would identify her."

"And did she?" He didn't answer, so I went on. "How about you explain to me why, having latex gloves in her pocket, instead of wearing them she left prints all over the crime scene and the weapon? How about you explain to me why, having panicked because Mrs. Meyer was going to identify her, she thoughtfully left the weapon with the prints all over it for the cops to find in the yard by the fence, instead of carrying it across the road and throwing it into Eastchester Bay? You beginning to get an idea what's so funny?"

I paused. Something had caught my eye. He must have noticed because he frowned.

"What?"

I looked him in the eye. "Sanchez was seeing a shrink?"

TEN

He stood, and I watched him walk to the window. His face said he was thinking about all the things he'd like to do to me if he had me alone in a warehouse with chains around my wrists and ankles. He turned and scowled at me, with the gray light of the window behind him.

"Nah," he said. "It was routine. He didn't need it. Brass wanted him to see a counselor. He got knifed breaking up a brawl. These days a goose says boo to you, you gotta see a counselor." He turned away again. "It was touch-and-go. He pulled through. You shouldn't read anything into that."

"Like hell I shouldn't! It says he was going to see her that night. So maybe Detective Dehan was not the last person to see him alive after all! That seems to me to be an important point. So how come he was at the club and not seeing the shrink?"

He made an ugly gesture, hunching his shoulders and pulling down the corners of his mouth.

"So maybe he met the shrink at the club."

"Shanna."

He didn't answer for a bit, staring out at the wet street. "Yeah, Shanna McLean." He turned to face me, waving a hand at me. "Like I said, don't read anything into it. They were old friends.

Everybody here knows Shanna. She's a great shrink, believe me. And Tony and her went back a long way. They were old pals. So they had an appointment and they had their session at the club. Then she went home, and he stayed behind with . . . Detective Dehan."

My mind was racing, making long movies. He didn't like the look on my face. He spoke loudly, as though by shouting he could beat those images out of my brain with his words.

"Either way, it makes no difference, because *her* prints were not found at the crime scene! He did not stay with her till the last minute, and she was *not* the last person to see him alive! Dehan was!"

"But he was *supposed* to see her. Was she at the club? Have you confirmed that?"

"Not yet."

"*Not yet?* You're so damned sure of a conviction you're not even going to talk to her?"

He didn't answer, so I read on, speaking as I went.

"Where does she live?"

"You can't go and see her!"

"Where does she live?"

"You cannot! You are not allowed . . ."

"Where does she live, Blakemore?"

He sighed and ran his hand through his hair. "Son of a *bitch!*" He kept taking steps in no particular direction, bending his knees and half-stamping his feet. "Go to hell! You cannot go there, Stone! You stay out of my goddamn investigation!"

I read on, talking half to myself, "I thought you were supposed to cooperate. So she goes home ahead of him. Then he comes home, but his wife is out celebrating a big contract. Where does he go? Does he go home, or does he go to see his old pal and shrink?"

"You have no grounds. That is pure speculation."

I dropped the file on the desk.

"So, Sergeant Tony Sanchez was an angel. An angel who

wanted more than anything in the world to help the kids. And he was so handsome, so charismatic, and so much darn fun, that most everybody did love him, especially the pretty girls. And maybe *especially* especially the duskier young maidens whom he rescued. And while his older, richer wife was out celebrating her business triumphs, our golden young hero was out providing guidance to the marginalized, the poor, and especially the young, pretty, marginalized, and poor. And his shrink, Shanna McLean, provided him with guidance in his ministries. You going to tell me the truth, or are you going to stick to the crock of shit that everybody else is peddling?"

"I don't like you, Stone."

"Well you just plain gone and broke my heart, Detective Blakemore, because I had honestly become truly fond of you."

His mouth was a twisted snarl. "I know you're here for one thing and one thing alone, to protect your Latina slut of a wife, and you'll destroy Tony's reputation to do it if you have to. Well, the fact is, Stone, Sergeant Tony Sanchez was a beautiful person. He was a good husband to his wife, and if there was gossip from time to time because of the age difference, and because he sometimes went out without her, neither of them ever crossed the line. This is a tight neighborhood here, and they were well loved and well liked. So you keep your wiseass comments to yourself."

I studied his face a moment. He actually looked sincere.

"Noted." I stood. "Thanks for all your help, Blakemore. I'll try to stay out of your way in the future."

He was frowning, confused. I leaned on the back of the chair, like I'd just remembered something. "By the way, I don't like you either. You are a disgrace to your uniform and to your badge. Either you're bent or you're incompetent. Either way, you're going down. And when this is over, you and me are going to find a quiet place, and you're going to tell me again what kind of wife I have."

I stepped out into the cold afternoon. A restless, ill-tempered breeze whipped cold specks of water into my face. I climbed into the Jag, turned the key in the ignition, and the big old engine growled. As I pulled away, I called Dehan.

"Hey, big guy. What gives?"

"Is there anything left of the sack?"

"A few shreds."

"Shanna McLean, that's the shrink from the club, right?"

"Yeah, why?"

"I need to know where she lives."

"How come?"

"Have you got her address? I'm driving now."

"I'm looking. How come you're going to see her?"

"She was Sergeant Sanchez's therapist."

She was quiet for a moment, then asked again, "How come?"

"That's what I want to find out. According to Blakemore he was receiving counseling because he was stabbed in a fight some time back. But I get the feeling it might have been more than his psyche she was tending to."

"Their behavior was not appropriate to a psychologist and client relationship. I always had the feeling that they had known each other for a long time. They were always a bit infantile in each other's company."

"So have you got the address?"

"Yeah, it's here. It's on Griswold Avenue." She told me the number, and I hung up. It was a mile and a half drive. I crossed the Throgs Neck Expressway and followed Shore Drive north until it became Stadium Avenue and then turned right into Griswold. It was a quiet, leafy street, and you'd be forgiven for thinking you were in a sleepy, New England holiday town on the coast. The houses were a jumble of styles, from severe '60s redbrick functionalism to seaside clapboard and mock Tudor cottages, each with their front and backyards. The right-hand side of the road, which included Shanna's house, backed onto the Palmer Inlet, and a number of them had small boats parked in the drive.

Her house was tall, narrow, and very long. It was faced in

white clapboard, with a black Dutch gabled roof, fringed with dormer windows. I pulled in and parked in front of the house, killed the engine, and climbed out. Muddy puddles peppered the sidewalk and her front yard.

I saw a movement behind the screen door, then the screen door opened and a woman you could not describe as attractive stepped out. You could not describe her as attractive because it would be an absurd understatement, like calling the Himalayas tall, or the Pacific quite big.

She was about five ten, with a slim waist and generous hips and bust. Her legs were long, shapely, and graceful, as were her arms. She was wearing faded jeans and a white cotton shirt—a man's shirt—undone to the waist and hanging loose. Her hair was what they used to call an Afro in the late '60s and early '70s. Not exaggerated, but enough to be cute. It framed a face that was astonishing in its beauty. The eyes were long and black, her cheekbones were high, and her lips, though full and generous, were also exquisitely shaped.

She didn't let go of the screen door but moved forward toward the wooden steps down from her porch.

"Are you Detective John Stone?"

I nodded a couple of times. "But I am not here on official police business."

"I know." She didn't seem in a hurry to get away and kept hanging on the door. "I've been warned not to talk to you."

I decided that was an invitation to get closer, so I put my hands in my pockets and strolled to the bottom of the steps.

"Yeah? Who gave you a silly warning like that?"

"Who says it's silly?"

I put my foot on the first wet, wooden step. She didn't complain. I said, "I do."

"Oh," she said, and then, "So if you're not here on official business, why should I talk to you?"

I took another three steps till I was only a couple of feet away from her, level with her chest, and looking up into her face. Her eyes were large and amused. I said, "Because you were in love with Sergeant Sanchez and you'd like his killer caught?"

Some of the amusement dulled in her eyes, and she took a step back. I climbed the rest of the way to the porch and stood looking down at her. "Am I wrong?"

She shrugged, tilting her head sideways and pulling down the corners of her mouth.

"Only a lot."

"Sure, are you willing to talk to me?"

"Well, that depends. If you want to talk nonsense about me being in love with Tony, then we'd be wasting our time. And I am not into wasting my time, Detective Stone."

"Saving an innocent woman from spending thirty years in prison, falsely accused of murder, sounds to me like a good use of time, especially if it helps to catch the real murderer."

She raised her chin in a silent nod. "So what's it to you?"

"The woman accused of killing him, Carmen Dehan, is my partner and my wife."

"Oh," she said, and after a moment she added, "What is she first, your partner or your wife?"

"My wife."

"I know Carmen. She's beautiful, and smart."

"Yeah, she's also a good cop and a sharp observer."

She arched an eyebrow. "Meaning?"

"Meaning that even though at the time she didn't know that Sanchez was supposed to be your client, she realized you were more than just old pals. And you can take, as a rider to that, that now that I know Sanchez *was* supposed to be seeing you professionally, as his counselor, I haven't the slightest doubt in my mind that you and he were lovers."

She nodded a few times, gazing down the street. "Wow," she said at last. "Is this some kind of subtle blackmail?"

I frowned hard. "I don't understand, Shanna. I am assuming that you and I both want the same thing: to know who murdered

Sanchez. That being the case, why would I want, or need, to blackmail you?"

She didn't meet my eyes. She gave a small shrug and stuck out her bottom lip.

"You're right."

"So can we talk?"

"Sure." She spread her hands, and there was amusement in her eyes, bordering on mischief. "It's what we're doing. You want a beer?"

"Sure. I could use a beer."

I followed her through the screen door into a very tasteful, elegant room with hardwood floors and cream, calico armchairs and sofas, heavy, polished wood occasional tables, and lamps that were more works of art than simple lighting. She had original paintings on the wall that were good, and a couple of bull skins scattered carelessly over the hardwood floors.

It wasn't so much a room as a space, and we crossed it into a second space which was a kitchen—the kind of kitchen you might expect to find in a sci-fi movie, with emphasis on stark, metal lines and highly polished steel. She pulled a couple of Grimms from the fridge and asked me, "You need a glass?" like she was going to judge me according to my answer.

"I don't need one, but I'd like one."

She took a glass from a cupboard and went out through a door into the backyard. There she had a thirty-foot turquoise swimming pool that was getting wet in the rain, a lawn, and a patio table under a brown-and-beige awning. She put my beer and my glass on the table and sat in a white chair with striped pink cushions. I sat too and poured my beer while she watched me.

"I like to sit outside in the rain. It feels nice on your skin."

"Sure. How long did you and Tony know each other?"

She made a soft explosion through her lips. "All our lives. We met in kindergarten. We stayed close after that. We went to school together, went to prom together, hung out together . . ."

"Did you make out together in high school too?"

Her face froze; her eyelids drooped. "That's pretty crude."

"No, it's direct. Did you?"

"Yeah, I also lost my virginity with him when I was fifteen."

"Did he lose it too, or was it just you?"

"I'm not sure what you're driving at with these questions, Detective? What are you actually trying to find out?"

"I'm trying to understand the victim. If I can understand the victim, maybe I can get a line on his killer."

"You think maybe he was killed by somebody he lost his virginity to when he was fifteen?"

"Are you going to keep trying to deflect me with questions of your own?"

She was watching the drops make circles in the luminous pool.

"There wouldn't be much point, would there?"

"I'm not sure why you'd want to try."

"You're right. It's a bad habit. It can help clients to focus their minds."

"It's helping me to focus mine. You're being evasive, which means you have something to hide. You're not making a great job of it, so you are climbing fast up my list of favorite suspects."

She arched an eyebrow at me, then threw back her head and laughed a deep, rich, resonant laugh.

"I know the compliment was unintentional," she said, "but thank you anyway."

"You think I'm bluffing?" I took a swig and set down my beer carefully on the table. "Let's see. You've been in love with Sergeant Sanchez since you were, what, twelve? But unlike most schoolgirl crushes, yours never wore off. It just got stronger. It didn't help that Sanchez, instead of becoming awkward and spotty in his teens and early twenties, just got more good-looking and more charismatic. You watched in silence, pretending you were cool, as he slept with one woman after another. After you lost your virginity to him, you hoped things would change, but they never did."

She drew breath to say something, but I raised my hand.

"It would have been okay if he had just moved on, right? But he never did. He always came back to you, because you were special to him in some way, but not in the right way. And every time he did, you thought this would be the one where he stayed."

She gave a little grunt and sighed, and looked away again.

"But here's where it started to get dark. When he got the brilliant idea of setting up the youth club. Not only would everybody love and admire him even more than they did already, but he would have an almost inexhaustible supply of beautiful young women to feed on."

She shook her head. "That's not . . ."

"But that wasn't the worst thing. The worst thing was when Detective Carmen Dehan came along. Because until then the girls who had come and gone in his life had been lightweight, passing fancies, not real threats. But not Dehan. Dehan was not only as beautiful as you, but she was also smart, focused on her work, and unavailable. That made her a real threat. And I'm going to go out on a limb and say that Sergeant Sanchez was becoming increasingly interested in her. And after three months, that was more than you could stomach. So you killed him."

"Very creative. You should write books . . ."

"You should quit giving me the runaround and start talking to me."

She took a deep breath and puffed out her cheeks. "Tony was very charismatic, *very* good-looking, and he and I became lovers when we were in our early teens. He wasn't a good lover, and neither was I. We are—were—both narcissistic, selfish lovers, with little concern for our partners. But I guess because we knew each other so well, we could just relax and enjoy our selfishness with each other. We didn't have to try. So in a bizarre kind of way, it worked." She paused, tipping her bottle this way and that. "But you're wrong about the jealousy. He could sleep with a hundred women or a thousand, I knew he would always come back to me. And as for Dehan . . ." She hesitated a moment, and I felt a lurch of heat and fear in my gut. "However much they might have been attracted to each other, I knew he couldn't cope with her. That girl is high-maintenance and very demanding. He was too damned self-absorbed, like I said. She'd chew him up and throw him out in a week."

I fought and resisted the temptation to ask about them. Instead I said, "That's a pretty damning assessment of him. Most people think he's a saint."

She shrugged, took a long pull on her beer, and set the bottle on the table, with a soft belch.

"That's because nobody knew Tony like I did. He had boundless energy, he kept himself in shape, and he was reasonably intelligent. And he learned at an early age that society loves a project, especially a charitable project aimed at ethnic children and youngsters. But what is more important, people adore—and I mean literally adore—people who start and run projects of that sort. Tony loved himself with a passion, but he could not do without people. He needed other people to love him too. So Tony was forever starting projects. They all failed because Tony was always fooling around. He didn't really give a damn about the projects. He was just feeding on the attention. Until he started this one. This one was a real success."

"What was different about this one?"

I knew the answer, even as I asked the question, and she looked at me like the answer was obvious.

"What was different about this one was Carmen. She showed up right at the beginning and pretty much took over. And while Tony and I fooled around, she made the thing work."

I thought about it for a while. The rain grew suddenly heavier, turning her back lawn into a quagmire, raising a spiky mist off the turquoise pool.

"Who wanted him dead, Shanna?"

"You mean apart from Carmen?"

"Why the hell would Dehan want Sanchez dead?"

Her smile was tinged with pity. "You're really in love with her, aren't you?" I didn't answer. "I don't want to hurt you, but you need to know the truth. She was into Tony in a big way. I wasn't always here, and I knew they were always the last two to leave. I always assumed they were making it at least a couple of times a week."

"How does that translate into a motive for murder?"

"Maybe he wanted to make it permanent, and she wanted to go back to you." She smiled. "I could understand that."

"Noted, who else?"

She thrust out her bottom lip in an exaggerated pout and shook her head.

"Nobody. I can't think of anybody else."

ELEVEN

I stood and looked down at my glass of beer on the table, practically untouched. I couldn't hide the bitterness in my voice. "Thanks for your help."

She didn't answer. She didn't look at me. I hesitated, about to turn and leave, but instead I went on.

"It's a question I have to ask myself. He must have been almost like a brother to you, only a lot more than that. Closer than any brother or friend could ever be, but closer than a husband or a boyfriend too."

Her eyes were lost in the sodden grass. Her face was expressionless, her expression trancelike.

"You'd think," I said, "that you would want the killer found and punished more than anything else on Earth. You know Blakemore isn't interested in the truth, you know Dehan didn't do this, and yet . . ."

She still didn't answer. "So I have to ask myself, what is it that makes you try to obscure the issue, withhold information, mislead me. What is it that makes you behave as though you were trying to protect the killer?"

She looked up at me. "Is that what I'm doing?"

"You're behaving as though you were trying to protect the killer, yes."

She stood and moved toward me. She was a bit too tall, her bosom was a bit too large, her hips were a bit too wide, but when it all came together, she was electrifying. She stood just inches away from me. I could smell her musky perfume and, mixed with it, the sweet scent of her skin.

"I think Dehan must have been crazy."

I fought to control my breath. "Dehan is anything but crazy . . ."

"If she chose Tony over you, she was crazy. You're ten times the man he was, and I bet you're a hundred times the lover."

She placed her palms on my chest and closed her eyes. "You don't know how long I have been searching . . ."

I growled, "What are you doing, Shanna?"

She let her hands slide down my chest and looked up into my face. Her eyes closed, and she took a deep breath, then let it out as a sigh.

"Forget it. Most men . . ." she said.

"Most men what?"

"Would want to get even."

"Most men," I said quietly, "would not notice that once again you had shifted the focus of the conversation. Now you're telling me that you want to hide the killer so badly you're prepared to hit the sack with a complete stranger?"

"God!" She slammed both her palms against my chest. "How can a man like you be such a prude!"

I snatched her wrists in both my hands and squeezed hard, dragging her so close our bodies were touching. I felt her tremble and saw her eyes open wide. Her mouth was a couple of inches from mine. I could taste the peppermint on her breath.

"Who?" I rasped.

She pressed her body hard against mine. It was supple and smooth. I snarled.

"Who wanted him dead?"

"I don't know." She rested her head on my shoulder, and I felt her lips brush my neck. I shoved her, and she stumbled back. For a second her eyes were dangerous.

"I don't know yet who wanted him dead. But I know one person who doesn't give a damn that he is."

"Jesus!" She turned away and put her palms to her forehead, driving her fingers deep into her hair.

"He'd grown bored with her! Okay? He loved her, but she'd become an old woman." She turned back to see how I was taking what she was saying. "She hadn't grown old in years, but in her attitudes, her mentality, her priorities. He was young, hungry, curious. She was a . . ." She spread her hands and shrugged. "She was a *Realtor*! The sexiest thing she ever did was sell a house. Then she'd get excited, get drunk, come home, and go to sleep."

"Why'd he marry her?"

"I told you. He loved her."

I couldn't keep the sneer from my voice. "What was it about her that he loved?"

"Jesus, you're cheap!"

"I've been around the block a few times, sister, and I think I passed you a few times going the other way. So don't play the injured idealist with me. Did he marry her for her money?"

Suddenly she looked exhausted. She held my eye, and her expression was one of sadness. Her voice was barely a whisper.

"John, I am so tired . . ."

"Of what?"

"Of pretending. Of lies and living this hollow, empty life."

"*Did he marry her for her money?*"

"*Yes!*"

Suddenly I was shouting. "*Then why the hell don't you tell me! Why do you keep dodging and weaving and avoiding?*"

I saw her jaw moving, like she was trying to form words. Then she closed her eyes like she had given up.

"You wouldn't understand."

"Well you'd better make me understand, Shanna, because you may be able to pull this shit with Blakemore. But not with me."

"Pig!" she said, without feeling.

"So he was having affairs."

"Yes." Vicious spite twisted her face. "Amongst others, with your wife!" I didn't answer, and she looked away. "I am pretty sure Astrid knew, but don't let your imagination run away with you, John. For all her flaws, she's a kind, gentle woman. She has no imagination, and no malice."

"Is this who you're trying to protect?"

She wouldn't meet my eye. "I'm not trying to protect anyone. I just lost my closest friend, my lover, the only real family I ever had. I'm confused, tired, and in pain."

"And you'd like me to leave now."

"No, I'd like you to stay and hold me, and make me forget. But I know you won't."

"The night he was killed, you left before him and Dehan. Did he go to you, or did he go straight home?"

"Do you mind if I smoke?" I didn't answer.

She pulled a pack of Camels from the breast pocket of her shirt. She shook one free, put it between her lips, and lit up. She inhaled deep, then let out the smoke in a long stream. "He was with me. We were going to go to an all-night club, Under the Clock, have some fun . . ."

"But you didn't go."

She shook her head. "We stayed and talked. He was upset. He didn't know what to do about Astrid. He had stopped sleeping with her."

"They had separate rooms?"

She nodded, trailing smoke from her nose. "He'd moved into one of the spare rooms. Made an excuse about sleep apnea. Astrid was in denial."

"There was somebody else. It wasn't Dehan, and it wasn't you."

"Talk about denial. Listen, John, your wife was sleeping with Tony. Accept it. It happens, and it has happened to you."

"Who's the other person?"

She shrugged, like she didn't care. "He frequented a club, I told you, Under the Clock, on Raymond Avenue, up by the depot. Sometimes I went with him. Other times he went alone. But the only woman I am aware of whom he took a serious interest in was Carmen."

I frowned. "So if he met a woman and wanted to have sex with her, they had to go back to her place? That must have been a real passion killer." I raised an eyebrow. "Or did he bring them here?"

She screwed up her face. "Jesus, John! No!"

"So what did he do?"

She shrugged, shook her head, stuck out her lower lip, and looked away. It was eloquent.

"Oh," I said, "he had an apartment which he used. A cozy studio. Did you both use it?"

Her voice had a bitter twist. "I have my own house, John. Aside from which you may be surprised to discover that I do not sleep around. The only man I slept with was Tony. That was it. He was the man I loved, for better or worse."

"Did he suffer from hypersexuality?"

"Yes, though I think what he really suffered from was a chronic lack of affection, which expressed itself in a craving for physical, sexual contact."

"So he came to you for help. It had nothing to do with the stabbing, had it? His appetite was getting out of control, and he turned to you for help."

"Are you telling me or asking me?" I didn't answer. I waited. "He came to me for help. He told the captain at the precinct a cock-and-bull story about the stabbing and got them to foot the bill."

"Have you got a large private practice?"

"I get by. So I advised him to create a space for himself, where he could disconnect emotionally from his marriage and make a wise, balanced choice about his future, about what he wanted to do with his life."

"Did you go there with him?"

"Once or twice, not often. It was his space. Don't ask me if he took lovers there. I just don't know. I assume he did."

"Where is this apartment?"

"It's a house, not an apartment. Soundview Terrace, right down on Locust Point, near the bridge, corner of Indian Trail. It's a small house, it has a backyard, it's right by the water. It was a perfect place for him to find his own space and decide who he was and what he wanted to do with his life."

"Do the cops know about this place?"

She stared at me a moment, then shook her head. "I don't think so. I haven't told them, and I was one of the few that knew it existed."

I thought for a moment, digesting this.

"What time did he leave you to go home?"

"It must have been ten thirty, ten thirty-five."

I had nothing left to ask her, but I knew she had a lot more to tell me. We stood a moment staring at each other, while she sucked on her cigarette and waited for me to say or do something.

Finally I said, "Thanks for the beer. You've been helpful. More than you intended to be, I think."

She followed me to the front door. There she stopped me before I opened it.

"If you think of more questions, or anything else you want to know, or talk about . . ." She slipped a card into my hand. "This is my home number. Call me anytime if you . . . you know, want to talk."

I studied her face and her eyes. I was struck again by how perfect they were. I nodded. She watched me walk down the wet steps, hunched against the rain, to my car. As I opened the door she said, "Call me."

I didn't answer. I got in the car, turned silently around, and headed back the way I had come.

I called Dehan and told her to meet me at Emilio's Pizza on Morris Park Avenue. It took me a little over half an hour to get there in heavy traffic and a mist of spray on the freeway, but when I got there and walked through the door, stamping my feet and shaking my coat, I saw Dehan sitting at our usual table by the open fire, nursing a beer. She smiled sheepishly. I handed Emilio my coat and told him I'd have a beer and we'd have a look at the menu. Then I joined Dehan at the table. I gave her a kiss, sat, and said, "I went to see Shanna."

She stared at her glass, tipping it this way and that. "Yeah? What did you think?"

"It seems Sanchez was not as happy in his marriage as most people seemed to think."

Her face remained impassive. "I was never under the impression he had an especially happy marriage. Neither did I think it was on the rocks . . ." She shrugged.

"Seems he was planning to divorce Astrid."

She frowned, seemed to have a brief internal dialogue, and finished off by taking a pull on her beer. As she set it down she said, "I guess that could be significant, but it cuts both ways."

I gave a single nod. "Let me run some thoughts by you. Then we'll try and make sense of them. First: when I went to see the crime scene, in the room where Sanchez was killed there was a hell of a lot of blood on and around the bed. There were four shots to the belly, and death would have come quickly. I would have expected the bleeding to stop shortly after that. But this was more blood than I have ever seen from that kind of wound."

She studied me a moment. "We can't approach Frank, Stone. The ME is out of bounds to us, and we would put him and Joe in an impossible situation."

"I know, so we have to rely on our own experience. And what I saw was a large bed, maybe king size, with a feather duvet, and the whole thing was saturated with blood, right down to the floor. That's a hell of a lot of blood."

She nodded agreement. "That is a lot."

"Then, the shots were accurate at about twenty feet, maybe a little more, and well grouped. But once he got downstairs our killer couldn't have hit an elephant. Astrid got home and disturbed him, and at thirty feet he fired twice. This time his shots went three or four feet wide and high of the target. That's hard to explain.

"He's just killed a cop at this distance, but now, faced with a forty-year-old female Realtor, he panics and runs. Astrid got off three rounds, but she was just as bad a shot as the killer was."

Emilio brought my beer, and we ordered a couple of pepperoni pizzas and an avocado salad. When he'd gone, I leaned back, took a long pull on my beer, and smacked my lips.

"So, how does this work, Dehan? I'm trying to make movies in my head. Sanchez has been out at the club. His wife is still out having dinner with colleagues. Sanchez leaves the club but—you don't know this—instead of going home, he goes to visit Shanna."

She slammed both hands down on the table, then shrugged and spread her hands.

"Well, there it is, Stone, goddamn it! That's my alibi! I'm not the last person to see him alive anymore!"

I smiled. "That's true, but it's not that simple either."

"Why not?"

"Obviously we will give this to Cohen, but we will have to convince Shanna to testify in court, and I don't know what she's hiding, Dehan, but she is hiding something, and she is very unwilling to talk. Plus, Blakemore is gunning for you. He wants you to take the rap. I don't know why."

"So what time did he leave Shanna?"

"Somewhere between eleven and eleven thirty."

"That makes events very tight at the house."

"I know, and if Shanna is telling the truth, it also raises a big problem. Let me run through it: it gives him about half an hour to get home, which is just five hundred yards away, get undressed, get into bed, and for the killer to show up and kill him, and then escape."

She was shaking her head. "The killer—or, more precisely, the killers—were waiting for him to get home. One of them was upstairs in one of the bedrooms, the other was on watch downstairs. One of them was a pro, accustomed to using guns and accustomed to killing. The other was an amateur who had never killed anyone before. That explains the poor shooting downstairs."

I winced. "Yeah, but what happens to the pro upstairs when Astrid gets home? It would take him ten seconds, fifteen max, to get down and plug her in the back. Instead he vanished. Where did he go?"

"He left before his accomplice. Astrid disturbed them just after he had gone out."

I grunted. "Yeah, it's possible, only the rounds are all from the same gun. They'd have to have swapped guns. Also, it leaves one major question unanswered."

"What?"

"What the hell was he doing in the master bedroom if they were not sleeping together and he had moved to one of the guest rooms?"

TWELVE

She sat staring at me and blinking.

Emilio brought the pizzas, and we ordered a couple more beers. Outside the afternoon was turning to dusk early under lowering clouds. A squally wind hurled handfuls of rain at the glass in the windows, and the fire guttered and flared. Emilio laid a couple more logs on among the flames.

Dehan went to speak a couple of times, but each time she returned to her pizza. Finally she tore off a wedge and said, "For the first time I feel hopeful, Stone."

I smiled and bit into a chunk of my own pizza.

"I don't want to put a downer on that, but you need to know this. Shanna stressed over and again that you were having an affair with Sanchez."

Her cheeks flushed bright pink, and her eyes sparkled with tears.

"Do you believe her?"

"I believe that if it were true you would tell me. I am not so naïve as to think it is impossible for you to fall in love with another man." Her look of shock turned to a scowl. I ignored it and went on. "But I do think that it is practically impossible for you, being who you are, to be dishonest and unfaithful. And from what I have heard today, I don't think Sergeant Sanchez was the man to make you do the virtually impossible. I don't think you go for infantile men, but Shanna says I am in a state of denial..."

"You're not!"

"I agree. She also tried to seduce me."

She froze with her mouth full of pizza.

"What did you do?"

"After I had asked her what the hell she was doing?"

"Yeah, after that."

"I asked her who wanted Sanchez dead."

She grinned, laughed around her pizza, and said, "I believe you. It must have been hard. She's as hot as a Tex-Mex picnic on Mercury, so I appreciate it."

I didn't smile. I didn't feel amused. I felt unhappy, and I was craving a hot shower.

"It wasn't hard, Dehan. There are no doubts in my mind about whom I want to share my bed with."

She paused in her chewing to regard me and smile. "Nor mine, big guy. You're the whom."

"Good. So, Dehan, we are left with one very important question among several others: Why was he in bed in the master bedroom? But that question begs another."

"How did the killer know which bedroom he would be in?"

I nodded. "Exactly. The killer was either very well informed or completely ignorant of what was going on at the Sanchez-Meyer household. I have to say that the latter seems very unlikely. How did he know Sanchez would be home? How did he know Astrid wouldn't...?"

"It's a bit of a mess..."

"And of course we have to add to this almighty mess the one detail that only you and I know to be a fact, that you are being framed by somebody with the skill and daring to steal your prints and frame you. That is pretty cold-blooded."

She was frowning hard. "So, this gets pretty deep. Are you saying that it was timed so Astrid would come home and find the killer?" I drew breath to answer, but she was still talking. "So that . . ." She wagged a finger at me across the table. "*That* would be another explanation for the shots. I gotta hand it to you, Stone. You are smart! Astrid was intended to see the killer get away. The killer deliberately missed the shots . . ."

"That wasn't all he missed."

"Uh-huh," she said, without really registering what I had said, "because she was supposed to see somebody who looked like me, escaping through the French windows and making for the wood, where they would find the gun with my prints on it."

"That is a possibility." I felt suddenly weary, like I was trying to untangle spaghetti with woolen gloves on. "But the main question, the thing we really need to know, is who benefits from his death. We are looking at somebody who will prosper when Sanchez dies, somebody who was familiar with the goings-on at the club *and* the goings-on in their private lives, someone able to plant traps for you to leave your prints, somebody who plans ahead, a good shot, and someone who is ruthless enough to use a gun and kill a person."

She grunted. "Or able to get somebody else to do it for them."

"Yes," I said, and nodded. "That too."

We ate in silence for a while. The fire crackled and spat, and its warm air filled my head with drowsiness. I was aware of heavy, dark fingers trying to close my eyes, and Dehan was saying, "Stone, Shanna is the only one who ticks all of those boxes."

I drained my beer and shook my head to try to clear it.

"How does Shanna benefit from Sanchez's death, Dehan?"

"She was jealous. She was sick of being taken for granted. You said she's convinced there was something between me and Tony. That might have been the straw that broke the camel's back. She had opportunity, motive, and access to Tony's revolver." She held up a hand. "Tony went to see her. What did they talk about? For all we know Tony might have been talking about divorcing Astrid. I told you myself they were a terrible match. So he doesn't go home alone. She goes with him. She tells him they should meet

Astrid together and lay it on her. But instead, when they are alone together, she shoots him . . ."

"In the master bedroom?"

She leaned forward. "You don't know what they were like, Stone. They were like kids, playing all the time. She might well have suggested they hit the sack in the master bedroom . . ."

"And she shoots him right there."

"Places the fingerprints . . ."

"We need to look into what's involved in doing that."

She arched an eyebrow. "You don't like her for it?"

"I don't dislike her for it. But the theory still leaves a couple of things unanswered."

"Like?"

I sighed and tried to gather my thoughts.

"Let's call this person X."

"Unoriginal, but I'll let it go this once."

"The crime starts about two or three weeks before the killing, the day you were going home early, or trying to, and they all started playing with balloons."

She grunted and nodded. "Okay."

"We can't prove it, but for the sake of the argument let's say the balloon covered in latex was the device they used to get your prints."

"Makes sense."

"Now, in the following two to three weeks our killer makes either finger pads or he or she imprints your prints onto the fingers of latex gloves, and seeks opportunities to place your prints at the scene in such a way as to suggest you were having an affair. So the person, X, had access to the house. Now, Shanna definitely had opportunity to fix up the balloon, but getting into the house to plant prints is going to be a lot more difficult for her. Astrid isn't exactly crazy about her. I doubt she had easy access to the house."

She grunted and sighed, and stared at the flames. "That is tricky."

"So our major problems: One, how did they get your prints into the house; two, how do we explain Sanchez's being in the master bedroom and in the matrimonial bed? Their sleeping in separate rooms is one of the few things Shanna told me that I feel I can actually believe."

Dehan nodded. "I agree."

"And three, equally difficult if not more so, why did he bleed so much? According to the report, he was shot four times in the gut. One shot you could bleed for a long time, but four? That would kill him almost instantly, partly from massive hemorrhaging, and partly from shock. So there would be considerable amounts of blood pooled in the legs and the arms. So, what made him bleed so much?"

She was watching me carefully. "There is obviously something on your mind, Stone, but I am not getting it."

I sighed. "That's it, neither am I. But the point is, Dehan, even if he had been exsanguinated . . ." I hesitated, unsure of my own conclusion. "I think there was too much blood."

She frowned. "Shit! Seriously? What would that mean? That it was somebody else's blood? That somebody else had been killed there? A bigger person? And he came home early and found the body?" I sighed, unsatisfied, but she went on. "Jesus, Stone, that would mean I wasn't being framed for his murder, but for somebody else's!"

"But we have no access to the ME's report on the blood. We need the report on that blood, Dehan."

"How the hell do we get that?"

I nodded and grimaced. "We'll have to wait and see." I drummed my fingers on the table. "That blood is all wrong. How does that movie play out?" I was squinting at my own thoughts, trying to make sense of them. "He shoots Sanchez, the bed is already drenched? Or . . . what? What the hell is Sanchez doing undressed in a blood-soaked bed? He had to be in the bed because the bullets go right through the duvet, him, and into the mattress."

I paused, trying to see it, failed, and went on.

"Then X goes calmly downstairs and waits for Astrid? And when she comes in he shoots twice at the wall and runs . . . It's so full of holes you could strain pasta with it." I pointed at her. "I'll tell you this. We work out why there is so much blood, and we have the case."

She took a deep breath. "I sure hope you're right, Stone. I sure hope you're right." She considered her glass a moment, clenched her brow, and looked at me. "You know, there is one angle we have not considered."

"Yeah?"

"Think about it. Everybody loves him. Nobody except Shanna, and she's a bionic bitch, has a bad word to say about him. Now, granted, I like my men a bit more mature and with a bit more gravitas, and he was a bit too childlike and enthusiastic, but I have to admit he was loveable and charismatic. You couldn't dislike him or hate him. Plus, he does good works for the community, the environment. I mean, who hates a guy like this enough to kill him? And four slugs in the belly, that is a cruel way to kill. That is a punishment killing."

"I agree. So what is it we haven't considered?"

"Well, at first I thought maybe there was a jealous lover, or a husband whose wife had strayed. But from what I can gather, his affairs were pretty limited in scope. It was either bad girls at the club, or girls he picked up when he went out at night. He was not into breaking up marriages or moving in on established couples. And Stone, whatever Shanna says, he never made a move on me."

I frowned. "Okay, so what am I supposed to be seeing here?"

She sighed. "Look, we are asking ourselves, what the hell was he doing in the master bedroom, right? Here is a guy without enemies who gets killed in a place where he wasn't supposed to be . . ."

I raised my eyebrows high on my brow. "Oh . . ."

"So, okay, maybe we're asking the wrong question. Just imagine, for the sake of the argument, that Tony leaves the club, goes to Shanna's, and they have a long, deep conversation, and—remember, this is a basically good guy—he has some kind of epiphany. You said yourself that Shanna was pretty bitter about him. Well, maybe the reason was because he had decided *not* to divorce her, but to stick with his wife."

I grunted. She went on.

"Stone, in the club he never shut up lecturing the kids about the value of family, being loyal and faithful, how parents influence their kids. I don't know, maybe he decided to have kids, maybe he started to repent for his promiscuous behavior. The point is, his presence in his own matrimonial bed need not be that complicated to explain. It may be perfectly normal and in character."

I nodded. "That is a very good point..."

"However"—she raised a long index—"like you said earlier, the killer's presence there is much harder to explain. Because if my theory is right, only he and Shanna knew about his epiphany. Unless the killer was not there for Tony. Maybe the killer was there for Astrid, a woman who might well have made enemies over the years. Maybe we've been barking up the wrong tree all along. Maybe Tony was never the target, maybe the target was Astrid."

"Son of a gun."

"She is a ruthless businesswoman; she is not loveable or charismatic. I'm not saying she is evil, or even worse than most, but her family has made a lot of money over the years, and people either love them or hate them."

"And it still stands that the killer chose you to frame because the gossip was that you and Sanchez were involved."

"I guess, yeah."

"So we are back to our small pool of suspects again, with Shanna popping up all the time trying to claim center stage."

Dehan leaned back and pursed her lips. "I can see her taking out Astrid a damn sight more easily than Tony. I always believed she was in love with him, and now from what you've told me, she has been in love with him for about fifteen years. She sees his marriage to Astrid going to pieces and dares to hope. But after their conversation, he tells her he intends to reconcile with her, maybe have kids. She flips and kills him."

"But what about your prints, Dehan? This was a murder that was planned well in advance."

"Sure, she could have been planning it for a long while, and finally came to a decision. 'If he divorces her and comes to me, he lives. If he goes back with her, he dies.'"

"What about the shooting? You see her as a marksman?"

"I have no idea. We could look into her background, but she wouldn't be the first girl to grow up with her daddy teaching her to shoot to protect herself. Besides." She shrugged. "Who *are* our other suspects?"

"Brainstorming, regardless of how realistic they are as candidates: first place always goes to the husband or wife, right? So Astrid has to be a candidate."

"Except that she did not know that Tony had returned home, and she exchanged fire with the killer in the living room."

I nodded. "And then there is the mysterious Mr. Tombs, whom we have been neglecting, Dehan."

"Yeah, that's true, and I have to say, Stone, he ties in rather nicely with the Astrid as intended victim theory. He was working for somebody, hunting for a hit man to take the fall, couldn't find one, and decided to put me in the frame instead."

I took a deep breath and sighed loudly. For a moment I felt that despite the seriousness of our predicament, and the efforts I had made so far, we had made virtually no progress. And I was acutely aware of not having the vast resources of the NYPD at my fingertips.

"Well, here's one thing you could do, Dehan . . ."

"I already decided I cannot sit at home another day doing nothing, Stone."

"Oh . . . ?" I tried to frown and raise an eyebrow at the same time.

"I called Saul and told him I was on his team as an investigator as of tomorrow. He was delighted and said if I made out, he'd offer me a job once the case was over. I'm going over to the Bay View tomorrow morning."

"Good, that fits in very nicely. Look into Astrid's background, her business interests and recent operations. Likewise her dad. Find out everything and anything you can about her. Obviously we are looking for any brush she might have had with organized crime, any deals where she might have upset the Mob, that sort of thing."

"What are you going to do?"

"I'm going to tail her. I want to see where she goes, who she talks to . . . Whether she is the prime suspect or the intended victim, I want to know who she talks to and whom she connects with in these next few days."

"I agree, it makes sense."

I stared into the flames for a long moment, watching the occasional spit and shower of sparks. Finally I frowned, looked straight into Dehan's eyes, and asked her, "What do you know about a property on Soundview Terrace and Indian Trail?"

She frowned. "What is that, Clason Point?"

I shook my head. "Throggs Neck, Locust Point."

Her eyebrows rose, and she shook her head. "You want me to check into it?"

"Yeah." I gave her the number. "It's the place he used to take his lovers."

She gave a small laugh and shook her head. "So, did I pass?"

I smiled and nodded. "You did, but I failed miserably."

"You did that, big guy. You did that!"

THIRTEEN

Dehan took my car to the Bay View after breakfast. I gave her a half hour start and took her car—an anonymous-looking dark blue Chevy Cruze—by way of Middletown to the Eastchester Bay and parked on the corner of Bayview Avenue and Watt, with a clear view of Astrid Meyer's drive. It was eight thirty in the morning, and I had brought with me a flask of coffee and a pack of croissants. Dehan had told me that the proper thing for a stakeout was donuts, but I don't like donuts.

Nothing happened until noon, except that it rained a lot. Then Astrid Meyer's dark blue Audi nosed out of the drive and turned right onto Bay Shore Avenue. I gave her a minute and followed.

I stayed well back, so even if Stuart, her driver, took the trouble to look in his mirror, he wouldn't notice me. I trailed them down to the Bronxonia Yacht Club and then across the Throgs Neck toll bridge to Queens. There they turned west onto the Cross Island Parkway and followed the spaghetti of expressways and interstates to Queens Boulevard, where the Audi pulled up outside a white, twenty-story building. I pulled in too, outside a Subway, and watched Stuart climb out and open the door for Astrid. Astrid climbed out and made her way through the sliding glass doors of the office block, and Stuart got back in his car and drove away.

I climbed out of the Chevy and ran along the sidewalk, skidded to a halt outside the plate glass doors, and strolled in like I went there every day. I spotted Astrid Meyer standing at the elevators and planted myself in front of a list of offices by floor, and some brass plaques on the wall. The elevator doors opened, and she stepped in with a couple of other people. The doors closed, and the LED panel above the elevator began to flash numbers. It stopped at three, then continued to seven, stopped, and went on to fifteen, then began to descend again. I looked at the list of offices. The third floor didn't give me much: an employment office, a literary agent, a dentist, and a gynecologist. The seventh gave me a financial advisor, a psychiatrist, and a shipping consultant, but the fifteenth floor held Freidland, Schneider and Gottlieb, attorneys-at-law.

I went back to the Chevy, dropped some coins in the meter, and sat and waited as raindrops accumulated on my windshield. At one thirty, three men in suits came out holding large, black umbrellas over a woman. The woman was Astrid Meyer. The other three I had never seen before, but they had that unmistakable look of attorneys about them. One was tall and stooping in a well-cut, charcoal-gray suit. The man next to him had steel-gray hair, a military bearing, and a double-breasted jacket, while the third was short, rotund, completely bald, and very emphatic in the way he spoke. They walked and talked and jostled their way through hunched, hurrying people and a bobbing sea of umbrellas, toward the parking lot in back of the building, pausing every few steps for the rotund guy to stress a point. I took a few pictures on my phone, then pressed the ignition and moved forward until I caught sight of them again, climbing into a dark blue Cadillac.

I called Cohen.

"Stone, what can I do for you?"

"What do you know about Freidland, Schneider and Gottlieb, attorneys-at-law?"

"Not a lot. They are a venerable firm of attorneys in Queens. They deal mainly in six- and seven-figure property deals. Why?"

They pulled out of the lot onto the boulevard, and I followed.

"Because Astrid Meyer just got into a Caddy with three attorneys from that firm." I sent him the pictures.

"Well, that's hardly surprising. They specialize in real estate transactions, property law, trusts, that kind of stuff. Which is precisely the field she works in. She probably uses them all the time. What do they look like?"

"I just sent you the pictures."

The wipers squeaked for a while as I moved through the traffic. After a moment Cohen grunted and said, "The short, fat one is Gottlieb. He owns the firm. Freidland and Schneider are just names on the letterhead now. The tall, stooping one and the one with the gray hair, I think I know them, but they are probably just junior partners."

I thanked him and hung up.

I followed the Caddy along the Union Turnpike as far as Lake Success, where they joined Lakeville Road and turned north, toward Kings Point. The rain remained steady, but as Lakeville Road became Middle Neck Road, it began to ease to drizzle again.

After about four and a half miles of winding among palatial mansions, each set in their own grounds, we eventually came to a large, ultramodern, three-story monstrosity at the very end of Kings Point Road. It was set right on the shores of the East River, surrounded by dense woodland, and seemed to be made of whitewashed concrete and vast sheets of plate glass, surmounted by tiers of slate-gray gables that had the look and feel of a nuclear fallout shelter, or a space-age fortress.

The Caddy turned in through the rolling steel gates and, as I drove slowly past, I saw it pull up at the foot of a short flight of granite steps flanked by exotic gardens. A flunky emerged and trotted down to the car. Then they all vanished from view. I cruised on, listening to the wet hiss of my tires and the squeak and thud of the wipers. Pretty soon after that I came to the end of the road. It petered out onto a beach where red and gray mud made a patchwork with green moss and lichen, bushes, ferns, and trees. I stopped, killed the engine, and rolled down the window. The smell of brine was strong on the air, and I sat for a while looking out at the sea.

I didn't know for sure why I was there or what I expected to find. I just had a vague idea that I wanted to know more about Astrid Meyer and her movements, who her friends were, who she met with and what for, and I was also aware there was an outside chance that if Astrid hadn't murdered her husband, she might well have been the intended target. And that meant the killer might still be stalking her. Though so far I had seen no sign of that. No sign at all.

I made a decision and pulled the Chevy in among the wet trees and the ferns, so it was largely concealed by the undergrowth. Then I took the field glasses I'd brought with me from the glove compartment and squelched my way through the forest, toward the house. After five minutes I came to the fringe of the woods, a little more than a hundred yards from the house. I hunkered down among the ferns and put the glasses to my eyes.

I could now see clearly that almost the entire rear of the house, overlooking the bay, was made of plate glass. It was a structure that took ugliness to a whole new level.

I found them on the top floor, which seemed to be a vast, open space with hardwood floors, a central, copper fireplace, and minimalist Scandinavian-style furnishings. It was like IKEA on steroids. I settled among the roots of a large chestnut, surrounded by ferns, watched them, and got slowly wet.

They all seemed to be very animated. They talked a lot, especially Gottlieb, who was on his feet pacing, pointing, and gesticulating. They were standing around and sitting, sipping what looked like champagne, and studying documents, which they handed back and forth while they spoke. You didn't need to be Sherlock Holmes to work out they were discussing a big deal, and that they were happy about it.

After maybe half an hour Gottlieb left the room and, a moment later, appeared in the next room, where he sat at a desk and made some phone calls. While he was doing that, Astrid and her pals started to relax. It struck me I had not seen her laugh before. She hadn't done a lot of that when we'd met. Now that I saw her do it, it wasn't something I was especially keen to see again.

A couple of hours crawled by toward midday. Despite my coat and the tree cover, the wet seeped in, and trickles of water began to run down from my hair, snake along my neck and down my back. In the house, a guy with a head as smooth and round as a billiard ball, dressed in black pants and a white jacket, entered and started setting what looked like a long, granite table on wrought iron legs.

By one o'clock the rain had become steady again, and I was soaked through, my kidneys ached, and I was getting cold. The smart thing would have been to leave, but something was telling me to stay. That something was in my gut, and said I was close. Close to what, I didn't know, but I was close.

By one thirty it was as dark as early evening, and the house formed an eerie, luminous spectacle against the pseudo-dusk. I watched Astrid and the three men rise from their seats and move to the glowing dining room. They ate and drank wine with the light of the fire dancing on the walls and making small pools of flame in the glass of the windows.

By three o'clock they were having cognac, and I was about ready to go home, have a hot shower, and join Dehan and Cohen at the hotel for an early dinner, when the four of them got up from the table and started making their way down toward the front door.

I scrambled to my feet and slid, staggered, and half-ran back through the woods to where I had concealed Dehan's car. I stamped as much mud as I could off my shoes and slid behind the wheel. Then, leaving the headlamps off, even though it was dark enough to warrant having them on, I cruised along Kings Point

Road, back toward Gottlieb's house. A hundred yards from the gate, I parked in the partial cover of some trees and waited.

Ten minutes later the gates rolled back and the Caddy emerged. It turned left and south onto Kings Point Road and moved off at a sedate pace. I followed. They took the Great Neck Road and, after a few miles, connected with the Northern Boulevard to cross over into Queens. At the intersection with Bell Boulevard they turned north, crossed the railway line, and turned right again into the tail end of 41st Avenue. There, they rolled into the parking lot at the back of a large, stand-alone building painted oxblood red. It had blacked-out windows and the sound of heavy throbbing coming from within. There was a guy standing on the door who, it struck me, was probably bigger than the door itself. I cruised slowly past.

A large neon sign outside spelled out *The Gasoline Club* in green script. Through it, as though growing out of the *l* in "gasoline," was a fairly accurate representation of a coca leaf. I drove on for a couple of blocks, did a U-turn, and drove back. I rolled into the lot, made like I was searching for a space, and saw the Caddy had gone. I figured Gottlieb's chauffeur had dropped them off with instructions to come and get them when they called. I found the darkest corner in the lot, under a large tree, beside a couple of dumpsters, tucked the car in there, and wiped myself off as best I could with a handkerchief. Then I crossed the lot with my collar turned up, climbed the steps, nodded to the vast doorman, who nodded back, and pushed inside.

It wasn't full, it wasn't even crowded. But still, the air was close and stale. There was a lot of dark wood but not enough light to see it by. There were small, round tables with padded stools and low chairs. The music was at a level where you could not hear yourself think, let alone hear other people talk, but there were a few scattered tables with five or six people sitting, drinking, and apparently talking. Perhaps, I thought, a new species of human was evolving, adapting to the new environment of perpetual, ugly noise with bionic ears. Against the far wall I could see a stage, but the music was coming over a sound system which was probably connected to an iPhone that belonged to a particularly depraved psychopath. I crossed to the bar, discreetly scanning the tables for Astrid Meyer and her pals. They weren't there.

I leaned on the counter, and a guy came over to me. He seemed to have every inch of his body tattooed, and so many piercings he looked like he'd been sprayed with pins in some kind of freak accident. He jerked his chin at me, and I ordered a beer. While he was pouring it, I asked him, "You got any private rooms, members only, that kind of thing . . . ?"

He flicked his eyes over my face and shook his head. I turned and looked around. At the back, past the empty stage, I could see a couple of doors. One of them led to the johns; the other said "Private." Two got you twenty that Astrid Meyer and her pals were not in the can.

I was wondering what to do next. One option was to storm through the "Private" door, arrest everyone and anyone who was snorting coke, and take them for a lineup to see if Dehan recognized Tombs among them. The idea appealed to me, but it didn't seem real practical. There were too many unknown quantities, not least of which was the possibility that I'd probably be met with an arsenal that would make Putin wince.

I mentally asked Dehan to forgive me and scanned the bar for a girl I knew would be there. As it was, she found me. She was in her midthirties and had a residual attractiveness that came as much from a general air of availability as it did from her looks. She had short, blond hair and blue eyes, skin that was good but tired, and legs that would look good in a bikini. She must have seen me looking around, because she came over, swinging her hips, and leaned on the bar next to me, smiling with hooded eyes. I said, "What'll you have?"

"They tell us to order champagne, but I need something stronger."

"How much stronger?"

She raised an eyebrow at me. "I have a radar for dangerous men."

I gave a small laugh. "Why?"

"Do you make a point of asking questions that nobody expects?"

"Are you going to answer my first one?"

"I'll have a Manhattan," she said, and it was almost a growl.

I called over Junkyard Jack, the Pierced Man, and ordered her drink. While he was mixing it, I could see she was trying to focus on my face.

"I haven't seen you before."

I smiled. "Are you sure you'd remember if you had?"

Her jaw dropped, but she was laughing. "My God! That is so rude!"

"But I see you laughing."

"I'm shocked! I'm laughing with shock."

"The Manhattan will help. What's your name?"

"God, my name!" She rolled her eyes. "I don't even know what my name is anymore. You can call me Zena."

"I'd rather not."

"Seriously?"

"Yeah. I'd like to call you something that reflected the person inside. Zena just says you look beddable."

"*Beddable?*"

"Sure. You are, aren't you? So where do you party around here, Zena?"

"Oh my God! Straight to the point, huh?"

"Time is infinite, Zena. But it's a finite resource, and I haven't got enough of it to waste."

She sidled up close to me and put her lips to my ear. "Through that door by the stage that says 'Private.'" She came away from my ear and gently took a hold of one of my lapels. "There's a whole different kind of club up there, on the second floor."

I smiled. "I kind of figured. So what goes on up there?"

"Parties, poker, roulette, parties . . . parties . . ." She threw her head back and laughed. It sounded strained.

I grinned. "So suppose a guy wanted to get invited to one of these parties. What would he have to do, and would he be guaranteed some *gasiolina*?"

She gave a fake cowgirl whoop and leaned against me, laughing. "You pays your money, and they lets you in. It's not cheap. But if I arrange you to get in, you have got to take me with you." She leaned close to my ear again. "They have got the *best* blow up there. I promise."

"Then I promise too."

"I'll talk to the boss. Maybe we can go tomorrow, or next weekend. You free? You got money?"

"Do I look poor?"

I regretted it as soon as I'd said it. Her eyes did the head-to-toe thing, and she arched a brow at me. "Honestly? You look like you've been sleeping in a ditch. What's all this mud? But you have telltale signs. Your hair, your shoes, your clothes. Above all, your manner."

"That's very acute of you."

She drew closer and took both lapels in her fingers. I felt her knee slide between my legs.

"Hey, you want to come to my place? We could get some blow, have a pre-party party. I'm a real fun kind of girl."

I looked into her eyes. The hunger was strong. "You know where we can get some, now?"

"Sure, Captain T always has some for me."

"I won't ask why."

She giggled and leaned on me. "You're so cute."

I looked across the room at the door marked "Private." They were up there, with the answers I needed, and they'd be there till gray morning brought the quiet despair of the hangover. I was tired, soaked, and hungry. I smiled down at Zena.

"So how will I know about the weekend?"

"Call me?"

"Give me your number."

She took the pen out of my pocket and wrote it on my hand. Then she craned her neck to look around the room. "He's always here, man. We'll get some stuff from him and go back to mine."

I took two bills from my wallet and put them in her hand. I bent over and kissed her cheek. "I'll call you Friday. Arrange it. You won't regret it."

I stepped out of the club and crossed the wet asphalt toward Dehan's car. I needed a steak sandwich and a cold beer as much as Zena needed her coke. But I needed a hot shower even more than that.

FOURTEEN

I took the Clearview Expressway and followed it all the way to the Throgs Neck Bridge. At the memorial park I came off onto the Throgs Neck Expressway, not really sure what I was doing. I stopped at the lights with Prentiss on my right and the Lawton Avenue bridge on my left. When the lights turned green, my automatic pilot made me spin the wheel left and cross the bridge, where I turned south again onto Pennyfield Avenue and followed it practically all the way to the water. But at Geranium Place I slowed, turned in, and cruised down Soundview Terrace to the very end, where it makes a dogleg and becomes Indian Trail. There I parked and sat awhile looking at the dead, empty house. As dead and empty as the man who had briefly owned it. For a moment I fought down the images of Dehan walking down that path, the door opening...

I climbed out, closed the door softly, and crossed the road. Wet light reflected across the blacktop and the sidewalk. I pushed open the gate. My steps sounded loud on the stone path as I followed it across the lawn to the small porch and the front door. There I pulled my Swiss Army knife from my pocket and hammered the screwdriver hard into the lock with the heel of my hand. I turned the knife, and the door swung open.

It was very still and very quiet, but small noises seemed to surface from the silence: the lap and hiss of the East River on the shore not far away, a foghorn moaning through the rain, the banal patter of rain falling from guttering, like it knew there was some kind of horror in the shadows of the house, but it didn't care.

I grabbed my imagination by the scruff of the neck and pulled it back into line. I also pulled the Sig Sauer Dehan had forced me to buy from under my arm and stepped over the threshold into the dark house.

No light penetrated, except the dim light from the streetlamps that filtered in through the open door, laying a crooked line across the hall, where my own shadow was silhouetted. I stood awhile, waiting for my eyes to adjust, listening for any movement, any sign of life. There was nothing, only the blackness that seemed to scream silently all around me.

I closed the door and pulled my flashlight from my inside pocket. The beam perforated the shadows and revealed, one by one as I moved it across the room, a kitchen area in back, behind a breakfast bar on the left. This was swallowed again by the darkness as I moved on to the heavy drapes pulled across what I guessed were glass doors onto the backyard; a dark green sofa, a dark wood and glass coffee table, two heavy armchairs, a TV, black and silent, on the wall opposite the sofa. On my right, at right angles to the sofa, was a low dresser with a tray of drinks: gin, whiskey, rum, and martini.

They were engulfed by a backwash of darkness as I moved the beam of light to the walls. Here there were watercolors and oils hanging, some in frames, others as bare canvases.

I pulled on my latex gloves and flipped on the switch. Four table lamps came on. Now I could see, in the corner, a small easel and a stack of canvases against the wall. Evidence of Shanna's attempts to make Sanchez expand his mind and break free from Astrid.

I crossed the floor and stood looking for a long while at the paintings. They were derivative and uninspired: still lives, landscapes, feeble, misguided attempts to recapture Paris in the '20s. Beside the easel there was a wooden tea trolley. It held a palette, stained cloths, a collection of brushes, tubes of paint, and dirty jars of turpentine. The smell was strong and strangely erotic. There was also a long white envelope that contained a stack of small, three-by-four photographs. Scrawled in longhand across the front was *CD Nude.*

There was one bedroom. The door was between the sofa and the easel. I opened it and stepped through. The light from the dining room made half a fan and lay across the foot of the brass bed. It was the same bed that I had seen in some of the nude paintings. It was neatly made, with fresh, fluffed-up pillows and a new, clean duvet. Something about it made me frown.

I snapped on the light. Like the living room, it came from two lamps, one on either bedside table. It was not a crime scene, but my eyes examined it like it was. There was an ashtray caught in the pool of amber glow from the lamp on my left. It had two butts in it. I went over and examined them. They were both Camels. Next to the ashtray there was a ring, left by a glass. There was another ring on the other table, but no ashtray. So Shanna slept on the outside. I wondered vaguely if that meant anything psychologically.

There was a small en suite bathroom. One tooth mug, one toothbrush, and more toiletries than you would expect from a cop in his early thirties. Maybe Shanna was right and there was something of the narcissist about him.

I stood and absorbed it for a bit, trying not to think. My first impression was about cleanliness. The place wasn't dirty, but it wasn't especially clean either. I knew that was important, but I wasn't sure why. I got on my knees and leaned over the bath to peer into the plughole. There was the usual matting of hair and soap gathered around the holes. I opened out my Swiss knife again and carefully scraped out the fluff and strands and dropped it in the palm of my hand. Then I sat on the floor and sifted carefully through it. Most of it was light, short, fine blond hair. There was no doubt in my mind that that belonged to Sanchez. There was other hair too, strong, black, and tightly curled, and that was obviously Shanna's. But there was still more, mainly short and black. I put it all in an evidence bag and slipped it in my pocket.

I stepped out into the living room–cum–dining room and crossed to the open-plan kitchen. There, on the draining board, I found two tumblers. Sanchez's last night in this house was beginning to take shape. The question that was nagging at my mind was, when was that night?

I went back to the living room, sat on the sofa, pulled out the envelope of pictures, and, with a sick feeling in my stomach and my heart pounding hard high up in my chest, I forced myself to go through the photographs. There were just six of them, three black and white and three in color. They were all of Dehan, nude, lying in sensual, provocative poses on the brass bed in the bedroom.

I wanted to throw them away, shred them and set fire to them. Instead I forced myself to examine and memorize each one. As I did so, an ice-cold calm came over me. It was a calm that was deadly and cruel.

I went to the dresser and poured myself a large whiskey. I swallowed it in one and went to the kitchen to wash and dry the glass. Then I set it back on the tray and returned to the bedroom with the photographs in my hand. I examined them one more time, forcing myself to visualize Dehan on that bed.

Then I put the pictures away in my inside pocket and got down on my hands and knees to examine the carpet under the bed. It was spotless. I stood, grabbed ahold of the heavy, brass frame, and dragged it across the bathroom door.

Hot rage welled up inside me, fogging my head. Where the legs of the bed had been positioned there were no marks, no indentations, nothing. The carpet was days old, if that. I tore the bedclothes off the bed and stared down at the mattress. It also was brand new. I grabbed the bedframe and heaved it on its side, knocking over the bedside table, smashing the lamp, and ramming the bed against the bathroom door. Then I tore the mat from the floor. They had been in a panic, pressed for time, and they had not done enough to the floor. It is hard to remove blood from wooden floorboards. It takes time. And time was what they hadn't had.

Or perhaps I should have said, *she* hadn't had.

I got down on my knees, pulled my Swiss Army knife from my pocket, and scraped the dry blood from the boards and into an evidence bag.

One .38 into a human belly on a soft mattress will not always penetrate through. A second one will, and the third and fourth will tear up the mattress. A lot of blood will seep through—not as much as I had seen in Astrid's master bedroom, but enough to soak through a carpet and stain the floor.

I stood and put the blood in my pocket, along with the photographs. Somebody had been killed in that bed. The carpet, the mattress, and the bedding had all been changed in a hurry. And that was what had been bothering me since I had entered the bedroom. They hadn't bothered to clean the rest of the bedroom, or the house. Whoever had done it had needed to get away fast; had not wanted to be seen anywhere near Sanchez's secret house.

I picked up the Camel butt and dropped it into another bag, then went to the dining room and opened the back door. The East River was just twenty or thirty yards away, and there were enough trees and bushes to shield anyone dragging a mattress and a rug down to the water from view. From where I stood I could see a small dinghy moored to the beach.

I stood, listening to the cold patter of the rain and trying to think through my rage. So the mattress and the rug, and the bedding, had been taken out in the boat, weighted, and dropped into the water, in time-honored fashion. Only, this time it didn't make any sense. If they had gone to all the trouble of dragging the mattress, the bedding, and the carpet down to the river, and rowing out to drop it into the dark depths, why the hell not do the same with the body and the gun?

Had they kept it for a second victim? Was Sanchez that second victim? I thought about the bloodstained mattress lying in the cold, salty depths, and I thought about that other bloodstained mattress left, rotting and stinking, on the bed in Astrid Meyer's mansion.

Astrid Meyer was at the Gasoline Club. Stuart was at his cottage. Sergeant Sanchez had been first with Dehan, then with Shanna, and then he had had his secret meeting, here, where he had paid the price for playing with dangerous women.

I didn't bother putting the bed back or hiding any signs of my presence. I took photographs of the whole place, left, and walked across the shiny, wet road to Dehan's car.

I sat awhile behind the wheel, thinking about the things I had seen and the things I had learned. I had killed. In the past, out of necessity, to save my own life or Dehan's. Killing, of itself, was not evil. I had come to understand that over time. What makes killing evil is the intent behind it. If you kill out of greed or the desire to cause suffering, then that is clearly evil. But what if you kill to protect the people you love from harm? Is that evil? I didn't have the answer. All I had was a deep, bloody rage.

I pressed the ignition and pulled out onto Pennyfield Avenue and crossed over again onto the Throgs Neck Expressway, headed north. I was going to the Bay View Hotel to meet with Saul Cohen, and Dehan. I would fill them in on what I had seen, and also what I had done. At least, part of it. Part I would keep to myself.

I needed to think. The game had changed. There were things I would have to do now, that I could not have done before.

Everything had changed.

It was almost eight by the time I arrived at the hotel. I found Cohen in the dining room. He was drinking a gin and tonic with lime and waved to me as I came in. I dumped my coat on a chair and sat. He eyed me up and down and said, "You badly need a bath."

"I've been busy."

"Good, busy is good. Are you hungry?"

"I'm not sure."

I pulled the envelope and my cell from my inside pocket and laid them on the table. Cohen eyed them absently while he spoke and I dialed.

"So far I have eaten very well here."

"Where is Dehan?"

"Upstairs, is there anything you need to tell me?"

I nodded. The phone rang a couple of times, and Dehan's voice, tired, said, "Hey, big guy. Where you been all day?"

"Busy. Did you eat yet?"

"Not what you'd call *eat*, no."

"I'm in the dining room with Cohen. Come down. We need to talk."

There was a brief silence, then, "Yeah, okay. I'm on my way."

I hung up. Saul sipped and cocked an eyebrow at me.

"You look pissed."

"That's because I am, very pissed."

"Have a drink."

"I'm not sure that's a good idea." As I said it I called the waiter over. "Give me a Bushmills, no ice. And a couple of steaks. Someone else is joining us. You'd better set another place."

The waiter hurried away, and Cohen sighed noisily through his nose.

"Something tells me I ought to know what's got you mad."

I chewed my lip and stared at Cohen.

"Sergeant Anthony Sanchez had a place on Locust Point that his wife didn't know about. In fact, nobody knew about it except his shrink, and lover, Shanna McLean."

He stuck out his bottom lip and nodded ponderously at his glass, like it had made a pretty good point.

"That would explain his reputation as the clean-cut boy next door."

I nodded. "That's exactly what it does. His sexual adventures were discreet and hidden from view."

I reached in my pocket and pulled out the evidence bags with the hair, the blood, and the cigarette in them. I dropped them in front of him and watched his face while I spoke.

"There were at least three kinds of hair in the bath: his, short and blond; Shanna's, black, strong, and tightly curled; and some others I could not immediately identify."

He picked up the bag like it might be infected. "You know we can't use this. It's illegally obtained."

"How do you know?"

"Excuse me?"

"In the first place you don't know how I got it. In the second place we have to assume that the title to that property has passed to Astrid Meyer, and she has begged me to find her husband's killer and given me free access to her property in order to do that."

He grunted. "You had better tidy that up before we let anyone know about this hair. John . . . ?"

"What?"

"You know that if we have this hair analyzed, it will have to be compared to Carmen's."

"I know. So what?"

"Have you thought . . ."

"Yeah, I've thought! And if she was screwing the son of a bitch then she'll get what's coming to her. And if she wasn't we have nothing to worry about."

His eyes narrowed to slits. "You'd better tell me what else happened today. This is not you."

I took the envelope and slammed it down in front of him. I watched him watch the waiter bring the drinks and set a third place at the table. Then he opened the envelope and looked inside. His face actually went pale and sagged. He sagged back in his chair, and his hands sagged into his lap. He shook his head and raised his eyes to meet mine.

"No," he said. "No, not Carmen Dehan."

FIFTEEN

He threw the envelope back at me.
"What do you intend to do with this?"
"I don't know yet."
He frowned. "Don't do anything crazy, John."
I watched him open his mouth three or four times. It was the first time I had ever seen him lost for words. Finally he picked up his glass and set it down again.
"John, we have never been friends, we have always been on opposite sides of the divide, but you should know that I have always held you and Carmen in the highest esteem. There are cops, a few of them, that I have worked with, and have cooperated with me, if you know what I mean. But you, you and Carmen, I have always known you both to be solid. Don't go off half-cocked. Keep your cool until you know for sure what has happened."
I looked at him like he was crazy. "For sure?" I held up the photographs. "This is not sure?"
He looked pained but didn't answer.
I left the envelope on the table, with the writing visible, and jerked my head at the evidence bag. "What about that?"
He eyed it a moment. "There are plenty of labs that can process it for us. There are a couple we use. I'll see to it."

"Listen," I said, glancing over at the door, conscious that Dehan was about to appear at any moment. "Is there anything I need to know about Gottlieb?"

He shrugged and spread his hands, like he was surprised at how stupid my question was. "Like what?"

I outlined what I had seen that day. He rolled his eyes. "What? They suspend you for a couple of weeks and suddenly you're some kind of amateur now? Come on! The maniacs in the upper classes of business survive on a diet of coke. If they didn't, they would go crazy. They build up unbelievable levels of stress, so they need these crazy things to relieve that stress. There is nothing to be read into that meeting, believe me. I don't do it anymore. It was never my scene, but when I was younger, if a Colombian or Mexican client came over, what were you supposed to do? You can't turn them down because that would offend them. So you play along. It's just business, John."

"Don't sidetrack me, Saul! The gun, the bedding, the blood, framing Dehan for crying out loud! None of it ties together! Whether she did it or whether she is being framed, either way, *neither way* makes sense. What is the motive here?"

He sighed. "Some people kill professionally, John. It's their job, they are experienced, and they do it for monetary gain. But those people are very rare. Nine times out of ten murder is not intellectual, it is emotional. The people most likely to murder each other are people who are in love. With love, logic goes out the window. I hate to say this, and in my heart I do not believe it, but if she was in love with this guy, and she killed him, you may be sure that she was out of her mind when she did it."

I didn't answer. I watched Dehan enter the dining room. She looked tired, but she smiled at me as she crossed the room, tying her hair into a knot behind her neck. She greeted Saul and gave me a kiss. She sat and gave me a narrow look that said she didn't want to lose her patience with me and was trying not to.

"What's up?" she said.

I waited till the waiter had delivered our food and a couple of beers. When he'd left, I said, "I went to Sanchez's love nest this evening."

She glanced up from cutting her steak. "Yeah? And? Did you find anything?"

I pointed to the evidence bag on the table. "That's hair from his bath and shower." I kept my eyes on her face as she glanced at the bag, chewing. "His hair is in there, but there are at least two other types of hair."

She frowned and swallowed, then shrugged. "I mean, that's good, right? Because it opens up our possible pool of suspects a bit, but it's not momentous. Did you find anything else?"

Saul coughed. "Carmen, I am your attorney. If you want to talk privately to me . . ."

She spoke with her mouth full of steak. "No, why?"

"I am going to send these samples to a private lab we use. Do you understand the implications of that?"

"I'm a cop, Saul. Of course I understand the implications!"

"Is it possible that your hair is in here?"

He picked up the bag and showed it to her. She sighed and rolled her eyes.

"No, Saul, it is not possible. One thing is stealing my prints from something I touched. A completely different thing is stealing my hair and getting it into a plughole."

"I have to ask you this, Carmen, were you ever at the house? Did you ever visit Sanchez there?"

"Again, Saul?" She turned to me. "Stone?"

"It's a serious charge, Dehan . . ."

She flashed. "Yeah, and I'm the one facing it, Stone! So don't patronize me. You got something to say, say it!"

Saul looked at me, like he was expecting me to say something. I shrugged. "I got nothing to say."

She stared hard at me. "What the hell is going on?"

"Why don't you tell me?"

"Quit the crap, Stone! We know each other too well! What the hell did you find at Tony's place?"

"What makes you think I found anything?"

"Because the man who left our house this morning is not the same man I am looking at now! Look at you!" She gestured with her hand at my face. "Your eyes! Your expression! Your whole manner! You look as if you'd like to stick that steak knife in my heart! Well go ahead! Do it! Things couldn't get much worse than they are! The whole damned NYPD believes I'm guilty of murder *and* adultery, and now the one person who I thought actually believed in me is turning against me too?"

Saul spoke suddenly. "Stone, why don't you leave us . . . ?"

Dehan was shaking her head. Her face was crimson. "No! I have nothing to say to you, Saul, that I am not prepared to say in front of my husband!"

He said quietly, "We are past this, Carmen. It's too late. You need to tell us."

"Tell you *what*? Tell me what you think it is you know, and I will answer!"

I was about to say something but kept quiet. Saul said, "The photographs . . ."

I watched her carefully. She frowned. "The photographs?"

"Yes, Carmen. We found them. And they could be very damaging for you. You should have told me about them." He glanced at me resentfully.

She frowned at me, then at him.

"That was . . ." She thought about it. "That was about three weeks ago, maybe four. He said he wanted to paint me." I felt a hot pellet of anger in my belly and tried hard to suppress it. "I told him not to be stupid, and then Shanna, who is a royal pain in the ass, started insisting too. I would be a great subject, I should do it, it would be great."

I asked, and heard the venom in my own voice, "Whose idea was it to make it a nude?"

She flashed a look at me and narrowed her eyes. "Tony's, but he was kidding. Then Shanna egged him on. But I already told you, Stone, when they got together they became like big kids. Anyway, how the hell would you know he suggested a nude?"

Before Saul could answer, I said, "Tell me about the photographs."

"What's to tell? He became a real pain in the ass and took like a dozen photographs of me. I told him it was getting on my nerves, but he wouldn't listen. In the end he told me to lie on the table in a suggestive pose, and I had to get serious to make him understand it wasn't funny anymore."

"Get serious how?" I asked with a bitter twist in my voice. "Did you wrestle him to the ground or something?"

Her eyes blazed. "I told him if there was any more of that kind of crap I'd quit! He stopped and apologized. It was that night I decided it was time to call it a day and hand in my notice."

"Why didn't you?"

She sighed. "I did. We had a serious talk, and I told him never to cross the line like that again. He was very apologetic and begged me not to go. He said the club needed me. I agreed to stay on a little longer, but also stressed to him that the club needed him, not me."

She looked at Saul for a while, then looked at me, trying to read my face. "What's this about?"

I glanced at Saul. "Excuse us for a moment." I turned to Dehan. "Come with me."

I led the way out of the dining room and into the cocktail bar. It was almost empty. I picked a table in the corner, and we sat. There was fury in her eyes, and she almost spat the words at me, "What the hell is going on, Stone? How *dare* you do this to me?"

I held her eye a moment, then asked, "Do you trust Saul?"

"Kind of, why?"

"Whom do you know, one hundred percent, that you can trust?"

She looked at me resentfully. "Until now, you. Maybe the inspector, a couple of others, maybe."

I nodded. "Yeah, well until this evening I was not so sure

about Saul. But actually, as of twenty minutes ago, I trust him more. But I am still not one hundred percent."

"You want to tell me what the hell this is about before I rip your head off and shove it up your ass, Stone?"

I smiled. "You know one of the things I most like about you?"

"Now? *Now?* This is the moment you pick?"

"You have a real cute mole, about an inch in from your right hip."

I tossed the photographs on the table in front of her. She went through them, and the color drained from her face.

"Jesus, Stone! This is not me!"

"The face is. And that is some very skilled Photoshop work. You can imagine how I felt for the first few seconds when I found them. Everything in my mind and body told me it could not be real, but there you were."

"It must have been awful . . ."

I nodded. "It only lasted a few seconds, but it was intense. They should have got a better model. She's not a patch on you. Plus, she's missing the mole. And I am very glad to know that Sanchez didn't know about it."

She reached over and thumped me hard in the shoulder with her right fist.

"Then why did you put me through all that in there just now?"

I picked up the pictures and waved them at her. "Because these were left there to be found, probably by the cops. To tell you the truth, I am inclined to trust Saul, but I can't be one hundred percent sure. So I played it safe, and let him know that I had them, and I believed they were real."

"What did he say?"

"He advised caution, and told me he had always respected you and didn't believe you capable."

She smiled. "Huh! Cool."

"Yeah, cool, but we are up against a very subtle, dangerous person, Dehan. If Blakemore had found these instead of me, we could be in very serious trouble. Moles can be airbrushed out of photographs. A jury might well buy those pictures, and they could provide a powerful motive for murder."

She nodded. "I know, Stone. What else did you find there?"

I told her about the bed and the bloodstains on the wooden floor. She said, "So either we are looking at two bodies, or Sanchez was killed at his love nest and transferred to the mansion."

"Which might go some way to explaining why he was in the wrong room. But it raises so many other questions, I'm not sure it gets us very far at all. I mean, what for? Why kill him in one place, go to the trouble of taking all the bedding out in a dinghy and sinking it, while keeping the gun and using it to make it seem he was killed somewhere else? It means whoever did it had to transport the body all the way from Locust Point to the north of Eastchester Bay, *with* the murder weapon, and drag the body into the house and dump it in the bed."

She gave a small laugh. "And the person who is going to all this trouble doesn't even know what bed he sleeps in."

I blinked at her a few times and said, "Yeah. There's that too."

She frowned and added, "Which kind of argues away from a jealous wife or even a jealous lover."

I nodded. "Because they would almost certainly know where he was sleeping."

"Exactly. So, if it is not a crime of love, sex, and passion, what is it?"

I sighed. "What are we going to tell Saul?"

"Tell him the truth, Stone. I think he's on our side."

I weighed it up, thought about his reaction on seeing the pictures, and decided I agreed. We made our way back to the dining room and found him eating a tiramisu, drinking black coffee and cognac.

He looked from Dehan's face to mine and back again, sniffed his cognac, and said, "Photoshop?"

Dehan said, "Of course."

He made a sad groaning sound. "There I was, believing myself to be one of just three men in the world who had seen Carmen Dehan nude. My dream shattered!"

"Take your medicine, Saul, it ain't never gonna happen."

"So, where does this leave us? In an unholy mess. We cannot prove any of the things you have discovered today. We may be able to use the hair and the cigarette, but the blood on the floor? What do we do with that?"

I thought about it for a moment. "We need to know if it's Sanchez's blood or somebody else's. Whoever killed Sanchez, Dehan, saw you both leave the club that night, and followed Sanchez to Shanna's and then, presumably, to Locust Point." I shook my head. "More to the point, whoever killed him had been watching you, knew your daily routine . . ." I pointed at her. "Somewhere in your head you know who this is."

She sighed. "I keep trying, Stone, but I get nothing. Nothing that fits and makes sense."

I leaned back and turned to Saul. "We need that house investigated by the crime scene team, but I don't want to hand it over to the Forty-Fifth and Blakemore. Can we bring a civil action against them alleging they had no grounds to arrest Dehan without a proper and thorough investigation? Maybe allege corruption and require a different precinct to investigate?"

"Leave the law to me, Stone, lest we shoot ourselves in the foot. If it comes to it *maybe* we can try to allege corruption and perhaps request a court order for another precinct to investigate. But we will need evidence. Right now we have a few very weak pieces of forensic evidence that show that the murder *might* have been committed at his love nest. We are still a very long way from clearing Carmen."

"Yeah, I know, but I think we might actually be closer to finding the killer than we are to clearing Dehan."

He scowled at me. "How? You're hallucinating!"

I shook my head. "No, I'm not. The behavior of the killer is unusual to the point of being bizarre. And if we can work out what drove him—or her—to that behavior, then we have a bead on them."

They were both frowning at me. Saul Cohen said, "You are deliberately shifting your focus. I am not so sure that's a good idea."

And Dehan said, "You're scared. You think this killer is a lot more dangerous than you thought to begin with."

I shook my head again but they both knew that I was lying. I shrugged. "I just think it's the fastest way to prove you're innocent," I said. "Take a more positive, aggressive approach."

Saul leaned forward. "John, do not even dream of going after this person."

I held his eye, and after a moment I said, "I'm going to have another talk with Blakemore tomorrow. Meantime, there's something I need you to look into, Saul."

He raised an eyebrow at me. "What's that?"

"I need to know the terms of Sanchez's will. I also need to know the terms of Astrid Meyer's will."

He frowned. "*Astrid Meyer's* will? Assuming she has one!"

"Yeah, Astrid Meyer. Who inherits if she dies?"

"Yeah, and something else. Check and see if any dogs have gone missing near Astrid's house."

SIXTEEN

We left her Chevy at the hotel, and I drove Dehan home through the shiny, wet, silent streets in my ancient burgundy Jag. We didn't speak. We climbed the stairs, showered, and brushed our teeth, and climbed into bed in silence. There, Dehan fell asleep with her head on my shoulder; and I held her, not tight, but secure, staring at the ceiling.

But it was not the ceiling that I saw, nor the shadows of wet ripple in the orange light from the silent street outside. I saw the gathering hyenas, half-concealed in the shadows, with hungry, evil eyes. Evil eyes informed by intelligence, a predatory intelligence that had sought a victim, identified her, and would not now stop until she fell.

I had not told Saul what I thought, what I feared. I had not told Dehan. They could not know. Because the law could not protect Dehan from these enemies. I didn't know if I could. But if anybody could help her, it had to be me.

The hours crawled by, the rain never stopped, the spattering gutter at two a.m. was the same at four and at six.

At six fifteen I rose and went to the shower. I showered hot, cold, hot, and cold again to wake myself up, then went down to make coffee while Dehan showered. She came down as I was putting breakfast on the table. She was in jeans and a sweatshirt, with her wet hair hanging loose down her back. She took the coffeepot from my hands and set it on the table. Then she put her arms around me and held me. I held her back, and we stood like that for a while. It might have been a few seconds, or a few hours. Time had no place in that moment.

She looked up into my face. "I know the answer, Stone, but I need to hear you say it. We're going to beat this, aren't we?"

I held her perfect face in my hands and nodded. "We are going to beat this, Dehan. Nothing else is an option."

"I couldn't..." She hesitated and shook her head.

I echoed the gesture. "Don't even bother thinking about it. It's not going to happen. It won't even get to trial."

She gave three short, quick nods. "You know that, don't you."

"I know that for a fact."

"And you're always right, right?"

She tried to hide it, but there was a glimmer of fear, of pleading, that she would not have let anybody else see. I smiled. "I'm afraid so. I am always right."

She gave me a gentle thump on the chest. "Pain in the ass. For once I'm happy about that."

I kissed her gently and whispered in her ear, "Coffee." I pulled out her chair, and she sat. I added, "I have a lot to do today, Dehan."

She looked a little scared. "Really?"

"Yeah, today I am going to rattle a cage."

THE 45TH PRECINCT WAS QUIET. It was like the incessant rain of the last week had robbed all the criminals of their motivation. The patrol cars sat immobile, glistening and pristine under the low, heavy ceiling of the sky. I parked the Jag, climbed out, and loped across the shallow puddles to climb the stairs for my third visit with Detective Blakemore. The desk sergeant looked up as I stepped in. Boredom got the better of distaste in the battle for control of his face and he said, "'Tective Blakemore?"

"Yeah, is he in?"

He jerked his head at the security door, and I heard it buzz. "At his desk."

I went through to the detectives' room and found him sitting typing at his computer. He looked up and eyed me as I approached.

"What the hell do you want?" The emphasis was on the "you," like other people could want things, but I couldn't.

I pulled out a chair and sat opposite him.

"My wife is accused of murdering Sergeant Sanchez, remember?"

"I don't know what idea you got, Stone, but having a wife who is accused of killing a cop does not give you the right to come in here and insult me. So if you're bringing me more of your attitude, you can get the hell out of here, wife or no fucking wife."

"I hear you."

His face contracted, like he had bad constipation. "*What?*"

"I understand, and I agree. I apologize for having insulted you. You're just doing your job."

"What the hell do you want, Stone?"

I scratched my head. "The blood. Sanchez's blood, at the crime scene."

"What about it?"

"There was too much. Did the ME comment on that?"

He shrugged. "Yeah, he said it was unusual. But Sanchez was shot four times in the belly with a .38 at close range. He took a long time to die and bled out. So there was a lot of blood."

I shook my head. I knew he was going to tell me to get lost, but I had to play it out. "With four .38 rounds at close range, he would have died almost instantly, and a good part of the blood would have pooled in the chest, in the arms, and especially in the legs."

"Yeah, thanks for your expert opinion. We also have experts in the Forty-Fifth. It didn't happen that way. He bled out. If I need your opinion again, I'll call you . . ."

"Did you have the blood tested?"

He got the same constipated look, but this time it was tinged with disbelief, like he couldn't believe he was that constipated.

"What the hell would I do that for? He was lying in a pool of his own blood, for crying out loud! Why the hell would I have it tested? *It's his goddamn blood!*"

I watched him a moment, then shook my head. "Yeah, you see? I don't think it is his blood. I don't think he was killed there at all."

"*What?*"

"I'm not one hundred percent certain yet, but I don't think he was killed there. I believe he was killed somewhere else and then taken to Astrid Meyer's house."

He sat forward and put his elbows on the table. He pointed at me with the index finger of his upturned hand. "You?" He glanced to the side, like he was looking for support from other people. "You, the big shot, John Stone of the Forty-Third? Well, let me tell you something, Sherlock, that is the *stupidest* fucking idea I have *ever* heard in my whole, entire, fucking *life!*"

"Just hear me out, Blakemore."

"*Hear you out?* You want me to *hear you out?*"

A few detectives were looking over from their desks and smiling. I was the asshole from the 43rd who was married to a cop killer, and I was getting my ass kicked by good old Blakemore. He plowed on, leaning across the desk, jabbing his finger at me.

"You come in here, playing fucking Sherlock Holmes on *my* time, exploiting the vulnerability of a woman whose husband was murdered by *your* goddamn wife! You insult me, you insult my precinct, and now you want me to *hear you out?* Check the fucking blood? Well let me tell you something, Stone, I listened, I heard you out, and I think you're an asshole and you're full of shit!"

"Take it easy, will you? I am telling you there is something wrong with the blood, and there is something wrong with . . ."

"Take it easy? You're telling *me* to take it easy? Get the fuck out of my sight! That's the second time I've thrown you out, and it's the last. Don't come back, Stone, I'm warning you."

"Okay, I'm leaving." I didn't move. I sat watching him for a moment, then asked, "What do I need to do to have you test the blood?"

"Nothing. It's a stupid idea. It's the most stupid idea I ever heard. I am not going to do it. It is not going to happen. Get out." I hesitated a moment, and he narrowed his eyes at me. "Do you have information pertinent to my investigation? Are you withholding evidence?"

I held his eye for a full five seconds, then sighed and shook my head. I stood. "No, no information, nothing more than I have already given you. You're probably right, he took a long time to die from four .38s tightly grouped in his belly. It's not like they were .44s, right?" I paused. We watched each other. I pointed my finger at him, like a gun. "But you should test the blood anyway. There's a lot of it. And I'm pretty sure Sanchez was not murdered in that room, or even at Astrid Meyer's house."

He made a face like I disgusted him and flapped his hand at me. "Yah, get out of my sight, you fucking clown."

Outside, a damp wind slapped me about my face a few times and tried to pull my hair off. I pulled up my collar and crossed the road to my car. There I clambered in and slammed the door. Specks of squally rain hit the windshield, and overhead, the blustery wind tore at the gray belly of the clouds.

I stuck the key in the ignition, and my phone rang.

"Detective Stone, this is Astrid Meyer. We need to talk."

"Sure, what's the problem?"

"There have been developments . . ."

I felt a jolt in my gut. I had expected this, but not so soon. "Developments? What kind of developments?"

"The DA has been in touch with me. She's an old friend. We have talked . . ." She sighed. "Just come over, will you?"

"Sure, I'm on my way."

I turned the key in the ignition, and the old car growled. This was going to be bad, ugly. But it was what we needed to go through to get to the other side. I slipped in first gear and headed east, toward the bay.

Fifteen minutes later I left my car at the foot of the mock Georgian steps and Stuart showed me into Astrid Meyer's study. She looked unhappy as she stood to greet me. She shook my hand in both of hers, like she was commiserating with me, and gestured me to one of her armchairs beside the fire. I sat, and she sat across the coffee table from me.

"Detective Stone, John. May I, John?"

"Of course, Astrid, go ahead."

"John, I told you on the telephone that the DA had been in touch with me. She tells me that they are ready to go ahead with the prosecution."

I frowned. "Already?"

"She is satisfied they have everything they need, and that it will be, in her words, a slam dunk." She sighed. "I don't know what to say . . . I put your concerns—*our* concerns—to her, but she dismissed them out of hand. I asked her for more time, but she believes I am being foolish. Blakemore feels the same way. Obviously they talk to each other. They say . . ." She shrugged and sighed again. "It's an open-and-shut case."

"Do you believe that?"

She gave a small, unhappy laugh. Like my question was an absurd one. "An open-and-shut case has nothing to do with truth or lies, right or wrong. It is just a matter of what evidence is available to whom. Let me ask you. Have you made any progress? Have you found anything?"

I nodded. "Maybe."

Her face cleared. "Then please, John, fill me in! Give me

something I can take to her; something we can adduce at the preliminary hearing, or before!"

I thought for a moment. "Give me a second, will you?" I pulled out my phone and called Saul Cohen.

"What?"

"Good morning, Saul. Listen." I stood and walked away, toward the window, with my back to Astrid. "Don't interrupt and don't ask questions, just answer. Can you legally get access to prosecution forensic evidence?"

"Like what?"

"Like a blood sample from the crime scene."

I turned to face Astrid. She was frowning at me. Saul said, "Access how?"

"To have our own tests carried out."

"Of course. But why would we want to do that?"

"I told you not to ask questions. I want the victim's blood tested."

Astrid went white and stood, staring at me with wide eyes. Saul said, "*What?* Have you gone *insane?*"

I held Astrid's eye. "I have my reasons. Can you do it or not?"

"Yeah, I can do it, but why the hell should I?"

"Because I'm telling you to, and I have just told you I have my reasons."

He sighed noisily. "I'll file the request."

I hung up. Astrid had moved to the window and was looking out at the wet, tossing trees and the wind-scattered drizzle.

"What is this, John? What possible reason can you have to test the samples of my husband's blood? What are you saying, that it wasn't his body I found up there?"

I slipped my phone in my pocket. "No, I am absolutely certain it was Anthony Sanchez you found in your bed. But I am equally sure he wasn't murdered there."

She turned from the window. Her face had changed from a pasty gray to a livid red. Her voice was choked with emotion, and there were tears spilling from her eyes. "How can you say that? He was... the bed..."

"I know, Astrid. I saw it, remember? But there are too many things that don't make sense."

She waved her right hand around erratically, and her eyes went wide. "Then what is the DA talking about? What is this open-and-shut case if there are so many things that don't make sense? To the DA and Blakemore they make sense!"

"Astrid, you forget that I have been a cop all my adult life. I know how this system works. As you implied yourself, the system doesn't care whether it is justice or rough justice, as long as the case can be successfully prosecuted. It's like a robot with artificial intelligence. It sees a critical mass of evidence capable of tipping the balance in favor of a conviction, and the machine kicks in to bring that person down."

She sat on the windowsill. Her hands were shaking, and she covered her face.

"This is exhausting," she said. "I still haven't been able to mourn poor Anthony."

"We all want this over and done with as soon as possible, Astrid."

"It will never be over for me."

"No, I guess not, but you can at least get some closure."

She dropped her hands into her lap. "I suppose so. However trite and facile that may sound, I suppose it is true."

I sat on the arm of a chair and watched her a moment. Finally I said, "Do you feel able to answer a few difficult questions for me?"

She scowled at me. "I hope they are not all going to be as strange and twisted as wanting a blood sample from a victim who has already been identified!"

She sighed, stood, and rose from the windowsill. Then returned to her chair and sat. "What are these difficult questions, John? It seems these days all questions are difficult and painful."

"If the answers were easy and predictable, you wouldn't need me. An ass like Blakemore would serve your purpose. But the very nature of this murder is telling you it is something out of the ordinary. The motive is not clear, the means are not clear—nothing about this case is clear. It is something out of the ordinary. You can see that, can't you?"

"What's your point?"

I was trying to read her, but she was inscrutable behind a sullen face. I waited a moment, then asked her, "Did you ever visit Anthony at his private apartment?"

Her jaw dropped, and she stared at me like she thought I was going crazy. "What in the name of god are you talking about now? What private apartment? Stone, I am beginning to think Blakemore is right! You're insane! Or you will do anything to protect your wife . . ."

I interrupted her. "The one he bought on Locust Point. The one he used to take his lovers to." I pointed south. "Down near the bridge."

Her mouth clamped shut. She looked oddly like a spoiled toddler refusing to eat. "You're talking rubbish!"

"Am I? What makes you say that?"

"There is no house . . . nothing on Locust Point! If he had bought some property, I would know about it! Obviously!"

"So you had no idea that he owned a small house on Soundview Terrace, where he used to take the girls he picked up?"

She shook her head. "I don't believe it. I *won't* believe it. This is *your* wife you are thinking about. Not my husband!"

"I was there last night."

She stared at me for a long moment, with dull, stupefied eyes. "How . . . ?"

"That's not really important now. The fact is that I was there."

"Why would he keep it a secret from me?"

I almost felt compassion for her, but I had no choice. "I just told you he took his lovers there."

"How can you know that? There is no way you can know that!"

"You were the one who was telling me he had an affair with my wife. So what's changed?"

She shook her head. "No."

"No? I think you need to come clean, Astrid. Things were not perfect between you and Anthony, were they?"

She averted her eyes, looked at the fireplace, where small flames wavered in the dull light. "All couples . . ." She seemed to hold the cliché in her mind, half-spoken, trying and failing to find comfort in it. "We had our small problems. He was German, but brought up like a Latino, without discipline or values . . . You can't live without values. We were discussing, he was learning."

"But it had gone beyond that, hadn't it?"

"No." She shook her head. "That is your assumption, based on nothing. We needed some time for him to adjust, and learn." She laughed and threw her hand in the air. "He was young! So young! But we adored each other. And we were moving toward the promised land!"

"Did you know he was thinking of divorcing you?"

Now she looked at me, and her face was ugly and distorted. "You're lying! *How! How! How!* How could you possibly know that?"

"He talked about it with Shanna the night he was killed."

"Shanna? Shanna is a lying, manipulating bitch! Just like . . ."

She stopped short, and I ignored it. I asked, instead, "Is she? What makes you say that?"

Her mouth worked, like the words wanted to come out, but she was fighting them. Eventually she looked away. "She is a black woman, primitive, with no moral constitution. Only sex, and drinking, and drugs. She tried to poison my Anthony's mind."

"So you think she was lying about Anthony wanting a divorce."

"In all probability."

"Either way, he had the apartment. It's full of his prints and his DNA, and the property register will show it's in his name. He painted there too."

"Painted?" She narrowed her eyes at me again.

"Sure, Shanna was encouraging him to paint. He wanted to paint a nude of my wife, but she told him no."

Her eyes were moving all around the room, like they were trying to find a North Star to guide her back to sanity. "This is madness," she said at last. She stood again and walked across the room, staring right and left, like she was searching for something, anything, that made sense. "I don't know what you're talking about. I don't know *who* you are talking about. This house, this man who paints now, it has nothing to do with me and Anthony. *Nothing!*"

I went on, like she hadn't spoken, "There was also a brand-new duvet on his bed, brand-new sheets, and a brand-new carpet underneath. It was so new the bed legs hadn't even left an imprint in the carpet."

Her breathing was heavy. She stared at me like she wanted to rip my head off and feed it to the fish in the East River. I said, "I'm guessing Anthony didn't smoke, right?"

She gave a tiny nod. "He didn't . . ."

"But there was an ashtray on the bedside table, with a butt in it. The butt was a Camel. You know anyone who smokes Camels, Astrid?"

She scowled at the floor. "I have no idea."

"Are you sure?"

"I don't notice that kind of thing."

"Something tells me you notice every kind of thing, and you know very well which of Anthony's friends smokes Camels. There were also rings on the bedside tables from where glasses had stood, one on each side . . . You want me to go on?"

She didn't answer. She buried her face in her hands, sank into an armchair, and sat rocking gently back and forth. She whispered from behind the barrier of her fingers, "*Please, go away . . .*"

"I can't do that yet, Astrid." I sat opposite her. "I found hair in the sink hole in the bath at Anthony's house. There was short blond hair, there was black, tightly curled hair, and there were other types of hair too. And I also found dried blood, on the floorboards."

Her mouth sagged open. "Why didn't you tell me sooner? You have to tell Blakemore. This changes . . ."

I waited, then asked, "What does it change, Astrid?"

She shook her head but said nothing.

I sat back and tried again to read her face. It said she was deeply confused. I said, "Somebody was shot four times, with skill, while they were lying in that bed. The mattress, bedding, and the carpet were removed and probably thrown into the East River, weighted down with stones. But traces of that person's blood were left behind, as were, I imagine, strands of their hair."

"You think Anthony was killed there . . ."

"If he was," I said, "then the lab will prove it."

I stood up then and left.

SEVENTEEN

The rain was holding off, limiting itself to small, cold spits carried on sudden, erratic gusts. But the wind was swelling, moving in off a dark, angry Atlantic, shaking windows, moaning down streets where people hunched and hurried, and whistling among power cables and treetops. I climbed in my car, pulled out my cell, and called Shanna. She didn't answer.

I turned the key in the ignition and drove the quarter of a mile to her house on Griswold Avenue. I pulled into her drive, behind her own car, and blocked her in. The wind wrapped my coat around my legs as I climbed the steps and hammered on the door. I rang too, for good measure, but nothing happened. So I hammered again. I was pounding a third time with my left fist, while I leaned on the bell with my right hand, when the door opened.

She didn't say anything. She just stared at me. She looked like she'd been sleeping.

"What do you want, policeman?"

"We need to talk."

"You need to talk. I don't need to talk."

"You don't know that until you've let me in and I have told you what I have to say. Let me in."

She turned and walked away from me, into the house. She was barefoot. I stepped inside, took off my coat, and followed her into her spacious, minimalist room with broad windows and low, modern furniture. It should have been airy and sunny, but instead it was gloomy and close. She dropped onto the sofa, and I couldn't help noticing that under her sweatshirt she had no bra.

"What do you want? I'm tired, sad, scared, and I want to be alone."

"Who was Sanchez's lover?"

She rolled her eyes and groaned. "Sweet Jesus, give me patience. I told you, he had no permanent lovers. They were one-night stands. Are you still stuck on that?"

"Yeah, you lied, and I want to know why."

On the lamp table beside her there was a pack of Camels. She picked it up, peered inside, and fingered out a cigarette. She lit it with a turquoise disposable lighter, which she dropped on the table as she sucked hard on the cigarette. I noticed her hand was shaking. She blew out a long stream of smoke at the ceiling.

"That's it? That's your argument? I lied?" She shrugged. "No, I didn't. Now what?"

"I went to his house yesterday."

She stared out at her garden. "I thought the cops had it sealed."

"I don't think they've found it yet. I let myself in."

"So?"

"There had been a woman there."

"How can you tell?"

"She had a shower and a drink. And she smokes Camels."

"That's me. I visited him there. So what? That means I killed him?"

I threw my coat on the back of a chair and sat on the couch, placing my elbows on my knees, studying her. She sighed, rested her head back on the cushion, and pinched the bridge of her nose.

"I don't think you fully understand," I said.

She kept her eyes closed and spoke like I was a tiresome kid and mommy had a hangover.

"I don't. Are you going to explain? I really hope you're not."

"I am going to explain the least you need to know." She still had her eyes closed but gave a single nod. I went on. "My wife is facing thirty years in prison for a murder she did not commit. This is the woman I love, and the partner I owe my life to, several times over."

She frowned but still didn't open her eyes.

"You know what?" she said. "I could do without the tearjerker romance meets *Brothers in Arms*. My best friend just got murdered. I am very sorry for your predicament, but frankly I can't help, and I am not even sure I want to. How do I know Carmen *didn't* kill him? I already told you I am sure she was into him and he was into her, if you'll forgive the *double entendre*. So for all I know she did kill him!"

"Cut the crap, Shanna. You and I both know you're lying, and we both know you're hiding something from me." I pointed at her. "But if you think I'm just going to stand by and let Dehan take the rap..."

"What? If I think that, what?" I didn't say anything, and she went on. "Well here's some news for you. That is exactly what I think you are going to do. Because you have no goddamn choice. Carmen was Tony's lover, she got jealous of me, and she killed him. Tough titty, policeman."

I leaned close to her and spoke softly. "There is nothing—do you understand me?—*nothing* I will stop at to save her life. You had better think this through, Shanna. Because you are about to make a bad mistake."

She raised an eyebrow and sucked on her cigarette. "That would be frightening, if I hadn't seen it done so many times, so much better, by so many cheap B-list actors on second-rate TV shows."

"Work with me, Shanna. What I am telling you is true. Try to frame Dehan and I will take you apart. I *will* make an example of you. And don't think that the law will limit me. If I have to spend the rest of my life behind bars to save Dehan, I will. Who was it? Who was his lover? Was it you?"

She rubbed her eyes, opened them to look at me, and sighed. "You son of a bitch . . ."

"Were you his lover?"

"I already told you he had more than one. Why do you keep on about it?"

"No! There was one special person. One who was above the rest, that he was in love with."

"I don't know what makes you think that!" She sounded exasperated.

"I *know* it! Who was it?"

"I don't know! He never talked to me about his lovers."

"Why?"

She frowned at me like I was crazy. "What the hell do you mean, '*why*'?"

I yelled at her, feeling my patience slipping. "Come on, Shanna! Wake up! You're his closest friend! You grew up together! You're intimate enough to have an on-and-off sexual relationship and stay that close! He tells you about his sex life with his wife, and that he's considering divorcing her. You're his damned psychotherapist for crying out loud! Why would he *not* tell you about one serious love affair among all the meaningless ones?"

Her skin went kind of pasty, and her eyes became moist. She opened her mouth as she tapped ash, and tears spilled from her eyes down her cheeks.

"It's not relevant," she said at last.

"I'll decide whether it is relevant."

"No! You will *not*!"

I raised my voice. "Shanna, I have the meanest son of a bitch in New York on my payroll as my attorney, and between us we will stop at *nothing* to get Dehan out of the frame. So if you have any sense in your head, you had better get with the damned program. Because when I give him the house on Soundview Terrace and Sanchez's string of lovers, the yellow press are going to have a feeding frenzy, and *you* will be the main course! Now *talk!*"

Her eyes blazed. "You piece of..."

"Yeah! *All that and more! Now who the hell was he in love with, Shanna?*" She turned away. I could see the muscle in her jaw working. I shouted again, "*Was it you?*" She stood and carried her glass to the window. I followed after her. "*Was it you?*" I saw the glint of a tear on her cheek. I grabbed her and spun her around, my fingers digging deep into her shoulders, and shouted into her face, "*Was it you he was in love with? Answer me!*"

Her lip curled, and she began to sob.

"I was very close to Tony..."

"You grew up together."

"No, it was more than that. I..." She stopped, hesitated, took a deep breath. "My family were middle-class intellectuals. I had a liberal education. We ate together as a family and we had conversations, played games together, like Scrabble, Clue, even chess. When I met Tony at kindergarten we just clicked right away. I guess I was too young to know it, but I loved him."

I let go of her shoulders, and she sat on the sill.

"His parents were immigrants, from Mexico. His dad was ambitious and a hard worker. He was a severe man and very strict. He worked hard and he became prosperous, but he didn't like Tony. He thought he was too delicate and effeminate. So Tony grew up with this weird contradiction, a father with strict morals and ethics who would then beat his mother and him with a belt for reasons as absurd as looking or answering in the wrong way."

I sighed. "You're losing me, Shanna. Where is this going?"

She spread her hands and shook her head. "I'm doing my best to explain something to you. Tony was lonely. He adored his mother. He clung to her. But that bastard of a father limited the amount of time they could be together. And if he ever found them talking privately, or quietly, he would whip them both. So as much as he craved his mother's love and attention, they both learned to stay away from each other. I was lonely too. My parents adored each other. They loved being with each other. They could talk for hours about stuff I just couldn't understand. Then Tony came along, and he filled a void for me . . ."

She crushed out her cigarette in a glass ashtray. "We were small kids, and miraculously his parents had no problem with him hanging out with me." There was a twist of irony in her mouth. "You know, ethnic groups who are discriminated against by whites also discriminate against each other. But Tony's parents were not like that. His mother was a beautiful, sweet, broken woman, and he was a son of a bitch who didn't care what went on outside, as long as Tony and his mother crawled on their knees before him indoors. So, as the months and then the years rolled by, Tony and I clung to each other, we moved up through school together, and I guess somewhere between twelve and fifteen I realized I was in love with him, and always would be. He liked me, he even loved me, but it became clear early on that he was not in love, the way I was."

"Did he know how you felt?"

She shook her head. "No. He had no idea."

I sat a moment, thinking it through. "So, how is this relevant? How does this answer my question?"

She covered her face with her hands and rubbed them up and down. Then dropped them in her lap.

"Oh, God," she said. "This is not easy. He, Tony, had no idea until recently, when his marriage to Astrid started to fall apart. He used to come over in the evenings to talk. Old pals. He used to joke that he was my heterosexual gay friend.

"Sometimes we'd go out. Sometimes we'd stay in, have dinner, get drunk. He began to say things like I was his best pal. He didn't know what he'd do without me. The things people say when they are drunk . . ."

"And usually mean, but can't face when they are sober."

"Yeah." She nodded. "Astrid was his mother figure, and I could never compete with that, despite my ample, black bosom."

She got up and went to her drinks trolley. There she dropped three cubes of ice into her glass, and a slice of lemon. Finally she doused it with a generous helping of gin and a dash of fizzing tonic. When she'd finished, she stood, staring down at her drink.

"He was very loyal in his own way, and he loved Astrid. She was his mother figure . . . I already said that. It was very traumatic for him to realize that he was no longer in love with her. He used to cry like a child, and I would comfort him. We hugged a lot . . ."

She turned to face me. "If I had been any other girl, I have no doubt we would have made love, even if he'd regretted it afterwards . . ."

I was frowning. "So this on-and-off sexual relationship you talked about . . . ?"

"It was not exactly a lie, but not exactly true either." She smiled. "You going to spank me, Detective Stone, for being a bad girl? I respond well to spanking."

"Cut it out!"

She sighed and returned to her chair, curled into it, and sat, chewing her lip, then started talking again.

"One night, maybe a couple of months back, we were a bit drunk. We'd just had dinner, and he was joking that I was a great cook and that I would make any guy a great wife. From there we got on to how come I was not married. I managed to maneuver the conversation away, and suddenly we were talking about how unhappy he was in his marriage, how something vital was missing, *and* how come I had never married." She sighed heavily. "He joked—half joked—that maybe me and him had always been meant to be together. I told him I thought so, and we kissed. Next minute he freaked and ran."

I ran my fingers through my hair. "Yeah, it was what I thought. It had to be you."

She snorted a small laugh. "Yeah, that's what I told him, but he didn't buy it."

"I'm sorry." I meant it. "What happened?"

"We made up. He came to see me. I apologized, and he said no way, it was him who should apologize. Then there were long, painful explanations and excuses, and nothing was ever quite the same again. He went a bit crazy. He started painting. He was never very good. He bought his little house, and shortly after that we became lovers. We had never been less intimate than when we became lovers. It was cold, like a steak sandwich. At the same time he also started picking up young girls. But, for reasons that must be obvious now, he never told me about them."

"He was protecting your feelings."

A flash of irritation. She closed her eyes and raised her face to the ceiling. "Oh, God! How can I ever explain? We had a closeness and an intimacy that few married couples ever achieve *because* he was not in love with me. Falling in love carries with it automatically the fear of loss, but Tony was so loving, so trusting, so naïve in many ways, he never feared that he would lose me. That brings an intimacy to a relationship that is deep and rare."

She stopped, and after a moment I asked, "What are you trying to tell me?"

"From the day we met, Tony sought refuge in me, and I willingly gave it. I protected him and cared for him. But I was not naïve. And from the beginning of puberty I was aware of deep and powerful feelings toward Tony." She paused, gazing out the window, shaking her head. "If he ever felt them for me, he displaced them, projected them, he never acknowledged them. So, when this happened, when I kissed him, it rocked his world. And not in a good way. Suddenly, trust was lost, his secure base was pulverized in a few seconds, the one person in his world who was rock solid was suddenly unknown to him and stimulating passions he did not understand."

A sudden wave of irritation made me snap. "Hang on a minute, Shanna! This guy was almost thirty! You're swinging from four years old to fourteen and twenty-eight like it was all the same thing. This man was an adult and a police sergeant."

She groaned. "You see? I knew you wouldn't understand! In many ways he was an adult, highly responsible and mature, and he was one of the few people I know of who genuinely *cared* about what happens to kids in our urban areas. But *emotionally* . . . ? Emotionally he stopped developing the first time his father took his belt to him and his mother; the day his father forbade him to go to his mother for comfort and consolation. Tony stopped developing emotionally when he was four."

I sighed. I knew what she was saying was possible. People are not just one thing. People are made up of a whole load of processes that are woven together to form an identity, and each of those processes can develop in a different way. After a moment I said, "He used you to replace the mother he was forbidden to see."

"Bravo."

I ignored her sarcasm and went on. "That was a sacred trust. And when you kissed him, you betrayed that trust."

"Yes."

She thought I was done and looked surprised when I continued.

"The problem was, you left him only two options: end your friendship, which wasn't really an option at all, because he needed you too badly, or become your lover. And that was what happened, wasn't it? You were the lover."

She looked at me for a long time with those huge, black eyes. It was impossible to tell what she was thinking or feeling. She transmitted nothing, except absolute attention. Finally she gave a slow blink.

"Yes," she said. "How did you know?"

"Because it's the only way any of this makes sense. Or *begins* to make any sense." I got to my feet again. Feeling a sudden weariness in my back and in my legs, I realized I had not slept more than an hour or two at a stretch for a couple of days. I went and stood at the window, watching the silent choreography of the trees and the wind, and the seagulls circling high in the chaotic air.

"What makes a man like Anthony Sanchez, who was so attractive to women, marry a woman like Astrid Meyer?"

"That is an incredibly sexist thing to say!"

"Is it?" I turned to face her. "Thanks for raising my consciousness. But you'll understand if, especially in this case, I don't bury self-evident truth under unthinking ideology. Astrid Meyer is an unattractive woman with a very unattractive personality. Now stop playing games and answer the damned question!"

She looked away. "Christ!" She took a deep breath and said, "She mothered and smothered him. He was a trophy for her. Aryan, with the Latin flamboyance, young, ridiculously good-looking . . . She decided she wanted him, and she took him. He was incapable of saying 'no' to any woman who showed interest in him. And if she made demands, he obeyed. Unconsciously, he was projecting his mother onto her."

"So she owned him."

She hesitated. "Yeah, up to a point. Emotionally he was like a slave. He wasn't a mommy's boy, because his father had never allowed him to be. But you could say that deep down inside, it was all Tony had ever wanted to be. His obsession with the project was a reflection of that. He wanted to save the children. He wanted to save himself."

"That's what I thought."

She snorted. "Sure."

Again I ignored her sarcasm. "He had found what he was looking for, and she had found what she was looking for. Left to their own devices, they might have carried on like that for years."

"I guess."

"He was not involved in any kind of criminal activity. He had too much integrity, and he was fulfilled, in many of the ways that Astrid could not fulfill him, with his project. He had attracted to himself like-minded friends, and he was satisfying that deep need.

So here was my big question. What makes a man like that a target?"

She looked vaguely startled. "I don't understand."

"Here is a man whose emotional needs are filled, he is not upsetting anybody's applecart, he is not rampaging through the criminal underbelly of the Bronx, making powerful enemies . . . He is just a nice guy, oddly but happily married, with the best friend he could ever hope for by his side. And to cap it all, he is able to fulfill his dream of the club and realize it. So how does this guy get on anybody's hit list?"

I waited, but all she did was stare at me.

"And suddenly, out of the blue, he buys himself a house where he can have affairs. Until now he has been attracted but he has been faithful. Now, suddenly, he is having so many affairs he has to buy a house to conduct them in! And each one is twenty-four hours, a couple of days at most. Wham, bam, thank you ma'am!" I smiled. She didn't return it. "The only way his behavior made any sense, and the only way he got onto anybody's hit list, was by having a love affair. Not an affair, an actual *love* affair." I shrugged and spread my hands. "That was, after all, why everybody thought he had fallen for Dehan. That was why everybody wanted him and Dehan to be having an affair. Because it was the only way to explain what had happened."

I returned to my chair and leaned on the back with my forearms, clasping my hands, watching her. Still she said nothing.

"But, you see, I knew it wasn't Dehan. And that left only one realistic candidate. You. And if he had started having an affair with you, things started to make sense."

Now she spoke, barely, in a raw whisper. "I didn't kill him."

"Really?"

"And you're wrong about Carmen. He was crazy about her, and she was about him . . ."

"Stop it, Shanna. I know you're lying, and so do you. Don't make it worse. By the time Sanchez was murdered, Dehan had begun to find him—and you—heavy going and childish. The ones who were always together, always clowning, were you and Sanchez. But you were trying to deflect attention onto Dehan, encouraging him to paint nude pictures of her, to have balloon fights..."

Suddenly there was fear in her eyes. "No, no, that's not..." She shoved her fingers into her thick hair, pulling the skin tight around her eyes. It made her look crazy. "No!" she said again. "*No!* You are not to think that way!" Her eyes locked onto mine. "I did not kill him."

EIGHTEEN

I stood and went to the trolley. I knew I shouldn't drink, but this case had me in near turmoil, and what the hell! I told myself. I was temporarily suspended, so I was not on duty. I looked at my watch. Eleven a.m. Somewhere east of where I was standing, out on the black Atlantic, the sun was over the yardarm. I took the decanter and poured myself a large whiskey. My ghost, excluded from the house, standing out in the wind and the rain, stared in at me.

"If Anthony didn't tell you about his one-night stands, how did you know about them?"

Her voice came disembodied from behind me. "When we had our heart-to-heart. When we discussed what had happened, he told me he needed to see other women. I think he hoped that would kill my feelings for him. He was wrong. It just made me want him more. The thing is, they were never more than one- or two-night stands, and he always emphasized how little they meant to him. So that always gave me hope that one day, he would grow out of it, lose the need."

I turned. "So you did talk about them."

"But never names, never anything that could be identified as a person, except . . ."

"Except what?"

She looked down at the floor. "You won't believe me. What's the point?"

"The point is that an innocent woman may go to jail for..."

"Except for Carmen!" Her eyes flashed with anger. "Except for the innocent, honest angel you trust so completely! The woman who would never betray you!"

"What about Carmen," I growled.

"Her he talked about."

"What did he say about her?"

"That she was beautiful, that she was intelligent, that she thought rings around him, without her his project would never have got off the ground . . . To be honest I got sick to the back teeth of hearing about little miss perfect Carmen Dehan!"

"Did he tell you he had been with her at the house?"

She wouldn't meet my eye. "I don't want to hurt you, John."

"Tell me the truth, goddamn it, Shanna! Did he ever tell you he'd been with her at the house?"

She stood, leaving her glass on the floor beside her seat, and came over to me. Her eyes were spilling over, and tears were trickling down her cheek to the corner of her mouth. She placed her hands on my chest. Her eyes searched mine. Her body pressed up against mine. I could smell the lime from her gin and tonic on her breath. She frowned at me and touched my cheek with her fingers.

"I'm sorry, John. I don't want to hurt you. I know how much it hurts. I wish I could soothe the pain . . . But they were together. More than once. She was the one he loved. And she loved him back..."

Her fingers went up into my hair. Her knee pressed between my legs. I took a hold of her wrists and pulled her arms down.

"You're a liar, Shanna. You're playing a dangerous game. You try to hurt Dehan, and you have no idea how damned dangerous your game can get."

I left her there. I went out and climbed into the Jag with anger twisting and thrashing in my gut. I took the Bruckner Boulevard north and crossed the freeway at the Westchester Avenue Bridge. Then I followed the avenue all the way down to the Owen F. Dolen Park. A right took me up East Tremont to the corner with St. Raymond, and on the right, surrounded by its own parking lot, was Under the Clock. A singles bar that opened late and stayed open till early. Right now I figured it would be closed, but there'd be somebody in there setting up for the night.

I parked in the lot and stepped out into the rain, then ran across the lot in long strides, avoiding the puddles in the blacktop. The roller blind was up, and I hammered on the door. There were glass panes in it, and through them I could see a fat guy in a black T-shirt behind the bar. He looked at me and shook his finger in the negative. I flattened my badge against the glass. He sighed and slouched over to the door to let me in.

He opened the door and said, "Man, I do not have time for this! You know how much I still have to . . ."

He sighed, gave up, and slouched his way back across the floor toward the bar. I followed.

"We're closed," he said. "But we are always willing to help New York's finest. You on duty? What'll it be?"

I leaned my elbows on the bar. "Give me a beer."

I showed him my badge. He glanced at it as he grabbed a glass and stuck it under the tap. I said, "Detective John Stone. You own this place?"

"For the last ten years. I run a clean operation. All my customers know it. You're comin' here to meet singles. You are *not* coming here to sell your body or to meet whores. Plenty of places online where you can do that, or you can take a ride down to Hunts Point, but two things I do not want in my bar are prostitution or drugs. So I keep a clean joint here, where singles can meet and maybe find happiness together. Hey? Why not? Right?"

"Sure. You know most of your regulars?"

He put the beer in front of me and leaned his elbows on the bar.

"I make a point of it. I ain't got a lot of time. Mind telling me what this is about?"

"You remember Anthony Sanchez? Young, blond..."

"Cop, sure. Got murdered couple of days ago."

"That's the guy."

"You investigating his murder?"

"What can you tell me about him?"

He shrugged, pulled a face. "Not a lot. He was a nice guy, friendly, popular." He grinned. "Real popular with the girls."

I took a pull on my beer. "How often did he come in?"

"Lately it was pretty reg'lar, two, three times a week."

"Alone?"

"Yeah, usually he was alone. Couple of times he come in with a black chick."

"Looker?"

"Man! You ain't never seen nothin' like this chick. She would blow you away."

"But usually alone, right?"

"Right."

I grinned, one dawg to another. "But he never left alone, right?"

"Not Tony! No way! Tony always left with some good-lookin' chick. Sometimes he left with two."

"Son of a gun. Apart from the black chick, did you ever see him come in with anybody else?"

He shook his head. "Nah. We was talkin' last night, bunch of the guys an' me: Did we ever see him with that cop?"

"The one who's supposed to have killed him?"

"Man! She's a looker too! I tell you, we all godda die, right? If I could pick a way to go, I'd go with that cop! Man, she could put the cuffs on me any day of the week!" He stopped, studying my face. "Hey, maybe you know her. Maybe I stepped outta line. No offense intended."

"None taken. I can tell you she looks even better in person, but she has a real bad attitude."

His face was expressionless. "Right. So, anyhow, trial by press, know what I'm sayin'? Point is, we never saw her in here. He never come in with that chick, for sure."

I pointed at the tap in an offer. He said, "I don't mind if I do. You're a gentleman, sir. Thing is, my own feeling, for what it's worth, he was a good-lookin' guy who was playing a dangerous game." He gestured at the empty bar behind me. "Women who come here? They're just like the guys. They take their ring off in the parking lot outside. They have their adventures, some screw in the lot, just before they put their ring back on, others can't wait and make out in the can. Others genuinely is single, but their partner is just playin', know what I'm sayin'? Those are the real dangerous hookups, because if the husband or the wife finds out what's going on, you don't know!" He stood, with his shoulders hunched and his hands spread open. "You just don't know what some people are capable of when they get jealous. I mean, *you* know!" He gestured at me with both hands. "You know, you're a cop! People will kill for jealousy more often than for money. I read that somewhere. Am I wrong?"

I shook my head. "You're not wrong." I eyed him a moment like I was trying to make up my mind. "Besides, Detective Dehan?"

"That's the cop? The one they're accusing of killing him?"

I nodded. "She has a third dan in tae kwon do, black belt in jeet kune do, five times Regional Tactical Police Competition winner, ten times runner up. That tell you something?"

He stared at me, walked away down the bar jerking his knees out, then came back and stood staring at me.

"Well, officer like that ain't gonna leave her goddamn prints all over the weapon and the house, is she? Goddamn!"

"Right. It stinks. So, listen. I am really interested in who he met here. Doesn't matter if they met here, he came with them, whatever . . . I need to know who he made contact with."

"Whatever I can do, man."

"So, first off, was there any one woman that he saw more than the others?"

"No." He was shaking his head before I had finished. "Not with Tony. It was strictly one-night stands with this dude. He was not getting involved." He hesitated then, raised his hands. "But then, there *was* that black chick. The one I told you about? I always had the feeling that she was sweet on him. I never really understood what the setup was there. And besides, end of the day, it's none of my goddamn business, right?"

"Sure, so what about people who were not chicks. People who were just interested in him?"

"You tellin' me this dude was *gay*?"

"No, just, did anybody else take an interest in him?"

His eyes became abstracted. "Yeah." He looked at me and nodded. "You know? You see so many people in a week, so many things happen, you don't retain everything . . ." He tapped his forehead with his middle finger. "But now you said that, there was a dude who came lookin' for him. I never seen him before. Never seen him since. He came in for about three nights, hung around, drinkin'."

"What was he like?"

"Ugly son of a bitch. Black. Tall, six-three? Six-four? Slim, but strong. Wiry, know what I mean? He had a weird name, like a nickname."

"He spoke to Sanchez?"

"No." He shook his head. "No, he never spoke to Tony. He asked about him. He asked me and a few other patrons, what was Tony like? Some other shit. He also asked about chicks who came in with him. Did he ever come in with a black chick, and did he ever come in with a Mexican chick. I told Tony about him. Tony asked me to point him out, but they was never here at the same time."

"It would be a real help if you could remember this guy's name." I waited while he strained his neurons. Finally I said, "Did it reflect any physical feature of his body?"

He frowned. "I think it might have."

"What were his teeth like?"

He snapped his fingers and pointed at me. "Man! You're good! Yeah! Tombstones. That was him. Tombs. Ugliest son of a bitch I ever did see. He hung around a few days, then disappeared. I didn't think much of it, tell you the truth. I thought maybe he was a snitch or somethin'."

"Any idea where I can find him?"

"I never seen him before. His accent was Bronx, but maybe he was from South Bronx or somethin'."

I finished my beer, thanked him, and left. The sky had darkened, and the eternal rain was coming down heavy and steady. I looked at my watch. It was lunchtime, but all I had in my belly was a sick hollow. I went to my car without hurrying, only vaguely aware of the water seeping in, soaking me through. I pulled open the car, climbed behind the wheel, and slammed the door closed. The windshield was awash, torturing and distorting the gray, liquid figures on East Tremont Avenue. I left the wipers off, staring but seeing only an imaginary figure in my mind.

Tombs.

Tombs was the element that was missing.

The guy who'd asked about Sanchez at the bar, the guy who'd offered Dehan a job, the guy who'd tricked Dehan into frisking him and searching his bag. That, and not the glue on the balloon, was how they'd got Dehan's prints. But where else had he shown up? Somewhere, but I couldn't remember where.

I fired up the engine and switched on the wipers. They set up a steady rhythm of squeak and thud, squeak and thud, as I rolled out of the lot, back onto East Tremont Avenue. I was going back to the hotel. I had to brief Saul Cohen and talk to Dehan. Then I needed a shower and some sleep, because it was going to be a long night.

I found Saul and Dehan having lunch in the dining room. Dehan got up as I approached, muttering through a full mouth that I was soaked. She took my coat, and I sat down.

I told the waiter I wanted hot soup, preferably chicken, and a glass of red wine. He went away, and Dehan was staring at my face.

"Something's happened. What's happened?"

"I need a hot shower after lunch, and then I need a few hours' sleep. Then, tonight, I need to go out. I need to buy some cocaine."

Dehan made a face like I just breathed ammonia over her. "*What?*"

Saul was shaking his head. "No, no, John. This is not the way to do things..."

"I know who killed Sergeant Sanchez." They both went quiet. "I know just about everything, except a couple of final details. And that, those details, are what I need to find out tonight."

Saul leaned forward. "Do *not* break the law, John! You could completely undermine our case."

"I'll try not to. I'll try even harder not to get caught. But believe me, unless I do it this way, there is no way of cracking it. They have it sewn up. It is airtight."

The waiter came with my soup and my wine. He set it down, wished me "bon appétit," and left. I drained half my glass, drew breath, and said, "I am going to need your help..."

But before I got any further, Saul raised a hand and said, "Wait, first I have to tell you, I got the sample from the prosecution."

NINETEEN

That changed things. I frowned. "That's too quick. It's less than twenty-four hours."

"I know. I called the DA. We play golf. I asked her what the hell she was playing at. She said violent crime rates are down and lab efficiency is up. Can you believe that. I told her bullshit, and she said that, as well as that, Astrid Meyer has influential friends and she is among them. She wants to expedite things to relieve some of the stress she is going through. Blakemore told her about your crackpot theory, and she wants you to prove to yourself that it's horseshit. Her words, not mine."

"What do you make of it?"

"I think they want us to get the sample fast because they don't believe it carries any weight. I don't know what *you* expect to find, but they obviously don't expect you to find it. They want the trial over quick and the conviction in the bag." He settled back. "So, what is your plan?"

I shook my head. "Not now. Where's the sample?"

He grunted and pulled a padded manila envelope from his pocket. He showed it to me. "What are you going to do with it?"

I took it from his fingers, opened the envelope, and looked

inside. There was a sealed glass vial with bloodstained cloth in it. Dehan echoed Cohen, "What are you going to do?"

I gave it back to Saul. "Get this to the nearest lab that will analyze it. I don't care how much it costs. Get it done now, along with the blood and the cigarette."

He called one of his paralegals and dispatched him with the items.

Dehan repeated, "What are you going to do, Stone?"

"Me? I'm going to buy some coke and have a party."

"Nice." Her tone was heavy with sarcasm. "Now would you like to tell me what you are going to do?"

"I am going to find the person who killed Sanchez, and it is best you don't know where or how."

"No, Stone! Absolutely not!"

"You know I'm not crazy or reckless. If I am doing this, it's because it is the only way I can see to do it."

"Stone, you are not to take risks. You have no backup!"

"I'll stay safe, I promise."

I stepped out into the early-evening rain, turned my collar to the cold and damp, and climbed into my car. I turned the key in the ignition, the engine roared, and immediately there was the staccato wail of a siren, and the cab was flooded with light. I killed the engine and wound down the window.

Blakemore was there in a rain mac with a couple of uniforms. "Get out!"

"You want to give me a reason why I should?"

"Come inside! We need to talk, and I'm getting wet."

I sighed, climbed out of my car again, and followed him to the entrance to the hotel lobby.

"What do you want, Blakemore?"

"Where are you going?"

"That's none of your goddamn business!"

"I can make it my business, Stone. If I look through your vehicle and find . . ."

I cut him dead. "It'll be the last thing you ever do as a cop. I have Saul Cohen just through that door, waiting for an opportunity to eat you alive. You want to know where I'm going? I'm going to Broadway, on Manhattan, to the Federal Plaza, to talk to friends in the bureau and have a sample analyzed."

I knew he was going to sneer, and he did. "What sample?"

I told him what he wanted to hear. "A sample of the blood you didn't want to have analyzed. A sample of the blood at the crime scene. You got any more questions, ask my attorney. Now get out of my way, Blakemore."

"Wait a minute." He put his hand on my chest and narrowed his eyes. He couldn't hide the smirk. "What the hell do you think you're going to find?"

"Too late, Blakemore. You had your chance to be a cop, and you blew it. Now you're just a thug with a badge. I told you before, but you didn't listen. When I bring your paymaster down, I'm bringing you down too." I went to step past him but stopped, my face a few inches from his. "And next time you put a hand on me, I'll break your arm. Now get out of my way."

I walked through the drizzle back to my car. In my head I kept going over the sequence of events leading up to and including Sanchez's death. There were still a couple of things that just didn't make sense. But then I reminded myself, as I climbed back behind the wheel, that they made perfect sense to somebody, somewhere —they made perfect sense to Sergeant Anthony Sanchez's killer. What didn't make sense to me was the way I was looking at it. I had to look at it in a different way. I had to try and see it from the killer's point of view. Then it would make sense.

I fired up the cat again and headed south toward the Throgs Neck Bridge. I'd been focusing too hard on the question of trying to prove Dehan had not killed Sanchez. But that wasn't the question anymore. I already knew the answer to that. I was trying to prove what I already knew.

The real question was, who killed Sanchez?

I stared out at the wet road and the steady flow of lights moving toward me through the dark. Somehow that didn't feel like the right question either. I asked myself what was wrong about it; what made it the wrong question? I leaned back and cracked my spine. The massive blackness of the East River approached.

It was wrong because...

I ran through it again. Shanna had said that Astrid and Sanchez were sleeping in separate rooms. But the body was in the master bedroom. Why hadn't Astrid mentioned that to the cops? Maybe she was in denial about the breakup of her marriage, wanted everybody to believe that things were fine between her and Sanchez. So she had made no mention of the fact that Sanchez had his own room. To do so would have been to admit they had problems. As well as that, perhaps she wanted to believe he had finally returned to their room that night for a reconciliation. Who knew? Maybe he had. But the fact remained, he should not have been in that bed.

She should.

Had the killer known that? According to Shanna, all of Eastchester Bay knew it. I knew that meant something. I just couldn't see what.

Shanna had insisted that Sanchez loved his wife, even if he'd stopped being *in* love with her. Had he then—after the crisis with Shanna, after the shock of discovering that the woman and friend on whom he had always relied emotionally as some kind of a sister was in fact in love with him—had he decided to attempt a reconciliation with Astrid? Had he gone willingly to her bed, to wait for her to return? Was that the reason he had gone home early and not gone out with Shanna?

If that was right, if he had willingly gone to the master bedroom, then those four shots were almost certainly not intended for him, but for Astrid. That had been Dehan's theory, and so far it made sense. And if it was right, the question became not who wanted Sanchez dead? But who wanted Astrid Meyer dead?

For a moment my mind strayed to the Gasoline Club, and Mr.

T, who sold blow. Two got you twenty that was Tombs. The coincidence was too great, and it was the only way it made sense. Did Astrid have associates there who had reason to want her eliminated? Had she upset people there? Had Tombs heard about Dehan's association with Sanchez and decided, if he could not employ her to eliminate Astrid, he would frame her for the murder he intended to commit himself? Had he, then, entered Astrid Meyer's house and, thinking he was shooting Meyer, killed Sanchez instead?

It was possible, but it left unexplained what had happened at Soundview Terrace. If Sanchez had been shot at home, who had been shot at Soundview Terrace? Whose blood was on the boards? Who had changed the mattress, the bedding, and the carpet, but left the ashtray?

It had to be the same killer's hand at work. Whoever had killed Sanchez, wittingly or not, was also responsible for cleaning up a similar crime scene at Sanchez's house.

Two crime scenes, only one body. One crime scene incompetently cleaned up, the other incompetently attempting to frame Dehan, with excessive amounts of blood, and displaying shots both highly accurate and incompetently wild.

I was over the black water of the East River, gliding toward Queens. What was the real question? What was the *right* question? The question I should be asking?

Not did Dehan kill Sanchez? Not who killed Sanchez? But was Sanchez the intended victim? Was Astrid Meyer the intended victim? Or, what happened at Soundview Terrace?

There was also one big, glaring coincidence that did not fit into any explanation I had come up with so far. It was that on the day I had tailed Astrid Meyer, she had wound up, late that night, secluded in a private bar at the very club where, if I was right and Mr. T was Tombs, he sold coke. Tombs, who had tried to recruit Dehan; Tombs, who had shown up at Under the Clock asking about Sanchez and Dehan: Tombs, who was rapidly becoming my number one suspect.

One thing at least was clear. Maybe I wasn't sure what to ask, but I sure as hell knew who to ask.

The Jag growled through the city streets under the amber glow of the streetlamps. The rain washed like amber blood across the blacktop and spattered the windshield under the relentless thud and squeak of the wipers. I cruised down the Bell Boulevard and slowed as I approached the intersection with 41st Avenue. There, on my left, was the Gasoline Club.

I pulled into the lot at the back of the club, aware that my heart was pounding. There were a few trucks and cars there, and a handful of Harleys. I took out my cell, checked it, slipped it in my jacket pocket, and climbed out of the car. The wind was not gale force, but it wasn't far off, and the rain was steady, enough to wet my face by the time I'd run across the lot toward the steps to the back door of the club.

That was when the door opened and the three guys stepped out.

They were not the kind of guys you'd want to be trapped in an elevator with. They came down the steps and spread out, with the rain glistening on their faces. I was wondering how they knew, who had told them. My money was on Blakemore. The guy directly in front of me was six foot with a big, muscular chest and arms that were massive and swollen from working out. But his gut was big and flabby, and his legs were thin.

One guy moved to my left. He was older and liked his beer. He also had a gut, and his hair was oiled and slicked back. Another moved to my right. He was slim and muscular, about five-five, with a bandana and a goatee.

I smiled and said, "What's up, guys? I'm just here to have a drink."

The guy with the gorilla arms answered, wiping trickles of rain from his nose with the back of his wrist.

"I don't like your face. You got a stupid face. To me, you look like a cop. And I got a message for you. Butt out. Go away."

I allowed the smile to become indulgent. "Who's the message from, genius?"

"You know who it's from, cop." He turned to his pals. "Come on, let's give this motherfocker a kicking..."

He took one step and the Sig Sauer Dehan had made me buy was in my hand. I pointed it by turns at the gut on the left and the muscular dwarf on my right.

"On the ground! Now. Facedown, hands behind your head. Do I need to shoot anyone to show I'm serious?"

I didn't. They shook their heads furiously, dropped on their bellies, and laced their fingers behind their heads. I pointed the gun at the gorilla and said, "Now you. On your knees." He dropped to his knees and put his hands behind his head. I stepped closer. "Close your eyes." He closed them.

I'm not proud of what I did next, but I figured my life was on the line right then, and so was Dehan's. So I kicked him in the head, hard enough to put his lights out for a long while and give him a headache the next day. I made the other two dump their pal in the trunk of his own truck then gave them a similar treatment. They joined him there for a cozy night among friends, gagged with their own shirts, wrists and ankles tied with their own bootlaces.

I climbed the stairs and pushed into the bar. It wasn't crowded. There was no band that night, but there were maybe a dozen people, perhaps a little more. The bartender looked surprised to see me. His eyebrows did a little dance: up with surprise, down to a frown, cocked into a "what the hell?" I smiled at him.

"That rain! Seems it's never going to stop. Give me a draught beer, will you? Say, is Tombs in yet?"

He stood for a moment, staring, apparently trying to make sense of what I was saying. Finally he cracked a bottle for me and put it on the bar. He was starting to look worried. "He's in back. But you can't go in there. It's private, members only."

I took another swig. A voice in my head was telling me to keep a grip, but there was something wild going on in my belly, and another voice—a louder, stronger voice—kept telling me that these were the people who wanted to destroy Dehan.

I leered at him and asked, "So, how do I become a member? See, I'm in the mood for a hand of poker or two." I beckoned to him with my finger and spoke very quietly. "Let me tell you what's going to happen. You are going to let me into the back room, so I can play cards with the boys. You're going to do that because, if you don't, I am going to tear your liver out with my bare hands and eat it while I blow your patrons' heads off their necks." I frowned at him while I smiled with my mouth. "Are you wondering where your three tough friends are? Let me tell you, they are at the gates of hell. Now, go tell Tombs I'm here. I promise you he will want to see me. Tell him Stone is here."

He stared at me for a long moment, then stepped out from behind the bar, went to the door, and gazed out into the rain. He turned back to me and said, "Where are they?"

I arched an eyebrow in reply. "Hell. Now, Tombs?"

I followed him past the quiet stage, to the door marked "Private." He opened it with a key, and we moved down a dim, narrow passage and up some stairs to a second floor. There, on a large landing, there was another door. He knocked, leaned in, and spoke quietly. I stayed close, but not too close, with my hand on the butt of my Sig, in my waistband. After a moment he glanced at me, jerked his head indicating I could go in, and pushed past me to go back to the bar. When he'd gone, I stepped through the open door.

The room was large, spacious, maybe thirty feet square. There was little light: a couple of wall lamps and a ceiling light hanging low over a table on my left. There was a bar, which was dark, and a number of gambling tables. Clearly tonight they were quiet.

On my right, four girls sat around a coffee table. They were drinking vodka, and they had a small, wooden box and a dusty mirror they seemed to be sharing. Maybe they were checking their makeup, or their hair. They watched me come in without curiosity.

On my left, under the low-hanging light, there was a round table with four men seated around it. Unlike the girls, they were watching me with real curiosity. Each of them had a tumbler with dark, amber liquid in it. Each of them was smoking: two of them Marlboros, one of them Benson & Hedges, the fourth was smoking Camels. On the table there was an ice bucket and a bottle of bourbon.

Tombs was easy to identify. He was exactly as Dehan had described him, like a snake. Long and thin and poisonous. Even in this poor light, he had black shades over his eyes.

The man on his right had his face set in that "I am a respectable businessman" frown, integrity tinged with outrage. He looked Indian, handsome in an expensive suit, with graying temples. The other two were WASPs, pillars of the community whose ancestors settled the area before the Tea Party. One was in his early sixties and had a gray pencil moustache. The other was younger, but his double-breasted jacket said he had less pedigree.

I took hold of the door and slammed it hard enough to make them all jump—all except Tombs, who just giggled. I knew the chances were high that I would die that night, but the chances were even higher that I would take Tombs with me and blow open the frame they were trying to set around Dehan, so I didn't really care that much.

I asked, "What's the stake?" Nobody said anything. I smiled. "You're gambling men, right? You don't want to gamble?" I jerked my chin at the black guy with the shades. "You're Tombs."

He was grinning like it was a chronic condition he couldn't help. "This is a private club, and you ain't got an invite."

"I'm going to ask again. What's the stake?"

He shook his head at his chips, making a hissing sound through his black, broken teeth. "You're a brave man, Stone. This is only ever gonna end one way, you know that."

"You don't want to tell me? Do these fine, upstanding members of the community know the stakes?" I looked down at the outraged Indian with the sophisticated sideburns. "Do you know the stakes? Do you know that Mr. Tombs here kills cops on the side, for money?"

They all three turned to look at him. I nodded and went on.

"You may have read about his most recent job. It was in the news, huh, Tombs? Sergeant Anthony Sanchez, husband to the well-known businesswoman and philanthropist Astrid Meyer. How much were you paid, Tombs? And why don't you tell us who paid you?"

The pencil moustache scowled at Tombs. "What the hell is this? You said we'd be protected from prying!" He scowled up at me. "Who the hell are you?"

I showed him my teeth. "My name is Detective John Stone, of the NYPD, and I will try hard to forget all your dirty, hypocritical faces, if you take your filthy money and get the hell out of here before my trigger finger goes into spasms."

Tombs said, "Wait a minute. Nobody move." To me he said, "Turn around, Stone, and go home to your wife. You'd better pray she makes it to trial. Pull another stunt like this and the only place you gonna see her is in fuckin' photographs."

I looked at the black lenses of his shades and saw myself reflected there, a dark form among shadows. I didn't flinch or hesitate. I am a good shot, with decades of experience, and I have seen death and mutilation often enough that it no longer makes me shake. The first round took an inch out of the wall two inches from the handsome Indian guy's head. The second punched a hole through the table three inches from the pencil moustache's family jewels, and the third sent the double-breasted jacket's stake fluttering around his ears and put a hole through his jacket pocket.

Chairs scraped and tumbled, and the three pillars of the community showed exactly what they were made of as they staggered back, clutching at their hard-gambled money. When the echo of the shots had died down, I growled, "Get out!"

They scrambled, and the four girls with runny noses went after them. The door slammed closed.

"Just me and you, Tombs."

TWENTY

THE DOOR OPENED, AND A GUY WITH DREADLOCKS AND a dirty T-shirt with a picture of a cannabis leaf on it stepped in. He said, "I hear shot a buss..."

He stopped dead, stared first at Tombs sitting motionless at his table, then at me, standing, holding the gun. I shook my head and grinned.

"You didn't hear shot a buss, pal, you heard the door slam." I kicked the door hard, and it slammed behind him. "Take your piece from your belt and place it very carefully on the floor. Do it right and it won't be the last thing you ever do. What's your name, pal?"

Most people can't multitask. Bozos like this guy find it hard to chew gum and walk at the same time. Thinking about taking his gun carefully from his belt and laying it down on the floor, while at the same time telling me what his name was, was about this clown's limit.

"I'm Delroy, tha's my piece, okay?"

It was a Taurus revolver. He laid it on the floor and stood with his hands up. I nodded. "Now, kick it under that chair and strip down to your shorts."

"Oh man." It was the whine of a kid being told he had to eat his spinach. He kicked the weapon under the sofa where the girls had been and started taking off his clothes. I said, "Stand up, Tombs." He didn't. He sat staring at me. I smiled. "You know how easy it would be for me to rig this as self-defense? You know how willing the cops and the jury would be to believe me?"

He sighed and stood. I said, "Come out from behind the table. Put your piece on the floor and kick it under the chair."

He did as I said and started stripping. As he took off his clothes, he spoke.

"Pretty soon, Stone, you gonna have ten bad bwai in here. They gonna cut your heart out. Then we gonna go a huntin' fo' yah ooman, and we gonna play with her till she cryin' out fo' more."

"Yeah? That what you're going to do, Tombs? Just give me the excuse I need, and you and your bad boys will never step outside the Gasoline Club. Now, how about we quit wasting time and you tell me exactly what happened to Sergeant Anthony Sanchez?"

"You out of your depth, Stone. You finally lost your mind."

"Tell me what happened to Sanchez, tell me what your connection is with Astrid Meyer and her attorney Gottlieb, tell me what happened at Soundview Terrace. Tell me what happened that night, and maybe I won't kill you both."

Delroy was sweating, swiveling his eyes from me to his boss. Tombs laughed a long, wheezing, graveyard laugh. Then flopped his head forward and giggled quietly.

"That little pig gonna take all kind of people down with he. Ain't nobody safe." Then he raised his face to look at me and his smile faded. "Get the hell out of here."

I gave a small laugh. My cell buzzed in my pocket. A message. I pulled it out and looked at the screen. Saul Cohen. "Call me. Urgent."

I called him. He answered, but before he could speak I said, "I'm entertaining guests, what is it?"

"You wanted me to find out who the beneficiaries of their

wills were. I had to pull some strings, but that's my specialty." He paused, then spoke like he was reading from notes. "Sanchez was the sole beneficiary of Astrid's will. If she had died before him, he got everything. I don't know what you were expecting, but these terms are what I would have expected. She is insane about him, so she leaves him everything. They also had substantial insurance policies on each other."

I could see him in my mind's eye, pausing and jutting out his bottom lip. "His will was not so straightforward. I had to call in favors but even so was not able to get the precise terms because the will is sub judice. It is being contested."

"Contested?" I frowned. "By whom? As I recall, the grounds for contesting a will are pretty limited."

"The grounds, and the people who are entitled to do so. They are either a person who would have inherited something if he had died without leaving a will, or a person seeking to prove that the deceased intended to include them in the will but was somehow prevented from doing so. Therefore the terms of the will they are challenging are invalid, and do not reflect the true wishes of the deceased."

"So . . ."

"You can't talk right now, can you?"

"No, talk me through it."

"Either Astrid Meyer is contesting a will in which Shanna is the beneficiary, or Shanna is challenging a will in which Astrid Meyer is the beneficiary. The chances of it being anybody else are nonexistent. Nobody else has standing."

"Agreed, so where does that leave us?"

"You're the detective! The way I see it, if he was taking women back to his house at Locust Point, it is at least even chances that one of his lovers got shot there, possibly by Astrid or someone working on her instructions. The body was most probably dumped in the East River, along with the mattress and the bedding, and will in all likelihood never be seen again."

Tombs was standing beside Delroy in his shorts. He looked

vaguely ridiculous and a little pathetic. I fixed him with my eye and spoke like I was reciting, watching his face as I did so.

"He's with a lover. Tombs, sent by Astrid, finds them and kills the girl. Tombs tells Sanchez to go home, while he takes care of the housecleaning. Sanchez leaves and goes home. For some reason, maybe because he is shocked and terrified, he goes to the master bedroom. Perhaps the horror of what has happened has driven him back to his wife. But Astrid is out to dinner, securing an alibi. Meantime, Tombs arrives intending to finish the second part of his contract, finds Sanchez in the master bedroom, and kills him."

Tombs spat elaborately on the floor. "That's bullshit, man."

In my ear Saul grunted. "Now all you need to do is prove it."

"Yeah. I'll talk to you later."

I put the phone in my pocket and sat staring a long time at Tombs. Finally I said, "What do you think happens now, Tombs?"

"I'll tell you, white boy. I think yo' bitch gonna go down for thirty years fo' killin' a white pig cop, and you gonna go down fo' ten years for kidnapping and ill treatment of a citizen, just because he was black."

"You think I haven't thought of that?"

"Oh, you thought of that? Because, I gotta tell you, boy. You sure as hell don't look like you thought about it!"

I trained the gun on Delroy and pointed at Tombs.

"Let me explain, Tombs. You are threatening to send my wife and my partner away for the rest of *my* adult life, and most of hers. Now, I know that empathy and sympathetic imagination are not your strong points, but in this case it would have been a good idea for you to try and imagine how I was going to feel about that, and how I was going to react. Because, I don't actually care what happens to me. But I *do* care what happens to her. So, what I am going to do is shoot Delroy here in the ankle, then I am going to shoot him in the other ankle . . ."

I was watching Tombs, but I was watching Delroy closer in

my peripheral vision. His eyes were wide, and he was swallowing a lot. I hated what I was doing, but I kept the image of Dehan in orange overalls, chained hand and foot, being led away for the next thirty years, firmly in my mind, and I didn't waver.

"He'll lose his feet, but he might save his legs. The next slugs go to his knees . . ." I gave a small laugh. "Now you're probably thinking, what the hell do you care, right? What do you care what happens to Delroy. He's not your wife, right?" I wagged my finger. "But you should care, because everything that happens to him is going to happen to you."

Delroy looked at Tombs, and there was hope in his eyes. Tombs was swallowing now, almost compulsively. I plowed on.

"But here's the clincher, Tombs. Here is the incentive to get a move on. Because whenever you decide to start talking, you still get to experience everything that Delroy has experienced up to the point where you say, 'I'll talk.' I think that's fair, don't you? So you say, 'Okay, I'll talk,' after I shoot off his left foot. You lose your left foot too. You wait until he has lost his arms and legs and is bleeding to death. You get to share that with him too."

Delroy was trembling all over. His eyes were wide, and he was staring at Tombs. I was praying that Tombs would not call my bluff, but I was also banking on Delroy becoming my reluctant ally.

I cocked the Sig and took aim at Delroy's left ankle. Delroy screamed like a little girl and held out both hands toward me, shrieking, "*No! No! I can tell you! I can tell you what you need! I'll testify!*"

At the same instant Tombs hurled himself across the room at me, and I turned and shot him in the thigh. He screamed too, spun and fell, clutching at his leg. While he thrashed and whimpered, I turned my attention back to Delroy.

"Talk!"

His mouth worked. He licked his lips, eyeing his boss on the floor clawing at his leg. "You want to know what it feels like?" I snarled.

"No! No! He had a contract. He had to take out the cop. I know that."

"Who gave him the contract? You're no damn use to me unless you tell me where the contract came from!"

"It was, it was"—he kept moving back and forth, taking tiny steps toward me and away, wringing his hands, speaking fast—"it was, it was a woman. A woman. I know it was a woman."

"*What woman, goddamn it?*"

A rage of frustration was building inside me. I strode to Tombs, knelt beside him, and pressed the muzzle of the gun against his good knee.

"*What woman?*"

He was sobbing. "Oh God, oh God, please, I need a doctor . . ."

"*What woman?*"

The door opened, and Blakemore stepped in. Behind him were two thugs. One looked Latino, with massive shoulders and a tattoo on his forehead. The other was black and built like a quarterback. They moved in, and Blakemore stood surveying the scene for a good three seconds before he said, "What the hell kind of mess have you got yourself into, Stone?"

I stood. "Why don't you tell me, Blakemore?"

"Oh." He gave a small laugh of genuine pleasure. "I think all the explaining here needs to be yours, Stone. Early retirement, minimum, but you'll be lucky if you don't do time."

"Yeah, you think?" I paused because I could hear Tombs trying to say something. He was reaching up toward Blakemore, his face an ugly, dark yellow.

"Jim, help me. Get me a doc. I didn't talk . . ."

Blakemore roared, "Shut up, Tombs!"

Tombs was choking. "You don't understand. I didn't talk. Delroy was gonna . . ."

"Shut up!"

"You have to help me, Jim!"

"*Shut up!*"

Suddenly his piece was in his hand and he shot Tombs through the head. The harsh detonation left a ringing silence in the room. Tombs quivered a couple of times and lay still. Delroy backed away a step, holding up his hands in front of him.

"I didn't say nothing, 'Tective Blakemore."

"You were talking when I came in."

"But, no, that was, I was lyin', and I was tryin' to stop Tombs from sayin' somethin' . . ."

I said, "He tried to keep you out of it, Blakemore, in all fairness to the boy."

He glanced at me gratefully and said, "Yeah, I never said nothin' about you . . ."

Too late he realized what he'd said, and Blakemore put two rounds through his chest. The two thugs in the doorway were looking worried, seeing their gang leaderless and being decimated.

I frowned. "You'd better stop soon, Blakemore. It's going to turn into a spree if you keep going. Who's next? Me? Are you going to shoot a cop, and live with that hanging over you for the rest of your life?"

He sneered, "No, Stone, I am just going to shoot a cop. And then you and Dehan will go down in history as a pair of rogue, twisted vigilantes who did too much blow and wound up dirty and bent." He trained his gun on me. "Put your weapon down, Stone."

"I don't think so."

"You're outgunned. Do the smart thing."

"I'm outgunned? What's wrong with this picture, Blakemore? You just shot two unarmed men, and you are using two gang members to hold me at gunpoint. What were Tombs and Delroy about to tell me about you?"

"Forget about it. Where is Detective Dehan? I went to pick her up and she's nowhere to be found. There's a BOLO out for her, and you. Do yourself a favor. Where is she?"

"Probably in Canada. When I saw this was a frame-up, I sent

her north for her own protection, while I requested a federal investigation."

"Bullshit, Stone. Where is she? And what have you done with Mrs. Meyer?"

I studied his face a moment. I said, "She was scared you and Gottlieb were going to cut her out and kill her."

He leered, showing all his teeth. "She was scared Gottlieb was going to kill her?"

"You and Gottlieb, Blakemore. Is that so hard to believe? Between you, you arranged Sanchez's death, didn't you?"

"You're fishing. Even at this stage of the game, you're fishing. If I didn't hate you so much, I'd admire you." He turned to the thugs. "Take his weapons and check him for a wire."

I swung my gun in their direction. They froze. "I have nothing to lose, boys, and everything to gain. I'll take at least two of you with me. Why'd you kill them, Blakemore?"

He stared at me a long time. "I should tell you shit! What I should do is kill you, like the rest of them, and dump you in the fuckin' river!"

"The rest of them? Who else have you killed? These two boys, unarmed and helpless. You act tough, Blakemore, but you're just a loudmouth. You didn't kill Sanchez. You arranged it, you conspired, but you got somebody else to do the work."

"You think you know, huh?"

"Yeah, I know. I know everything. I know about the will, I know Tombs was the triggerman, I know who ordered it . . ."

There was a loud yell, and suddenly the big Latino was charging across the room at me. He smashed into me like a steel battering ram and hurled me against the wall, knocking the wind from my lungs. Next thing he had his right hand over the barrel of my gun and he was levering it from my hand. I bellowed and pounded my left elbow into his ribs. I heard him grunt and saw the huge black guy hurtling across the floor to join the fray. He grabbed the Sig in both hands and yanked hard. I knew if I didn't let go he'd break my fingers. I let go and simultaneously smashed my instep into his balls. He backed away, staggering, and fell to his knees. Then I heard Blakemore's voice, loud and authoritative.

"Freeze, Stone. It's over. If you know that much, then you know too much. You have to die."

He raised his gun and trained it on my head.

There are some things you just can't prepare for.

The Latino who'd taken me down was standing a few paces from Blakemore, sneering and laughing, feeling pretty good about himself. The black giant was dragging himself to his feet with tears in his eyes. My eyes were fixed like microscopes on Blakemore's hand, holding the weapon, his finger on the trigger. And there was an absolute, undoubting certainty in my mind that I was about to die. I only hoped I had done enough.

And then, as though in slow motion, the Latino seemed to snake. His head moved to his right, making his body whiplash in slow motion, then his head moved violently back to the left as a pink-and-black plume erupted from his temple. He seemed to dangle on tiptoes for a moment and then collapse to the floor. Blakemore was momentarily distracted, and that was all I needed. I screamed and charged inside his guard, grabbed the barrel of his gun in my left hand, and powered my fist into the side of his jaw with all my two hundred and twenty pounds, fueled by rage, frustration, and other primitive emotions my mother would not have been proud of.

I felt the gun come loose from his grip and delivered two more crosses, left and right, before he collapsed in a heap.

I looked for the black guy. Saw him lying on the floor with his hands over his head, when a figure burst through the door and roared, "*Hit the deck!*" I dropped the gun and complied.

TWENTY-ONE

A SURPRISINGLY SMALL FIST GRABBED THE BACK OF MY collar, and a voice snarled, "We have to get the hell out of here! The cops are a couple of minutes away!"

We sprinted down the passage and out into the bar, where people were stubbing out rollups and making hastily for the door. A quick flash of a couple of Sig Sauers and they made way for us. We ran across the asphalt in the parking lot, with the rain spattering our faces, and a couple of seconds later we were rolling out onto Bell Boulevard, heading south and west, in the general direction of Brooklyn and Manhattan, with sirens wailing behind us.

I looked over my shoulder, satisfied nothing was following us. Then I turned to Dehan and roared, "What in *hell's name* are you doing here?"

"*Saving your dumb ass!*" she shouted. "*Now shut up until I'm sure we're okay!*"

"Fine!"

We spent about half an hour doing loops and fancy maneuvers while we made sure and double sure that A, we were not being followed and B, there was no BOLO out for my Jag. So some of what Blakemore had said was BS. But right then, in that moment, my head was in such a turmoil I had no idea what was what.

We gradually made our way onto the Northern Boulevard, headed west. At the water we turned right and north onto the Whitestone Expressway and began to relax. She kept the pace steady. There wasn't a lot of traffic, but the lights headed south on the far side of the freeway created a silent, vaguely hypnotic rhythm. We passed Flushing and came to Powell Cove on the left without speaking. And then we were out, over the water.

Her voice was quiet when she eventually spoke.

"What do you think my life would be like, if you died? And especially if you died trying to save me from prison?"

I took a while to answer, then answered equally quietly. "Can you tell me how I can answer that question without sounding like an arrogant narcissist?"

"I'm serious, Stone!"

"I imagine it would be hell. But let me ask you a question. If our roles had been reversed, and you knew the only way to . . ."

She interrupted me. "Yes! I would have done the same! But Stone! You can't do that kind of thing! What use is staying out of jail if every day I have to live with the fact that you're . . ." Her right hand waved around in the dark for a moment. She didn't finish the sentence.

"I can't let them do that to you, Dehan. I won't let them. Whatever the price is, I cannot live knowing that you are a prisoner in jail, for the rest of your life. That we will never again eat breakfast together, take a walk, solve a crossword. That I will never again wake up and see your face on the pillow. Whatever the risk, Dehan, it's worth it."

"Jesus!" she said and looked away from me out of the window. "Don't! Don't make me cry when I'm driving, for crying out loud!"

I nodded. "Keep your eyes on the road. And dry." And after a moment I added, "Bit of a mess, huh?"

"We've known worse. What's the plan?"

"We have?" I snorted. "News to me. They kept asking where Astrid was. She seems to have disappeared. I think I might know, though. I think maybe I have been stupid."

She looked at me in the dark. "Where?"

"I think she might be at Locust Point. And I think we should go and ask her why Blakemore and Tombs were so keen to find her."

She looked skeptical. "I didn't think she even knew it existed . . ." Then, "We'll have to loop around. Why don't we take a look at Astrid's house first, then swing by Shanna's? It's not a big detour."

I nodded. But I felt uneasy.

We stopped at the Bay View on the way, checked in with Saul Cohen, and deposited the recordings I'd made on my cell. I put him up to speed, briefly, on what had happened. He frowned a lot, and by the time I'd finished he was flapping his hand and saying, "We need to go over this slowly. I understand now you need to find Shanna and Astrid Meyer. Go, then, and do it. Where is Detective Blakemore? We don't know. Recovering from severe brain damage no doubt. Keep me posted, and come back when you have found the women."

We left him settling down to a bottle of brandy and the recordings in the cocktail lounge.

It was a short drive through the dark and the squally rain, with the black East River indistinguishable from the black sky on our right. We stopped at Shanna's house first, with the rain lashing at the windshield and our headlamps illuminating amber needles that peppered the stygian air.

As we climbed out of the car I saw light in her windows. There was an arrhythmic hammering among the gusting wind. Dehan said, "The front door is open."

We ran across the sidewalk and up the steps to her front porch. The wind was slamming her door, slowly opening it, and slamming it again. I bellowed her name, but the wind snatched it and hurled it out over the trees, into the blackness.

Dehan pushed through over the threshold. I closed the door and locked it. There was an unreal stillness to the house. I shouted her name again, and Dehan moved into the open space of her living room. The lights were on, and the black glass in the windows looked back at us from behind the reflected glare. On a coffee table, a tall glass held a single cube of melting ice and a slice of lime. I raised my voice. "*Shanna!*"

In the kitchen a pot of cold rice stood on the cooker, beside it a pan of meat in tomato sauce. I heard Dehan's steps as she ran up the stairs to the bedrooms. I followed.

They were all empty. In her room the bed was still unmade.

Her study was beside her bedroom, overlooking the backyard and the creek. The door was open, and I flipped on the light. The blond wood held textbooks on psychology and psychoanalysis. A cold coffeepot. A stained cup.

Dehan stood beside me, and suddenly I was on my knees, wrenching open the drawers in her desk, pulling out the papers, packs of staples, envelopes, and instruction manuals, throwing them on the floor, scattering them.

I heard Dehan: "What the hell are you doing?"

A filing cabinet stood against the wall. I stood and hauled open those drawers too, ripping out file after file, patients and case studies. What I was looking for was not there.

And then, in the bottom drawer, I found five files of correspondence with her attorney. I threw it on the desk, sat in her chair, and started going through it. It was the fourth document from the top. I took hold of it and flopped back in the chair. I heard Dehan whisper, "What the hell . . ."

Anthony Sanchez's last will and testament. It was a photocopy. The original would be with his executor, probably his attorney. It was dated less than two months back. I read it slowly, carefully. It stated that this document revoked all prior wills and codicils, and that, being of sound mind, and without coercion, he left everything that he owned, both realty and personalty, to the only woman he had ever truly loved, Shanna McLean.

There followed a comprehensive list of everything that he owned, and it began to dawn on me that Anthony Sanchez had been a very rich young man. There was not only a substantial amount of cash, there were also stocks and bonds held in trust by his family in Mexico, and property holdings: land in the U.S.A. and Mexico, apartments and houses that ran into several million dollars.

I put aside the will and started going through the correspondence with his attorney.

"I was wrong..." I muttered to Dehan.

"About what?"

"There had been no reconciliation. These letters..."

The letters and emails from Gottlieb were not only aggressive, they were downright threatening. Property and money that Sanchez had given to Astrid, they said, were not loans, but legal transfers of title, and moneys and properties that had been promised were due to her by law. My head was reeling. One thing stood out above all others, and I spoke it aloud to Dehan.

"If there was no reconciliation," I said, "then he was in the wrong bed."

Images flashed in my mind: the light streaming from the windows, the door unlocked and banging in the wind and the rain. The house, empty; the glass, empty—the melting ice and the lime.

"Damn!" I said. "I think we're too late!"

I grabbed the will and ran, clattering down the stairs while Dehan took them three at a time. She wrenched open the front door and clambered into the Jag. Just at that moment my cell rang. I answered, wiping the rain from my face.

"Stone!"

"It's Joe, I have the results from the sheet you asked me to collect. I have no idea why you sent me a second sample via the DA. I almost didn't run it. I'm glad I did. I don't understand anything, Stone, but brace yourself..."

I climbed slowly into the car, my hair matted with rain, scowling. When he'd finished, I fired up the engine, rammed in first, and hurtled down Griswold to fishtail as we skidded into Outlook Avenue. There I floored the gas. The huge old car surged and growled, and we did a quarter of a mile in fifteen seconds. I slammed on the brakes as we neared the iron gate to the mock Georgian manor. We skidded to a halt, and Dehan's door was open before the Jag had stopped. I followed her at a run across the gravel. She was shouting over her shoulder, wiping the lashing rain from her face.

"*What the hell is going on? You wanna let me in?*"

His door was also open. Protected by the gabled porch and the white columns, it was not banging. It was just creaking to the sullen rhythm of a dirge. But this door had not been left unlocked. This door had had the lock shot out.

Outside, the wind coiled and whipped around the house, howling and moaning, playing eerie panpipes with the chimneys and stairwells, like a gang of wailing banshees . . .

Banshees . . .

I had my piece in my hand. So did Dehan. I called his name. My voice echoed, then died. Our footsteps were startling and loud. I crossed the floor to his study and pushed through. The flames were burning in the grate. His glass of bourbon was still on his small table by the Chesterfield.

Dehan called from across the hall. In the drawing room the fire was also burning in the grate. It was the only light in the room, and it washed the walls with a dying orange glow. It was enough to see his body by. There was not much blood, because he'd died instantly. It had been a quick, efficient death. Expedient.

James' wide eyes stared but did not see. The shot had come from directly in front of him. It looked like a .22. No exit. His right hand was extended forward, cupped around the butt of a Colt revolver.

"We should have gone straight to Locust Point."

"Astrid and Shanna? But who . . . ?"

I drew breath to answer. But a voice from the door—barely a

voice, more a rasp—said, "You killed Stuart. Why the hell did you have to kill Stuart?"

We turned, and I stood. Blakemore, with his face grotesquely disfigured, purple and swollen, stood swaying in the doorway. He said, "You didn't need to kill him. He thought it was a banshee." He gave an ugly, gurgling laugh and raised his gun. "Where is Astrid? What have you done with her?"

I said, "Give me the gun."

"So you can kill me too?"

"No, you asshole. So I don't have to. I didn't kill you last time, did I? You think about pulling that trigger and Dehan will plug you right between the eyes."

He frowned, trying to focus on her. "You're not allowed to carry a gun. I'm gonna put you away."

While he was talking, I had taken three steps forward. Now, aware that I was closer than before, he swung his weapon back toward me.

"Watch your step, cowboy," he slurred. "Now you better tell me where Astrid is . . ."

Dehan's voice cut across him, in a respectable imitation of Mickey Rooney. "Should I plug him, boss?"

The gun wavered. A long stride had me level. I snatched the barrel and levered hard down, while I delivered a massive right cross to his jaw. His legs attempted a complicated jive while his eyes rolled into his head and he slumped to the floor. Dehan was already hunkered beside him, pulling out his laces. "I enjoy doing that," I growled. "I should do it more often. Should we take him home and hang him in the garage?"

"I think you're disturbed, Stone."

She finished tying his wrists, and we made for the car. She spoke as we ran.

"You want to explain? If Blakemore is tied up in there and Tombs is dead, clearly either Astrid has Shanna at Locust Point, or Shanna has Astrid . . ."

I said, "Uh-huh . . ." as I clambered behind the wheel and

took off, slamming both doors through sheer momentum and hurling Dehan back against her seat.

I fishtailed onto Watt, wiping rain from my eyes, and then hurtled down Mac Donough as far as the Country Club Road. The wipers were thrashing furiously at the heavy rain. I skidded across the bridge, weaving from right to left lane, then fishtailed again onto the Bruckner Boulevard, slipped onto the I-695, and floored the gas, sending streams of spray from the wheels high into the air.

We finally came off at Harding Avenue, spun the wheel into Pennyfield, and skidded to a halt outside Anthony Sanchez's house on Soundview Terrace.

There was light in the window, filtering through the drapes. It reflected off Astrid's dark Audi.

I said, "There's a back door that leads down to the river."

She nodded. "I'll take the back. You knock on the door."

She slipped around the side of the house, and I crossed the front yard to the door. I rang the bell and hammered a few times with my fist. A shadow moved inside. I hammered again and the shadow resolved itself into a silhouette, moving steadily toward me.

The door opened. Shanna stood frowning at me. "John? You look terrible. What happened? What on Earth are you doing here?"

"I went to your house. You weren't there. The door was open. Looked like you'd left in a hurry, on an impulse." We stood a moment staring at each other. "What are *you* doing here?"

She drew breath. Did a kind of wincing smile, like she didn't really want to talk. Over her shoulder I saw the back door open silently, and Dehan slip in. I smiled at Shanna. "You going to keep me out here all night in the rain? Can I come in?"

She ran her fingers through her hair. "Oh, you know what? This is a really bad time . . ."

I laughed. "Really? *This* is a bad time? Are you with someone?"

She gave a short, humorless laugh. "Of course not. Why did you come here, Stone?"

I drained all expression from my face and gave her the dead eye.

"Let me in."

She sighed heavily and dropped her arms by her side. She muttered "Jesus!" under her breath and walked away, leaving the door open. Dehan had disappeared. I stepped in and pushed the door closed behind me.

"What's going on, Shanna?"

She answered without looking at me. "It's none of your goddamn business."

"*Really?*" She caught the disbelief in my voice and turned to face me. I said, "It doesn't *concern* me? Does it concern my wife? Does it concern a woman who is likely to go to jail for twenty to thirty years?"

She shut her eyes and raised her hands to cover her face.

"Shut up, Stone. Shut up. I *know* your wife is accused of Tony's murder. And I am *sorry* about that. And I am *sorry* that I have developed some feelings for you. I didn't mean that to happen. But none of that *matters*! This, *this*, what is happening here, now, *tonight*! This has *nothing* to do with you, and you should go."

"What is going on here tonight, Shanna?"

"Go away, Stone."

"Come on. You know I can't do that."

"You don't *understand*!"

"Then make me understand. Maybe I can help?" She shook her head. I pressed her. "Where is Astrid?"

"*Go away!*"

"Where is she?"

She reached behind her back, and suddenly there was a .22 in her hand. It wasn't a surprise. I'd expected it.

"Is that the gun you used to kill Stuart? He didn't deserve to die. You shot him in the back."

"Whatever, Stone. I won't let you stop me."

"Do you know how many people have died tonight, Shanna, because of this madness?"

She shook her head. "I don't care."

"I don't believe you. You're a doctor." I stepped toward her, and she backed up a step. "Caring is what you do. You're a healer of minds and souls. That's why Sanchez loved you." I shook my head. "Too many people have died already. It has to stop."

She took another step back and gripped the gun with both hands. She was trembling badly. Her eyes were wild, and I knew she was close to breaking. What she would do when she broke, I didn't know.

I sighed. "You know I am never going to back down, Shanna. I know what happened now. I understand. I am on your side. Just tell me where you have Astrid."

I could see her jaw muscles bunching. "If you try to stop me, Stone, I swear to God I will kill you both. She has to *pay*, Stone! She can't get away with this!"

Dehan appeared again over her shoulder. She said, blandly, "She's here, in the bedroom, tied to the bed."

TWENTY-TWO

She swung around in a panic, pointing the gun at Dehan. For a second I thought she was going to fire, and my heart lurched. But Dehan looked at her blandly and said, "Hey, Shanna."

I said, "I'll tell you what we are going to do."

She swung the gun back at me. "Stay away!"

I ignored her and went on. "We're going to sit there at the table and have a drink. And you can explain to us what this is all about, and what it is Astrid has to pay for." I shrugged. "Maybe the DA will agree with you. Okay?"

"The DA is a friend of hers!"

"The DA's only friends are the electorate."

While I was talking I walked toward the dining table and pulled out a chair. Dehan did the same. I glanced toward the bedroom. Shanna ran, still holding the gun. Her voice was shrill. "No! *No! No!*"

But it was too late. I had seen her. Like a grotesque parody of the photographs of Dehan, Astrid was on the bed, stretched out, stripped down to her underwear, with each ankle and each wrist bound tightly to a post, and a gag in her mouth. Her eyes were wide and terrified. I shook my head.

"This isn't you, Shanna."

Her scream was shrill. "*She has to pay!*"

"For *what*?"

"For what she did to Tony!"

I shouted back, "What did she do to Tony, Shanna? Tell me so I can understand!"

"Don't fucking patronize me! Don't play me! Don't try to *fucking* manipulate me!"

I repeated the question more quietly. "What did she do to Tony?"

Her rage was subsiding into grief and exhaustion. Tears were starting to spill from her eyes. "She killed him. She *killed my only love*..."

I shook my head. "No, she didn't."

The rage returned to her eyes, and she screamed, baring her teeth, "*She killed him!*"

"That is not what happened that night." She stared at me, breathing heavily, but she didn't answer. I pressed her. "That's not what happened that night, is it?"

She didn't answer, so I went on.

"She was out, dining with colleagues. She was seen by lots of people."

"She killed him."

"Why don't you tell me what really happened?"

"No, go away, stop it."

"He was shot in that bed, wasn't he?"

"I didn't know..."

"Is that why you brought Astrid here, so she would die in the same place, in the same way?"

She spoke with a wet, twisted face. "All I know is she has to pay..."

"You didn't know that he had been killed here?" I stood and walked toward her. She waved the gun at me, limp and helpless.

"Get back! Sit down!"

But the moment had passed. Her resolve was gone. I took

hold of the gun and gently levered it out of her fingers. "I am not a threat to you, Shanna, and you are not a killer."

Her face crumpled. She stared at me, with horror in her eyes. "*No, Stone! She has to pay . . .*"

I held her in my arms. Dehan came round and took the .22 from my hand. Shanna sobbed into my chest. I maneuvered her to the table and sat her down. Her face was sodden and twisted with grief. She repeated, mindlessly, like a mantra, "She killed him. She has to pay, Stone. You can't. You can't take this away from me."

"Quit saying that. You know it's not true."

"*It is!*"

The exhaustion overwhelmed me for a moment, and I snapped. "*He was shot in that bed, Shanna! She wasn't here!*"

She suddenly screamed at me, "*And neither was I!*"

Her meaning became clear. I glanced at Dehan. She went into the bedroom. Shanna made to get to her feet. "What are you doing?" I stood and took hold of her. She clawed at my shoulder, trying to get past. "Don't let her go! *Don't you let her go!*"

"*Shanna!* Settle down, goddamn it!"

We both stared into the bedroom as Dehan approached the bed, leaned down, and removed the gag.

Astrid lay and stared at us in silent, sullen terror.

I went to stand beside Dehan, looking down at the prone woman on the bed. Rain lashed the glass beyond the drapes. Finally Astrid spoke, and her voice shook.

"Stone, for God's sake, you're an officer of the law. This woman is out of her mind! Her mind is full of fantasies. She is going to kill me!"

"I know. But right now I am exhausted, and badly in need of a beer and twelve hours' sleep."

"*Stone!*"

"Don't worry, nobody is going to kill you." I glanced back at Shanna. She was slumped on the sofa with her hands over her face. I called to her.

"Shanna, come here."

She rose and came and stood in the doorway, staring at Astrid. I said, "I am confused. There are things that confuse me. For example." I turned to Astrid again. "Why did Blakemore try to kill me? And why were he and Tombs so desperate to find you? I keep asking myself, if Shanna hadn't come and dragged you off for an evening of bondage and murder at Tony's place, what would have happened to me, when you had joined Blakemore and Tombs at the Gasoline Club?"

"No, you're wrong. You are very wrong. I have no idea about any of that! I am a *victim* here! My husband is murdered, and now this bitch wants to kill me too!"

My brain was tired. I needed sleep. I knew I was missing things. I said, "Here's something else that confuses me. It confused me from the start. The blood."

"What blood?"

"When I saw the bed, the bed where Sanchez was supposed to have been killed . . . I have seen a lot of men shot, but I have never seen as much blood as I saw on that bed, not from a bullet wound to the gut. I kept wondering why. So I asked my pal Joe, at the lab, to go and collect the sheet . . ."

Astrid went pasty and pale. "You did that? I thought Blakemore was . . ."

"Was what? Cleaning up the crime scene?" She shook her head but didn't answer. "No, I did that. But out of sheer curiosity, you know what else I did? I requested a sample of the blood to be handed over to my attorney, by the DA. They are both being analyzed right now at the lab, along with the blood I found on the boards under this bed."

The room had gone very still and very silent.

After a moment Astrid said, "Analyzed for what?"

"To see whose blood it was."

"It was Tony's! Who else?"

I gave a dry laugh and shook my head. "Here's the confusing thing, Astrid. The sample that was sent to me by Detective Blakemore, via the DA, was Sanchez's blood. But the blood I collected from the bed . . ." I watched her face carefully. I gave a small shrug, pulled down the corners of my mouth. "Hazard a guess."

Her voice became hysterical. "This is my husband's murder you're talking about!"

"Was your husband a dog, Astrid? Was your husband a German Shepherd?"

She screwed up her eyes and screamed. Her face turned crimson, then violet. She drew breath and kept screaming. A moment later Dehan pushed past me with a cooking pot in her hands. I wondered what she was going to do. What she did was upend it over Astrid's face. Cold water plunged onto her head, making her gasp and choke.

Then Dehan turned and stared at me, frowning and squinting like she couldn't quite see me. She said, "*What?*"

"The blood that drenched Sanchez's bed was the blood of a dog, a German Shepherd. It was not Sanchez's blood."

Astrid had started sobbing. Shanna gave a small scream and covered her mouth with her eyes. She was shaking her head and whispering, "No . . . Oh God . . . *Why?*"

I turned back to Astrid. "Then I remembered something Stuart had said to me. Something else I didn't understand. On the night that Sanchez was killed, he heard a banshee howling near the house, late at night. I saw the possibility then but didn't want to believe it. The dog was sacrificed to provide the blood that Sanchez could no longer supply."

I pointed at the bed where Astrid was lying. "Because he was shot, by Tombs, right there, where you're lying, and that is where he bled out. Then he loaded the body into a vehicle and took it to your house, where he placed it in your bed. To make it look like he was killed there, he went and slaughtered the dog, collected the blood in a couple of buckets, and soaked the bed with it. He knew the blood would never be tested, because the investigation would be conducted by his pal, Detective Blakemore, and the weapon would be found with Detective Dehan's prints all over it. It would be a slam dunk."

I frowned and shook my head. "But what confused me was, why. Why would Tombs go to all that trouble? Why would he risk getting caught at your house? How did he know you'd be out? And, if he'd gone to all the trouble of getting Dehan's prints days before, why did he kill Sanchez here? If he had a grudge, or a beef, he could have killed him anywhere!"

Shanna spoke suddenly, and her voice was shrill, near hysterical. "*You killed him! You murdering bitch! If you didn't do it with your own filthy hands, you had that snake Tombs do it.*"

Astrid screamed back, her face drenched with tears, her voice close to despair. "*Why? Why would I do that? I loved him! I adored him!*"

"*You lying bitch! He told me! He told me himself that he was through with you! With your greed and your manipulation! He couldn't stand you anymore! He loved me!*"

"*In your sick fantasies, you thieving bitch!*"

"*He was fucking every woman he could get his hands on, just to forget you!*"

Astrid turned to me. Her expression was desperate. It was hard not to feel compassion. "Stone, please! Tony and I had our difficulties, like any couple. I was older than him, we had different interests. But we loved each other, and we were working to fix it. He was coming back to me."

I gave a small sigh. "He'd changed his will, Astrid. He'd left everything to Shanna."

I pulled my cell from my pocket and called Inspector John Newman, the chief. A sleepy voice answered.

"Who the hell is this?"

"John Stone."

"John? What in the name of . . ."

"I need you to listen very, very carefully, sir."

"If this is about . . ."

"It is not about Dehan."

"Oh . . ."

"It is about a very complex web of deceit and corruption. The first thing is that you need to contact Joe and Frank at the lab and the morgue. Joe is going to tell you that the bed in which Sergeant Anthony Sanchez was found was not saturated with his blood. It was saturated with the blood of a German Shepherd dog."

"Are you insane?"

"If you don't call them, sir, I will have them call you."

"A *dog*?"

"Have I got your attention, sir?"

"Yes, goddamn it, Stone! Of course you have!"

I ran through everything, and when I was finished I added, "So, I need you to get a court order and send a detective and a couple of patrol cars to Gottlieb's house and offices. I want all the documents relating to the sale and/or development of Sanchez and Astrid's properties—agreements, contracts, negotiations, minutes, emails, letters—everything! If I'm right, Gottlieb has been party to a conspiracy to murder, to framing an officer of the law for that murder, and the wholesale theft of land."

"Dear God."

"I'm not sure how the DA stands on this, sir, but we have at least one corrupt detective at the Forty-Fifth."

"I'll have it covered, don't worry."

I turned to Astrid and Shanna.

"We're going to the Bay View Hotel. There we are going to meet with the chief of the Forty-Third and the chief of the Forty-Fifth, as well as, I should imagine, the district attorney and a large number of police officers. You, Astrid, will go cuffed. You, Shanna, will not. But I warn you, I am very tired and in a very bad mood. So you try anything, and I promise you I will shoot you. Is there anything we are not clear about?"

Nobody answered. So we untied Astrid and led her and Shanna down to the waiting Jag. Far off I could hear the wail of sirens, patrol cars from the 43rd. It was an anomaly, an irregularity. It was not done. There were questions of jurisdiction, but the 43rd would protect its own, when the need was clear and unambiguous, as it was now. Move in, sort out the legal niceties later.

I didn't want to be there when the cavalry showed up, so we climbed in the car. I drove with Shanna in the passenger seat, and Dehan sat behind with Astrid, where she could hit anyone who misbehaved.

I had called ahead, and we met Saul Cohen in the dining room. He looked disgruntled, but when he saw us, and the state we were in, he toned it down and even rose, frowning, to meet us. He had gathered the night staff and either promised them money or threatened them with some obscure legal procedure, but they were in the kitchen making hot rolls and coffee.

"What the hell have you been doing?" he said. "You have a reputation for causing trouble, but this is ridiculous."

Dehan sat Astrid and Shanna at separate tables and was pouring coffee.

I sat, and Saul sat with me.

"I need you to listen with great care, Saul, because I am about to describe to you exactly what happened, and as we speak, Blakemore is being picked up and arrested, and the homes of Astrid Meyer and Shanna McLean, as well as the Gasoline Club, are being sealed off as crime scenes, and all the documentary evidence you will ever need is being confiscated by the cops of the Forty-Third Precinct, from Gottlieb's offices and his private residence."

He smiled with the pleasure only a lawyer can know on hearing the word "documentary." "I am listening," he said.

"The thing that was missed, right from the beginning, because Sanchez himself was at pains to conceal it, was the simple fact that Sergeant Anthony Sanchez was in fact very well off in his own right. He had his defects, and like a lot of beautiful, young people, he had a touch of narcissism and vanity, but basically, at heart, he was a good, kind, and above all charitable person, who was embarrassed by his own wealth. And that was, in a roundabout way, what killed him..."

TWENTY-THREE

I took a generous slug of old, Irish whiskey and allowed it to spread its warmth through my aching body. Saul Cohen was sipping old cognac. Dehan had a Bushmills, while Astrid and Shanna had both opted for more coffee. I guess they didn't feel like celebrating.

"I have to admit," I said, "that I was pretty confused myself for a long time. The thing was, when Astrid and Sanchez met, they fell in love. He was naïve, idealistic, embarrassed by his own wealth and privilege. Though it wasn't huge, for the Bronx, and compared to most of the people he knew, it was considerable. The way Astrid came across to him, she was prosperous, but also a philanthropist who was keen to help the less privileged. The fact was, she played him. She manipulated him and persuaded him that between them, together, they could make a real difference in the eastern Bronx. He thought she genuinely cared, and that went a long way with him.

"For Astrid, Sanchez was the kind of trophy husband most middle-aged businesswomen dreamed about. He was young, good-looking, honorable, and idealistic. Unfortunately, there was another great love in your life, right, Astrid?" I didn't wait for an answer. "The love of wealth—not just money, but wealth! Land, houses, things that generated more wealth, and above all beautiful things of incalculable value, like those paintings in your living room, which the killer was so careful to miss. I am guessing that love of art and treasures was something handed down to you through your father, and his father before him.

"Of course Sanchez ticked boxes in both of those categories, because as well as being good-looking, he was also a commodity that would keep generating wealth, just so long as you controlled that wealth. And as he had no interest in money, he was happy for you to administer what he had.

"That was fine, except that at some point along the way, you stopped caring about him as a person. And he noticed. And with Shanna in the background, that became an untenable situation. It was just a matter of time before the inevitable happened. But you were just too greedy and stupid to notice."

Astrid was engrossed in her coffee, but Shanna was watching me like a hawk. I paused and sipped.

"There were two great loves in Sanchez's life. He had pretty much lost his mother at an early age, robbed from him by his father. Family was important to him, though he had never really had one. He loved Shanna as though she were the sister he had never had. She was also his closest friend. So she was his first great love, but it was not at first romantic or sexual.

"His second great love was his wife, though with time that love would also become nonsexual. He began to see you as a mother figure, a guide, and a protector. And that was the position seized on and abused.

"He was probably substantially richer than you were. That is something you never told me. At first, because of your skill and his lack of interest, you both agreed that you, Astrid, would administer a joint estate.

"But there came a point, a few months back, where Sanchez wanted to do something more. He wanted to put something back. He wanted to create this youth club."

Shanna had stopped staring at me and was scowling at Astrid, who exploded with sudden rage.

"It was this *bitch* who made him change! She filled his head with crazy ideas about personal fulfillment! *Bullshit!* All *she* wanted was to get her hands on *our money*! She manipulated him and twisted his mind!"

Shanna got to her feet. "You mean I helped him to escape from your *fucking Auschwitz!*"

Astrid turned on her savagely. "*I should have killed you when I had the chance!*"

Dehan stood, and they both shut up.

I went on. "The fact is, Sanchez began to spend more time with Shanna because you two were drifting apart. He didn't feel that you were both seeking the same dream anymore. He had a dream; you had a portfolio.

"Two gets you twenty, he kept trying to tell you that what he wanted was to fund the youth clubs, maybe even make them a chain across the country. I am guessing here . . ."

I glanced at Shanna, and she was nodding.

"But you didn't listen. Instead you told him how it was going to be. And day by day he watched his dream die. The only option left for him, the only person he could turn to for support, was Shanna.

"That is when things started to get complicated. Because Sanchez and Shanna almost inevitably became lovers. It was an easy transition for Shanna, but difficult and traumatic for Sanchez, who was loyal to his wife, and saw Shanna as a sister.

"Whatever the ethics or morals of the case, the simple fact was that Shanna's love for Sanchez flowered. She encouraged him to buy the house at Locust Point, to place some distance between himself and his wife."

I sighed and took another sip.

"Then something happened that made the situation irretrievable. From that point on, murder was almost inevitable.

"Originally, Shanna, you had encouraged Sanchez to go out

alone, to break free from Astrid. He was known and respected in this neighborhood, and well liked. Plus he was discreet. Nobody batted an eyelid.

"But eventually you started going out with him. You figured you were just friends. And after a few drinks, with the good feeling of companionship, of conspirators contra mundum, you both began to enjoy it.

"And then one night it became too much to control. You made a pass at him. If he had not shared your feelings, that is probably where it would have ended. He would probably have sunk into a depression, and back into his wife's control.

"But that wasn't what happened. He did love you, but he'd lied to himself for years about his feelings. Then, he gave in and went on a kind of sexual rampage, but always, in the end, he gravitated back to you.

"It didn't take long for Astrid to hear about it. Who told you? Was it Blakemore? Or was it at one of your poker games at the Gasoline Club?"

She didn't answer.

"The rampage was short-lived. Because he was coming to terms with his feelings for you. And as he realized how he felt, and what he had to do, so he changed his will. Perhaps he had an intuition of what was going to happen, or perhaps he knew deep down the real nature of his wife. Whatever the case, he wrote a new will and filed it with his attorney, making Shanna his sole heir. Did he tell you, Astrid? Or did he just tell you he was planning to do it?"

"It was a threat. If I didn't release funds for the clubs, he would alter his will and leave everything to this black bitch."

"So you spoke to your friends at the Gasoline Club. Tombs said he and Blakemore would take care of the situation, for an appropriate fee, and you sentenced your husband to death.

"At the same time, Tombs decided he needed a fall guy. He'd heard from Astrid about the beautiful cop who was helping out at the club and had become close to Sanchez. That made her the ideal candidate. So he set up the elaborate visit to the club, where he got her to frisk him and search his bag. He acquired her prints and converted them to silicone patches to be transferred to the murder weapon. With that, and the investigating detective as a coconspirator, it was, as I was so often told, a slam dunk."

Saul Cohen stirred. "Can I order anybody a refill?"

Dehan stretched. "I wouldn't say no."

Shanna raised a hand like a kid in class. "Am I allowed a gin and tonic?"

Astrid stared sullenly at the wall.

Saul said, "The blood..."

"That was part of it. There was too much of it, which suggested very strongly to me that it was not his blood, and, by extension, that he hadn't been killed there. But that raised questions which were just nuts: Why would you kill somebody and then go to all the trouble of taking them home and dousing their bed with somebody else's blood? There were other things.

"The disparity of the shooting, upstairs and downstairs. You have a tight grouping of shots upstairs in the dark, and downstairs in the light, this same shooter goes wild." I smiled. "That was when I first started to suspect you, Astrid. With all that crazy shooting going on, every shot managed to miss all your priceless works of art.

"And then there was what I found at Locust Point. Again the crazy question: Why dump the mattress, all the bedding, and the carpet into the East River, but take the body all the way back to the house?

"But the amount of blood on that bed was really nagging me, so I got Saul to request a sample from the DA, ostensibly so that we could run our own tests. What nobody but Joe at the lab knew was that I had asked him to come and take the bedding, claiming he had been asked to do so by the investigating officer. So when he analyzed the blood in the sheet, I got him to compare it with the sample Blakemore had given us. Blakemore's sample contained Sanchez's blood, but the sheet at the house, as you know, was canine. That was conclusive. Blakemore was crooked.

"Then I remembered what Stuart had told me, about the banshee, and it made sense. So Sanchez had been murdered at Locust Point, his body had been brought home and dumped in his bed. His killer had then gone and slaughtered the dog, collected the blood, and doused the bed and the body with it, so that the uniforms, the press, and anyone else who saw the scene would see that the murder had taken place right there, in the master bedroom.

"Tombs had then gone downstairs and fired some carefully placed shots and left by the back door, depositing the gun with Dehan's prints by the woods. All this time Astrid was celebrating a deal in town. She got home just in time to disturb the killer and get shot at."

I shook my head. "Not only did it make no sense to bring the body home and go to so much trouble to make it seem he was murdered there. It also made no sense that, having been so methodical in his planning, he was then so ham-fisted as to murder him somewhere where he had to take the considerable risk of moving him. Why not just murder him at home?

"And then I remembered something you said right at the beginning, Astrid. You said that the reason you did not pursue the intruder was because you ran upstairs to check on your husband, and you found him dead." I smiled and shook my head. "It was so simple, yet I had completely missed it. I had been turning it over and over—he was in the wrong room—but what I had never stopped to think was, *you went to the wrong room*! Which meant that you knew where he was!

"Of course, you had told Tombs to take him to the room you shared because in your vanity and your arrogance you wanted the world to believe you still shared a room. But in your arrogance and your stupidity you ignored the fact that everybody knew already that you no longer shared a room.

"And there it was, the reason why his body could not be

found at Locust Point, the reason it had to be brought back at so much risk. The myth must be preserved that you were both deeply in love. Not just for your ego, but also to support your challenge against the new will."

There was some restless shifting of asses.

I waited, then went on. "It was the one thing that I just couldn't get to fit. If Tombs had planned the murder so carefully, to entrap Dehan, if he had gone to such lengths to get her prints so he could transfer them to the gun—why did he not simply kill him at home, in his bed? It would not have been difficult. Why did he not do it the way he made it *seem* he'd done it?"

Saul Cohen was frowning. "And?"

"That night, Sanchez was due to go out to a club, Under the Clock, with Shanna. But things were reaching a crisis point with Sanchez and Shanna. After he'd left Dehan at the youth club, he went to Shanna's to pick her up. But instead of going out they got talking. I imagine he had recently confessed to you how he felt . . ."

She spoke into her gin and tonic. "I begged him not to go to the club, not to pick up any more girls. It was surprisingly easy. He agreed. He told me he was tired of the whole fake scene. It wasn't him, at all. We decided to spend the night together, but he said that before going any further he had to end it with Astrid. I told him I wanted us to do it together."

"So you went together. It was still early, probably no more than eight or eight thirty in the evening at the latest."

Astrid went suddenly puce and screamed at me, "*You fucking idiot! These animals threatened to kill me! Me! After everything I had done for him! After all the love and care I had given him! I adored him! I loved him! I made him rich, for fuck's sake! And they threatened to kill me! Me!*"

She folded her arms on the table and buried her face in them. She looked oddly childlike, convulsing in her chair, making ugly wailing noises.

To Shanna I said, "You pulled your .22 on her, didn't you?"

"Yes. I told her it was over, to stay away from us. Tony begged me not to do it. He said it could all be resolved by talking. He hated violence." She snorted with contempt. "After all the years he had been married to this slug, he still didn't get it. He didn't realize what kind of a greedy, racist, fascistic pig she was. I knew that she would never let go of him, and the more they talked and the more they negotiated, the more she would insinuate herself into our lives. She would never give us peace, unless it was in fear for her life. So I told her to leave us alone, or I'd kill her."

"But you miscalculated. You misjudged her, and you misjudged his influence in this neighborhood. She went for you. She pulled a gun on you—both—and you had to run. Because you didn't have the stomach to kill her.

"You believed still that she didn't know about Locust Point. So you sent Sanchez to Locust Point and you went home, to wait for Astrid. I can imagine that by then you were half hoping she would turn up, so you could kill her and claim self-defense. Meanwhile, Sanchez made the last in a long string of fatal mistakes. He took your advice and went to spend the night at the house on Locust Point, Soundview Terrace.

"By this time Astrid was out of her mind with rage. She called Tombs and told him to do it then, that night. To find Sanchez and kill him. Whether Astrid knew about the property, or whether Tombs had done his homework and followed him there previously, we can't know. The thing is, he knew where to find him.

"He broke in. He killed Sanchez, using the gun he had already covered with Dehan's prints, loaded the body into his car, and brought it here. The rest we know already.

"Astrid pretended to find the body, reported it to her friend Blakemore, and Dehan was arrested."

Shanna was still staring into her gin and tonic. "So what happens to me, now?"

I was quiet for a long time before answering.

"For my part, I think you paid a high price for your stupidity.

You were childish in what you did—a psychiatrist and a police sergeant; between you you should have been able to muster a grain of responsible maturity. What you did was to provoke an unstable woman into homicide. But the price you paid was unimaginable."

I turned to Saul Cohen. "But I suspect the DA will be glad to get this case over and done with. What do you think?"

He looked at Shanna. "If you are prepared to act as a witness for the prosecution, there's a good chance they won't press charges against you. The evidence is very thin."

Astrid made a noise of disgust. I studied her face.

"A lot of people are dead because of your greed and your vanity. Frankly, Astrid, you're lucky to be alive."

Shortly after that the chief turned up with the DA and a couple of detectives. Mo wasn't among them. We offered them coffee, and they eyed the whiskey and the brandy. And once again I prepared to tell the story.

Several hours later, Dehan and I staggered out into the endless rain. Dawn was turning the horizon a pale gray, and there was a hint of an insinuation that one small patch of sky might soon peer through.

It seemed wise to call a cab and come back for the Jaguar at a later date. On the wet curb, with the early traffic hissing past, I put my arms around my wife and said, "Please forgive me for doubting you."

She put her arms around my waist and looked up into my face with an unmistakable expression.

"If there were something to forgive, I would. But you, you must forgive me, Mr. Stone, for neglecting you. I foolishly forgot that you are the most important thing in my life."

"That's kind of nice to hear. Because, y'know, it's kind of mutual."

What followed was private and too mawkish and sugary for print. Let me just say that it ended, eventually, several weeks later, on Espiritu Santo, in Vanuatu.

Don't miss FALLEN ANGELS. The riveting sequel in the Dead Cold Mystery series.

Scan the QR code below to purchase FALLEN ANGELS.

Or go to: righthouse.com/fallen-angels

NOTE: flip to the very end to read an exclusive sneak peak...

DON'T MISS ANYTHING!

If you want to stay up to date on all new releases in this series, with this author, or with any of our new deals, you can do so by joining our newsletters below.

In addition, you will immediately gain access to our entire *Right House VIP Library,* which includes many riveting Mystery and Thriller novels for your enjoyment!

righthouse.com/email

(Easy to unsubscribe. No spam. Ever.)

ALSO BY BLAKE BANNER

Up to date books can be found at:
www.righthouse.com/blake-banner

ROGUE THRILLERS
Gates of Hell (Book 1)
Hell's Fury (Book 2)

ALEX MASON THRILLERS
Odin (Book 1)
Ice Cold Spy (Book 2)
Mason's Law (Book 3)
Assets and Liabilities (Book 4)
Russian Roulette (Book 5)
Executive Order (Book 6)
Dead Man Talking (Book 7)
All The King's Men (Book 8)
Flashpoint (Book 9)
Brotherhood of the Goat (Book 10)
Dead Hot (Book 11)
Blood on Megiddo (Book 12)
Son of Hell (Book 13)

HARRY BAUER THRILLER SERIES
Dead of Night (Book 1)
Dying Breath (Book 2)
The Einstaat Brief (Book 3)
Quantum Kill (Book 4)
Immortal Hate (Book 5)
The Silent Blade (Book 6)
LA: Wild Justice (Book 7)

Breath of Hell (Book 8)
Invisible Evil (Book 9)
The Shadow of Ukupacha (Book 10)
Sweet Razor Cut (Book 11)
Blood of the Innocent (Book 12)
Blood on Balthazar (Book 13)
Simple Kill (Book 14)
Riding The Devil (Book 15)
The Unavenged (Book 16)
The Devil's Vengeance (Book 17)
Bloody Retribution (Book 18)
Rogue Kill (Book 19)
Blood for Blood (Book 20)

DEAD COLD MYSTERY SERIES
An Ace and a Pair (Book 1)
Two Bare Arms (Book 2)
Garden of the Damned (Book 3)
Let Us Prey (Book 4)
The Sins of the Father (Book 5)
Strange and Sinister Path (Book 6)
The Heart to Kill (Book 7)
Unnatural Murder (Book 8)
Fire from Heaven (Book 9)
To Kill Upon A Kiss (Book 10)
Murder Most Scottish (Book 11)
The Butcher of Whitechapel (Book 12)
Little Dead Riding Hood (Book 13)
Trick or Treat (Book 14)
Blood Into Wine (Book 15)
Jack In The Box (Book 16)
The Fall Moon (Book 17)
Blood In Babylon (Book 18)
Death In Dexter (Book 19)
Mustang Sally (Book 20)

A Christmas Killing (Book 21)
Mommy's Little Killer (Book 22)
Bleed Out (Book 23)
Dead and Buried (Book 24)
In Hot Blood (Book 25)
Fallen Angels (Book 26)
Knife Edge (Book 27)
Along Came A Spider (Book 28)
Cold Blood (Book 29)
Curtain Call (Book 30)

THE OMEGA SERIES
Dawn of the Hunter (Book 1)
Double Edged Blade (Book 2)
The Storm (Book 3)
The Hand of War (Book 4)
A Harvest of Blood (Book 5)
To Rule in Hell (Book 6)
Kill: One (Book 7)
Powder Burn (Book 8)
Kill: Two (Book 9)
Unleashed (Book 10)
The Omicron Kill (Book 11)
9mm Justice (Book 12)
Kill: Four (Book 13)
Death In Freedom (Book 14)
Endgame (Book 15)

ABOUT US

Right House is an independent publisher created by authors for readers. We specialize in Action, Thriller, Mystery, and Crime novels.

If you enjoyed this novel, then there is a good chance you will like what else we have to offer! Please stay up to date by using any of the links below.

Join our mailing lists to stay up to date -->
righthouse.com/email
Visit our website --> righthouse.com
Contact us --> contact@righthouse.com

 facebook.com/righthousebooks
 x.com/righthousebooks
 instagram.com/righthousebooks

EXCLUSIVE SNEAK PEAK OF...

FALLEN ANGELS

CHAPTER 1

It was dark.

I sat a moment in my car, with the windows down, thinking about Billy Crystal in *Throw Momma from the Train*. The night was hot, the night was muggy, the night was oppressive and sticky. The night was sultry.

I was parked on Bolton Avenue, near the corner with Lacombe, outside a large, blue-gray clapboard house that stood in its own plot of land with a small garden in the front yard. Its porch lights were on, and Dehan was standing in the middle of the road with her hands in her pockets, looking back at me, frowning slightly among a smile. She was wearing a T-shirt and a bun, low on her neck. She also looked more than a little sultry.

As well as Dehan, there were three patrol cars making red lights dart here and there against the walls of the houses, there was an ambulance from the ME's department, and Frank the ME's car. Then there was the crime scene team's van and Sam Epstein's Jeep.

Dehan said, "You coming, or do you want to video conference?"

"I was thinking," I said, and climbed out of my ancient

Jaguar. I slammed the door and joined her, and we crossed the road together. She sighed and shook her head.

"So soon? We just got here and already you're thinking? How am I supposed to compete with that?"

"Compete? Why would you want to compete with me?"

Sergeant O'Brien was at the gate talking to a rookie. He greeted us and raised the tape for us to pass under, then pointed toward the steps up to the porch.

"'Tective Epstein's inside. Vic's in the dining room at the back." He shifted his pale eyes to Dehan and gave his big Irish head a twitch. "It ain't nice."

She shook her head. "Such a letdown. Last murder I was at rocked."

He leaned back and wheezed a laugh as we walked away. "She's a one!" I heard him say. "I tell you, she's a one!"

We climbed the steps and moved across the threshold into a brightly lit living room with a staircase rising to the second floor on the left, a fireplace, comfortable armchairs and a sofa, bookcases with real, well-used books, and lamps on lamp tables. A couple of Joe's boys were going around on their hands and knees, dressed like spacemen, dusting and spraying and picking minute things off the carpets. One of them was taking photographs.

But the real action was through the arch, in the dining area. Dehan stopped dead in her tracks and whispered, "What the hell . . ."

Epstein was standing with his hands on his hips and an expression on his face like he'd just found the Bolognese sauce he'd made six months ago and forgotten about. On the floor I could see Frank's hunched back, and just beyond it a man. You couldn't say he was lying on his face, because he had no face left to lie on, but he was lying on his belly, and the floor and the carpet where his head should have been were awash with blood and gore.

A couple of paces away from him was the dining table, which had apparently been moved from its habitual position, and on it was a complicated arrangement with a box and a drip-stand.

There was also a cat box, and by the sound it was making, there was a cat inside it.

I gently propelled Dehan forward, and we both looked in the direction the shot had come from. There was nothing there but a large painter's easel with a shotgun clamped to it by means of a couple of vices. Detective Epstein turned to look at us. He didn't say "good morning," even though it was three o'clock in the a.m. Instead he said, "Boy, am I glad to see you two!"

Dehan glanced at me. Her face said she was bewildered. "I don't think anybody has ever said that to me before. And I know for damn sure nobody has ever said it about . . ." She indicated us both with her finger, back and forth, and Epstein frowned at her, like she was speaking French to him.

I said, "I'm guessing this case relates back to a cold case, that's why we have been from our beds untimely ripped."

Frank turned and looked up at me from the mangled corpse. "Seriously? *Macbeth?* At three a.m.?" To Dehan he said, "How do you live with him?"

Epstein winced. "What?"

Dehan pointed at what was left of the body and said, "Cold case connected?"

He nodded, said, "Yeah," then frowned at me and said, "Who's Macbeth?"

"A Scottish regicide. You wouldn't know him. Tell me about the case."

"Chief says to hand it over to you guys. I tell you, I'm glad to. It's been get'n on my nerves." He clenched his fists to show just how much it had been getting on his nerves. "You done, Doc? I want to show John and Carmen here just what went down."

Frank snorted and said, "Good luck. Be very careful where you tread. I want as much of that brain matter and blood as I can get back at the lab. Make it snappy and let Joe's boys in."

The gurney rattled in. They put the decapitated corpse in the body bag and lifted it onto the trolley, then wheeled it out to the ambulance. Frank went with it, and as it passed through the door,

Epstein beckoned us into the dining area. We stepped in, avoiding the gore, and looked around. There was a threadbare, Persian-style rug where you could see the impressions made by the four table legs over many years. But the table had been moved over to the left, in front of where the corpse had been lying.

Epstein said, "See? Whoever it is does these things, he's come in and he's tied this poor bastard to a chair, right there..."

He pointed to a chair that was lying on its side, about six feet from the table, and a couple of feet in front of the easel with the shotgun.

"Wait, stop." It was Dehan with one hand raised. "Let me see if I get this. Who is this guy, the victim?"

"Reginald Jensen, sixty-six, retired bank manager."

"So the intruder ties Reggie to that bentwood chair, places this table in front of him, and the easel behind him..."

"That's what I said. But here's the crazy thing. Reggie could have sat there all night and nothin' would have happened. When the postman came, or whatever, he could have shouted and hollered and *somebody* would have heard him. The only reason the damned gun went off was because he moved forward. He had a string in his hand. He pulls the string, the knots come undone, and he can move. But if he moves, he has a string around his neck, on a pulley... see? So whichever way he goes, forward, backward, sideways, it pulls the trigger and blows his head off. But if he waited, he'd be okay."

I was looking at the table, thinking that if the killer put him looking at the table it was because there was something on the table that he wanted him to look at and think about, possibly to make him move. Dehan was frowning, staring at the chair on the floor. "So...?"

Epstein was nodding big nods, with his mouth sagging open slightly and releasing small, single laughs. "Right?" he said, and then again, "Right? Well get this. Jensen loves cats, he's got like a hundred books on cats, but the cat he is most crazy about is Siddhartha here." He pointed at the cat basket on the table where a tabby and white cat was lying, gazing at us with detached interest.

"How do you know he's called Siddhartha?"

"It's on his bowl in the kitchen. Anyhow, the son of a bitch killer knows this. So he ties Jensen to the chair, with the contraption behind him tied to his neck, and he gets Siddhartha and he puts him in that box . . ." He pointed to the carton on the table. "But that ain't no ordinary box. It's like that guy who wanted to prove things are only real when you see them . . ." He snapped his fingers a few times.

I said, "Schrödinger."

"Yeah." He leered at Dehan. "I knew it, if anyone is going to know the name, it'll be Stone, right? So it's like Schrödinger's cat. The box is set up with a timer and a small detonator that, after fifteen minutes, is going to release something into the air inside the box. Joe's already bagged it for the lab. My guess is it's going to be some very painful nerve gas . . ."

I interrupted, pointing at the box, which had a long, blood-soaked string attached. "That string . . ."

He gave a few more of his exaggerated nods while he interrupted me back. "Exactly, it was a few inches from his right hand. If he reached for it and pulled it, it killed the timer, but it also triggered the shotgun. I think that's what you'd call diabolical, right? Son of a bitch. But the weirdest thing, thing that makes your blood go cold, was the music. Pen drive stuck in the sound system playing classical music."

I suppressed a sigh and raised an eyebrow. "Classical?"

He grinned and pointed at me. "I knew you'd do that. I said, Stone ain't gonna be satisfied with 'classical music.' So I asked Frank what it was. He said it was Italian, sacred, ren . . ."

"Renaissance."

"That's it. That's what he said."

I nodded. "So he's giving Jensen a choice: save your cat and die, or let your cat die in pain, and save yourself."

Epstein held up both hands like I'd pointed a gun at him. "A guy like you or me, no contest, right?" He laughed. "But for a guy like Jensen." He shrugged, tilting his head on one side. "Guys like him, lonely, sensitive . . . you know what I'm sayin'?"

Dehan muttered, "Son of a bitch," and then asked, "So what's this got to do with us?"

I interrupted before he could answer. "You said earlier, 'Whoever it is does these things . . .' So he, or she, has done this before, it's gone cold, now you think it's gone hot again and you want us to take it."

He winced and shrugged at the same time. "The chief. Me? I'd take it, see it through, know what I mean? But the chief figures you guys got a feel for cold cases . . ."

Dehan looked at me and pulled down the corners of her mouth. "The Schrödinger's Cat Killer?"

I smiled. "No."

She arched both eyebrows high. "The You're-Only-Dead-If-They-Find-You Killer?"

I shook my head. "Actually, Schrödinger was trying to prove the opposite. His thought experiment was intended to show how stupid that view was, but as it turned out that view was right, and he and Einstein were wrong."

Epstein was staring at me with his mouth slightly open. He turned to Dehan. "See? Nobody likes him, but you have to admit he's smart."

Dehan squinted at him and then at me.

"Nothing is real unless we look at it? Somebody put Pink Floyd on the record player, I'll get the acid. Where's the maharishi when you need him? It's a good job there are nearly eight billion of us, or the whole damn planet would disappear!"

"Which was kind of Schrödinger's point. But I don't think that's what this killer was about. This killer is about salvation. Are you connecting this case with the Georgina Cheng case a year ago?"

He spread his hands at Dehan. "See, this is why nobody likes him."

"It was on TV, but I remember you and Hank talked about it. She was a vivisectionist, and she was vocal about how we needed to perform vivisections for medical reasons."

"That's the one."

Dehan was nodding. "She was fed curare and tortured while she was conscious. Frank said she died of shock."

I added, "There was a pen drive in the sound system playing sacred music, but as I recall, that was English Tudor music, John Tallis, I think, 'Kyrie.'"

Dehan grunted. "Hell, some religious nut trying to get people to repent."

I asked Epstein, "How many victims are you attributing to this killer?"

"With this one, a total of six. One a year for the past six years."

Joe approached us. "Okay, guys, gonna have to ask you to move somewhere else. Let's go!"

We moved out to the living room. Epstein stood in the open doorway, and Dehan sat on the third step leading to the upper floor. Epstein was talking, but he had one foot out the door.

"At first it didn't look like a serial killer. They were just kind of random. It was the third one that got us thinking, you know, there is some kind of a link between these cases. I'll leave the file on your desk with all the details."

"Just give me an outline of the other four before you run off, will you?" I gave him a smile that wasn't much of a smile, and he sighed.

"First victim, September 2015. Ana Orcera, single mother. She'd just taken her kid to school. On the way back she'd been to her local church. Her boyfriend was out. He was some kind of bum, from Sudan or something. He was a suspect for a while. So when she got home the killer was waiting for her. Broke her arms and legs, stabbed her in the gut, and left her to bleed to death, listening to classical, sacred music.

"Second victim, February 2016, Mathew Cavendish, a financier and a philanthropist. Tied to his dining table, with the gas turned on, but this time the music was weird Japanese music, some kind of flute, jerky kind of stuff."

"Zen."

"Yeah, that's it. Weird, jerky."

I grunted, and he went on. "Third victim, November 2017, Saul Arender, criminal attorney, defended some very bad people and got a lot of them off on technicalities. He was hanged. It was elaborate, a bit like this case, the killer used ropes and pulleys in such a way that the victim's own attempts to escape caused him to be choked and decapitated. He used a piano wire as a noose. That was nasty. That time it was Tibetan bells.

"Fourth victim, June 2018, Judge Jeremiah Jones, known as Three Jay, the hanging judge. He handed out some pretty severe sentences along with a few lectures and sermons—he was an evangelist—but I gotta say I never thought he went too far. He was impaled with a decorative, ceremonial sword he had in his office. He was bound on the floor, and the sword was suspended from a rope over his chest. It was tough because he could see the rope being burned by a candle, and he couldn't move. With him it was, uh"—he snapped his fingers—"Gregorian chants."

Dehan asked him, "What about suspects?"

He winced and shook his head. "We never really got a solid lead on anybody. We thought about . . . uh . . ." He looked up at the ceiling. "Abdo Deng? Something like that. It's in the file. Ana Orcera's partner. But he didn't fit the profile at all. Then we had Reverend Morton Wells on our suspect list, but we couldn't really tie him to anything. There was no forensic evidence, and there were no damned witnesses."

"What made the reverend a suspect?"

"He was a priest, I forget what kind, I'm not big on religion. Must have been some kind of Protestant because he worked as a teacher in a Protestant school, but he was kicked out—of the school and the church—over allegations of child abuse. The allegations were never proven, but the shit stuck, and they preferred to get shot of him. He later opened his own ministry down on Leland Avenue and Soundview. Ironic, his big thing is the sanctity of the family, the power of forgiveness, and the 'divine grace in rebirth.' Thing is, Ana Orcera, the first victim, was in his congregation for a while, then switched to the Catholic church one block away on Thieriot. A few days before she was killed, he was seen visiting her. It ain't a lot to go on, but it was about all we had. The day she was killed she dropped the kid at the school on Thieriot, crossed Randall to the church a hundred yards away, spoke to the padre there, then went home. Now, her shortest route home is right past Morton Wells' mission."

I grunted. "Any other connections to her or any of the other victims?"

He sighed, pulled a pack of Lucky Strikes from his pocket, offered us a cigarette, and asked if we minded. I shook my head, and he lit up. Blowing smoke into the predawn darkness, he looked away down the road.

"Nah . . . I mean, they was tenuous links. Know what I mean? But they made you feel there was more you weren't seein'. He was at Drew University with Mathew Cavendish, the second victim. They were both part of the debating club. Cavendish was a committed atheist *and* a philanthropist. Apparently they had a few debates, in and out of the club." He flicked ash. "Saul Arender was known to him, and he mentioned him in a few sermons, along the lines that as a criminal attorney and a Jew, he was a servant of Satan. He also preached against Georgina Cheng, the fifth victim."

Dehan said, "That leaves the judge and Jensen."

He shook his head. "No links that we ever found with the judge." He shrugged. "This case? What can I say? Aside from the fact that Morton's church is . . ." He stuck his arm out rigid, pointing at the house. "Exactly there, one hundred and fifty yards away, two houses away—aside from that, my gut tells me the connections are there."

He took another drag, dropped the butt on the ground, and,

with his hands shoved in his pockets, ground it into the concrete. Then he smiled at us.

"You guys have fun with the case. Maybe you're the ones to crack it. See you around."

With that he turned and slouched his way out of the gate toward his Jeep.

CHAPTER 2

WE DID THE ROUNDS OF THE HOUSE, INCLUDING THE rooms upstairs, and found very little other than evidence that this was a man who lived alone and his only real companion was his cat, Siddhartha. But you didn't get a feeling of real loneliness from his home. Real loneliness carries with it despair, and despair expresses itself most often as either excessive order or chaos. There was neither in Jensen's house. It was clean, tidy, and well ordered, but not obsessively so.

In his bedroom, Dehan picked up a couple of books from his bedside table. "Looks like he was interested in Buddhism."

I had also noticed the books, and the small statue in the living room. I nodded, inspecting the inside of his wardrobe and his few clothes.

"Theravada."

"Isn't that a planet in *Star Trek*?"

I smiled but didn't let her see it. "You know it's not. It's the oldest form of Buddhism, practiced mainly in Sri Lanka, I believe."

"Is it important?"

I got to my feet from where I had crouched to inspect a drawer. "I don't know. Maybe. Some people say that Theravada, amongst the different styles of Buddhism, is most concerned with karma, or as they call it, *kamma*."

She thrust her hands in her pockets and frowned. "Retribution?"

"Not exactly." I shook my head. "There is no retribution in Buddhism. It's much more complex than that. It's more to do with cause and effect, but state of mind and intention are central to the doctrine. A very simplistic example would be . . ." I searched my mind. "If you are habitually absentminded and fail to be present in the moment, for example, and you get up from your chair and carry your glass to the kitchen, knock your hand on the corner of the table, and the glass falls and breaks. That is not retribution, it is simply a consequence of your mental attitude."

"Okay, and when you sweep it up, you continue to be careless and leave shards on the floor. Next morning when you come down barefoot you cut yourself, so the consequences can project into the future."

"Add to that the Buddhist ideas of reincarnation and that everything is, so to speak, mind, and you wind up with a surprisingly complex theory."

She grunted and narrowed her eyes, which meant she was thinking deeply. "So we have a victim who believes in karma, and a killer who seems to want to bring retribution . . ."

"Quite a coincidence, I agree."

She sat on the corner of the bed with her hands between her knees. "And the cat," she said. "They believe people can be reincarnated as animals, right?"

"Something like that."

"So it might have been really important for him to save the cat because it was his mother or something?"

I didn't really buy it, and I screwed up my face to show it. "I'm no expert, but I don't think it's quite like that. Maybe he just loved his cat and he was prepared to make that sacrifice to save it."

She shrugged. "Maybe. We are assuming a lot from a couple of books and a small statue. We don't even know for sure that he *was* a Buddhist, or whether that was relevant."

I agreed and nodded. "Anything else you need to see here?" She shook her head, then said, "Yeah, I want to see how this killer got in. The windows are all closed and intact. The back door is locked from the inside, which only leaves the front door. I want to know if he broke in, or if Jensen let him in."

"Yup, let's go have a look."

We found Joe, the head of the crime scene team, dusting the lock and taking photographs of it, inside and out.

"Did he break in, or was he let in?"

He laughed. "I can't tell you that, John. But I can tell you that this lock was not forced. Did he have a replica key? Was the door open when he arrived? I don't know. But I can tell you that he did not pick this lock."

We thanked him and walked down to where my old burgundy Jag was waiting for us. Dehan opened the passenger door, but I rested my ass on the hood and sat looking at the house. A breath of cool predawn air touched my face and made me shudder. Dehan's voice came from over my shoulder.

"What? First you didn't want to get out of the car, now you don't want to get in. You turning temperamental on me, big guy?"

I smiled over my shoulder at her, and she came and rested her ass next to mine. "I am just trying to visualize what happened." I shook my head. "If Reverend Morton Wells killed everyone in New York who had a different religion from his own, there would be a ten-year waiting list to get murdered by him."

She gave me a quick once-over with her eyes. "That is a very dark notion, Stone."

"My point is that what this killer does . . ." I sighed. "That's a lot of attention to pay somebody. There must be thousands of people in New York who are interested in Buddhism, and at least half of those probably have a cat."

"Why?"

"I don't know, it just seems to work that way. Buddhists have cats. It's a thing. The point is, what made *this particular* Buddhist with a cat different to all the rest, and worth killing in such a cruel way?"

She grunted. "Cruel and..."

She screwed up her face, and I said, "Cruel, and well-informed, and..."

I shook my head, and she said, "*Accurate!*"

"Yes," I said, and nodded. "Accurate. He had him down to a T. Even the little touch of Schrödinger. Everything is mind, which was pretty much what Schrödinger was trying to disprove with his thought experiment."

We were quiet for a moment. Then she put her hand on my shoulder. "Most serial killers are stupid, Stone. But I have a bad feeling we have a smart one here."

"Is he, or she, a serial killer?"

"Whoa! Seriously?"

"I'm not sure he's killing without motive. There's a lot about his actions that suggests motive. Also, if you look at each case, assuming they were all committed by the same person, the victims are not selected by type, by sex, by profession—in fact there seems to be no common feature to the victims at all, but in each case he kills them in such a way as to give them time to think about their death, and he plays sacred music designed to make them reflect on it. That definitely suggests a motive to me. But more than that, it suggests a fairly deep knowledge of each victim's personality." I hesitated, not wanting to go too far. "Or at least of the victims and their *moral* life."

She was silent, thinking about it. Then she said, "That's pretty far-fetched."

I nodded. "I agree, but it's no less true for that."

"So, what? We are looking for some kind of spiritual vigilante?"

"Or a fallen angel."

By the time we got to the 43rd it was almost six a.m. As

promised, the file was on my desk, with a copy for Dehan. I went to get a couple of buckets of coffee-like black liquid, and we sat and started going through the files.

There were profiles on the victims, crime scene photos which were mostly pretty harrowing, forensic reports, and details of interviews with Reverend Morton Wells and Abdo Deng, Ana Orcera's boyfriend. Outside the window there was a strip of luminous blue-gray skirting a black sky, and here and there, dappled orange streetlamps peppered the black glass through restless leaves. My head ached and my eyes wanted to sleep. I said aloud, "Abdo Deng, why are we discarding him as a suspect?"

She did something between a growl and a sigh, which was distracting, and said, "Our friend Epstein hasn't done a great job of putting this all together. He's a street cop, not a collator of evidence. Abdo Deng first shows up in Ana Orcera's profile. He was a short-term boyfriend-cum-lover of hers shortly before she died. Had a reputation for violence. Seems like they called him in mainly on the strength of that, just to talk to him."

I found the place and nodded as I read. "Uh-huh, interviewed him and didn't like him much, so they did a background check. Seems he was suspected of violent crimes in the Sudan . . ."

"Including rape and the murder of several young girls and women. Entered this country as a refugee, had ties with militant Islamic groups, but seems not to be active. Now works as a taxi driver."

"Interesting," I said. "A taxi can form a matrix of connections which, unless you know about the cab, seems utterly random. I wonder how he comes across in the interviews."

She was staring at the file in front of her. "I'm just reading through them now. So far he comes across as a miserable, surly bastard." She glanced at me over the page. "You're thinking that maybe he's really chatty in the cab and gets to know people that way?"

I gave a small shrug. "Maybe he connects with them, gets their addresses, is able to follow them . . . Maybe he's a lot more sociable when he's not being interrogated by cops."

"Yeah, maybe. That seems to be about it. A few people were looked at, but all had alibis for one killing or another. Morton and Deng did not have alibis, but there was nothing beyond slim circumstantial evidence connecting them to the victims." She was reading through the first interview while she talked. Suddenly she asked, "You think this guy has a subtle understanding of karma?" I eyed her a moment, searching for traces of humor. Before I could say anything, she went on. "But it could be a religious thing. We have here three of the four major religions of the world, and Buddhism is the fastest growing."

I shook my head and looked back at the list of victims, then made an ugly "Nah" sound. "This is not religious. It is moral, ethical, philosophical. Our first victim is religiously undefined, the second is an atheist, the third is Jewish, though we don't know if he was practicing, fourth was Judge Jones, a Christian evangelist, fifth was another atheist, and the last was a Buddhist. This has nothing to do with Buddhism, or religion even. These people were killed to make them repent . . ." I trailed off and shook my head. "No, scrub that, not repent. They were killed to make them *aware* of some perceived flaw in their personality. That was the purpose of the music. The only thing Islam wants you to repent for is not converting to Islam, and the only thing you need to be aware of is that there is only one god, and Mohamed is his prophet."

"Harsh," she said absently to the file as she read it. I shrugged. "Find me a mullah who will tell you something different."

"So you don't like Abdo Deng for this?"

I dropped the file on the table, feeling suddenly frustrated and bored. "I wouldn't go that far. It's within the bounds of possibility. But I like Reverend Morton Wells better. What I *really* feel, though, is that Epstein boxed himself into a corner because he got tunnel vision. I think he thought, 'serial killer,' and tried to apply classical serial killer criteria and methodology to the cases. But this is not a standard serial killer, even if such a thing existed."

She sucked her teeth and made a face like I'd put too much sugar in her coffee. "You sure about that?"

I spread my hands wide and sighed. "Standard murder: a relationship is established between K, killer, and V, victim. That relationship gives rise to a motive for killing: K feels jealousy, greed, frustration . . ." I waved my hand in an et cetera. "That motive gives rise to K's desire to kill V, and K acts on that desire. In serial killers that is reversed. The desire to kill arises out of K's psyche for no apparent reason, K then seeks a victim and establishes some kind of relationship, even if just as stalker and prey, and then K kills V. But I don't get the impression that is happening here. I get the impression that our killer connects with these people somehow first, establishes some kind of relationship with them, and from that relationship, from his knowledge of them, arises first the motive, and then the desire, as in a normal murder."

She puffed out her cheeks. "And that motive is?"

"Ethical, philosophical, moral . . . K sees in his victims something that he wants them to reflect on *while* they are in the process of dying. And he, or she, selects the music to stimulate a reflective, spiritual state of mind."

"Jensen was a Buddhist, but K selected Christian music."

The best I could offer to that was, "Hmmm . . ." and then, "Arender was a Jew and he got Tibetan bells."

She looked up at the ceiling. Outside the gray was leaching from the rim of the sky into the dome. Cars were pulling up outside, and there were voices of people greeting each other and laughing. Dehan shook her head at the ceiling.

"Either K doesn't care about denomination, only about spiritual . . ." She spread her hands and shrugged slowly. ". . . merit? Development? Growth? Or, he wants to convert people."

"Cavendish was played Japanese Zen music, Arender had Tibetan bells, and with Georgina Cheng it was . . . Tallis. That

IN HOT BLOOD | 245

makes two out of six non-Christian, and the other four are three Catholic and one Anglican Protestant."

She said, "That feels like a blind alley."

"The whole case feels like a blind alley. I want to start by going to visit Reverend Morton Wells to see if Epstein simply developed a prejudice against him or if there is actually something there. After that we go and talk to Abdo Deng. Meanwhile we need to be getting background on the victims to see how they connect with each other. Somewhere in their background there is some way in which they all connect with each other and with the killer. That much, at least, we can take as a hard fact."

She nodded. "A congregation is a pretty good place to connect with people."

I stood and stretched. "Not if it's a Christian congregation and you aim to meet atheists and Buddhists."

She stood too and touched her toes a couple of times. There was a dog whistle from one of the few desks that were occupied, but she ignored it. I saw who it was and grinned. "Don't try it at home, Alvarez, it's not a good position to get cardiac arrest in, and that Great Dane of yours might get all excited."

"It ain't a Great Dane, wiseass, it's a Doberman!"

"I wasn't talking about your dog. I was talking about your wife."

We left the detectives' room among a barrage of obscenities. As the door closed, I leaned back in. "And, Alvarez? Those little blue pills? They can cause cardiac arrest in a man in your condition."

On the steps outside, dawn had arrived, and it was beginning to smell and sound like morning. I looked at my watch. Eight o'clock was not far off.

Dehan said, "You want to walk? It's twenty minutes, we'll clear our heads."

I nodded, and we made our way through early light down Story Avenue toward Soundview, and the Church of Divine Grace and Rebirth.

CHAPTER 3

The Church of Divine Grace and Rebirth was a two-story house that had been converted and expanded. It was a flat-fronted building with a flat roof, painted a nasty shade of sickly beige, with peeling red double doors and red bars on the windows. When we arrived the doors were closed, and so were the drapes behind the glass in the windows. I couldn't find a bell, so Dehan hammered with her fist, and while she waited, I took a stroll round back.

Round back was a parking lot with space for maybe a dozen cars, but he also had an area sectioned off behind a fence where he had a garage and a bit of lawn. The garage was open, and I could hear a lot of grunting coming from inside, also an occasional thump. I approached and peered in, unsure what I was going to see.

It turned out to be a man in his late forties or early fifties beating the hell out of a sack he had suspended from the ceiling. You could tell he was in good shape because he was wearing only tracksuit pants and sports shoes. His upper body was that of an athlete, and he moved fast and aggressive, delivering high kicks to the sack that made it quiver and swing. Then he would lay into it with combinations of four, five, and six punches.

I said, "Good morning."

He turned quickly and stared at me. He wasn't exactly hostile, but he wasn't warm and fuzzy either.

"You can't be here. This is my private area. Service is at ten thirty."

I pulled my badge and showed it to him. "The house of the Lord is always open," I said, facetiously, "but not necessarily the house of his minister. Detective John Stone, can you spare a couple of minutes?"

He reached for a towel. "My apologies. As you pointed out, some members of the congregation seem to forget that, where God is divine, His ministers are only human. They expect us to be imbued with the perfection of a deity. How can I help you, Detective?"

I called Dehan, then turned back to the pastor. "Are you Reverend Morton Wells?"

"Yes, I am. Why?"

Dehan appeared at my side and eyed the garage, which was in fact more of a gym, and the reverend.

"Detective Dehan," she said, and showed him her badge. "We were wondering if you would be willing to talk to us about Ana Orcera."

He smiled in a way you could describe as rueful, sighed, and then nodded. "Yes, of course, *again*." He sat on a bench and gestured us to a plastic chair and another bench. I took the chair, and he said, "What do you want to know? I answered Detective Epstein's questions back in 2015, and since then Sam and I have *almost* become friends."

I returned the smile and nodded. "I know. We genuinely don't want to harass anybody. Detective Dehan and I are the cold-cases unit at the Forty-Third, and the Ana Orcera case has been passed to us. I'm afraid the obvious place to start is . . ."

I gestured at him with my open hand. He was drinking water from a bottle while he listened and watched me. He set the bottle down and dabbed his mouth with a towel.

"I understand. I believe poor Ana's case has been absorbed into a wider case?"

I nodded and offered him a smile as rueful as his own. "What can you tell us about Ana? Detective Epstein was interested in you; we are more interested in Ana. If we can understand her, maybe we can understand how her killer came to select her as a target, and those that followed."

He grunted and stared at the wall awhile, thinking, with the towel hung between his hands. "It's a long time ago, and we were never what you'd call close, despite what Sam Epstein thought. I always thought of her as a lazy, dissolute woman. She was forever either failing to do things she had committed to doing, or she was leaving them half done. I had the impression of a woman who saw her responsibilities as burdens, rather than objectives to be achieved."

Dehan leaned forward with her elbows on her knees, frowning. "Can you put that into context for us? Give us some examples of what you mean . . . ?"

"Yes." He said it like she had asked a question she was going to regret, but now she would have to suck it up. He had his eyebrows raised, and he was nodding. "Yes, I can. She was fat, not grotesquely obese, but definitely overweight to an extent that was unhealthy. She must have promised me, and the congregation, that she was going to tackle that problem a hundred times. Every Sunday she would repeat the promise, but every time I saw her and her son, she was stuffing her mouth with a cake, or a burger, or some item of fast food. I called her out. I called her out *several* times, and she always repeated her promise that she was going to try harder. 'Don't try,' I told her. 'Do it or don't do it. There is no try!'"

Dehan smirked. "Yoda; the Chinese have Confucius, the Europeans have Aristotle and Kant, good old US of A, we have Yoda."

She laughed out loud and slapped her thigh, then punched

me on the shoulder. Wells' smile became strained. "Forgive me," he said. "Yoda?"

I shook my head like it wasn't important. "Oh, a guru-like character from *Star Wars*. He said almost exactly those words to his disciple."

"Oh." When he looked at Dehan again his eyes were cold. "Believe me, I was not quoting from *Star Wars*. I have better authorities than that to quote from."

I ignored the comment and moved on. "So, your overall impression of Ana was of a lazy woman, lacking in will and commitment."

He nodded. "I would say that was a perfect description of her, yes." He paused, reflecting for a moment, and then went on almost apologetically. "The ability to learn places us between the animal kingdom and the divine, but an essential aspect of the ability to learn is the willingness or . . ." He seemed to search his gym for a better word. "The *commitment* to pursue one thought beyond the next, the *desire* to go not merely from A to B, but to follow through then to C and D and perhaps even E!" He sighed. "Ana's son was a consistent underachiever at school. The boy was not particularly stupid, nor was he especially smart. He was average, which meant that with appropriate guidance and teaching, his performance at school might have been slightly above average."

He paused, and I prompted, "But his mother did not help."

He shook his head. "No, she did not, but that is not the point. The point is that she continually came to me, and to the congregation, asking *us* for help. She could not manage her son, she could not get him to do his homework, she could not get him to obey her. So we offered her first advice and then help." He spread his hands. "And she *consistently* failed to take either the advice *or* the help. She had no ability to learn, because she was incapable of taking her failures and using them as lessons." He held out his hand toward me, palm up, as though he was showing me something. "My son has failed in his exams, my pastor and my friends in the congregation are advising me to sit with him an hour a day and help him with homework, and several friends have offered to take him for extra lessons. I will take their advice..."

He shook his head. "No, she would weep and moan, beg us for help, and then go right back and make exactly the same mistakes again—and get exactly the same result. The intellectual processes for learning anything but the simplest lessons were missing from her brain."

Dehan pulled a face. "Isn't that what used to be called plain stupid?"

"No. Because when you spoke to her, she was perfectly coherent and perfectly able to understand. She just wasn't able to turn her understanding into learning. She was not stupid, she was lazy. Chronically lazy."

She nodded like that made sense to her. "Can you tell us anything about the kid's father, or any other men in her life?"

"Not very much, Detective Dehan—the boy's father had disappeared long before she joined my congregation. By all accounts he was a waster, a drug addict, and an alcoholic, not to mention a thief. It is a sad fact about certain women that all too often they choose men who hurt them, in many ways, physically, mentally, and spiritually, not to mention morally and financially. And, referring back to my earlier point about Ana, she, like many others, failed to learn and constantly gravitated back to the same kind of man. Shortly before she left my church to join the papist franchise up the road, she had taken in a Sudanese waster who enjoyed getting drunk, smoking pot, and beating her and her son until they could barely walk."

Dehan, suppressing a smile, asked, "Did you ever try to dissuade her from joining the..." The grin broke out. "I assume that by 'papist franchise' you mean the Catholic church on Soundview?"

"That's exactly what I mean, and yes, I did indeed try to dissuade her. I even went to her house. Detective, there are two evil religions on this Earth. In my opinion they are truly Satanic, in that they embody all that is evil and dark in the human soul, and they are Catholicism and Islam. They spring from the same desert root, and they both advocate abject prostration and the abdication of choice and personal responsibility. Have you read the Jefferson Bible?"

Dehan shook her head, but I said I had. He went on.

"Then you will realize, Detective Stone, that Jesus' mission in this world was to shine the light of His Holy Grace on a path that led away from the brutality and ignorance of the Old Testament, toward a doctrine of personal responsibility, compassion, and forgiveness. That is what I teach and what I have always believed. When Ana took in that barbarous man and joined the Catholics, I tried very hard to persuade her that she had made a mistake. But it was to no avail. She was lost, and her death was horrible. She did not deserve to die that way. And I confess I have always believed that she died at the hands of her boyfriend."

We sat in silence for a moment. I was thinking hard about what he had said. I glanced at Dehan.

"I'm not sure now what details were released to the press..."

He laughed. It was the first time I had seen any sign of humor from him. It seemed to change him into a human being. And that made me think that the overall impression he gave was that of an avenging angel.

"I am quite sure, Detective Stone," he said, "that you remember very well what details were released to the press, and you would love to trip me up on some piece of information that only the killer could possess. But I did not kill Ana. In fact, I pray every day for forgiveness, that I did not do more to save the poor woman.

"What I know is that the killer seems to have been waiting at her house." He shrugged and spread his hands. "Or he was simply *at* her house, where he himself lived, and that shortly after she arrived he broke her arms and legs, stabbed her with a knife, and left her to bleed to death while classical music of some description played in the background. A terrible, barbaric way to die. She must have been in indescribable pain. We can only hope that unconsciousness overtook her soon and she passed out."

"In your opinion, Reverend Wells . . ." I paused for a moment, trying to think of the best way to phrase the question. "In your opinion, was Ana Orcera forgiven because of the way she died?"

The expression on his face told me he thought I was insane.

"*Forgiven?* For what? And by whom?"

"Sloth is a mortal sin. So in Christianity as a whole, she would need forgiveness from God, wouldn't she?"

He rolled his eyes and shook his head. "This is precisely the kind of bullshit that Jesus was trying to get away from. Thomas Aquinas defined sloth as 'sorrow about spiritual good.' He also said that it was a 'sluggishness of the mind' which prevents one from beginning 'good,' which became evil in its *effect* if it drew a man away from performing good deeds. But this is Catholicism, and the Catholics love to take human weakness and turn it into sin."

Dehan surprised me by asking suddenly, "But isn't that *exactly* what sin is? Sin is a daily part of life, because all human beings have human weaknesses. As soon as you hit puberty, you are wanting to sin."

The reverend chuckled. "Dehan, Jewish, right? I like the Jewish view of sin. It is more understanding of the human condition, and ultimately more forgiving. The Catholics got stuck in the Old Testament. It's as though they are forever trying to forget Jesus and his teachings on forgiveness, and they use him only as a symbol of guilt—a cross to beat their followers with. My own view, for what it's worth, is that God is omnipresent and all powerful. That means that He is literally—not figuratively, *literally*—everywhere, and that He is literally able to do *absolutely* everything and anything. Now, you only need to think about this for a fraction of a second to see that all we need in order to achieve forgiveness from God is to know ourselves, *understand* ourselves and our fallibility as humans, and then *forgive ourselves*. His forgiveness is implicit in our own forgiveness, *because* He is omnipotent, *because* He is everywhere, even in our hearts. So, did Ana achieve forgiveness for being lazy? I have no idea, but I hope that as she lay there, bleeding to death and unable to move, she was able to forgive herself for allowing this to happen to her and her son, and then I hope that she forgave her killer."

I nodded slowly a few times. "You have certainly given us a lot to think about. I hope you will forgive *me*, Reverend, but I would be negligent if I did not ask you about your expulsion from the school where you worked, and from your previous church."

He sighed. "It would not be negligent, Detective, because the whole thing is thoroughly documented, and I have been over it numerous times with previous detectives. So everything you need to know is available to you, in your file, without having to ask me. But, you want to see my face and my eyes when you explore the subject."

I nodded. "Yes."

"It was a group of three boys from very privileged WASP families in Manhattan. The school, St. George's Anglican School, as I am sure you know, is in Manhattan. Privilege in this world is inevitable. It happens, and there is nothing we can do about it. But what we *can* do is to ensure, by good education, that privileged children understand the responsibilities that come with privilege. These three boys did not understand their responsibilities toward the rest of society, and I did not miss a single opportunity to draw their arrogance, their conceit, and their bad manners to their attention and that of their parents. I felt it was *my* responsibility. My thanks for my efforts was to be accused by the boys of having molested them sexually. I was summarily dismissed and defrocked. Both the school and the church offered me compensation to the tune of several thousand dollars to keep my mouth shut about what had happened. What had happened was precisely nothing, except that I was accused of something I had not done."

"You accepted?"

"If you've read your file, you know I did. But I think you have lived enough to know, Detective Stone, that there are temporal powers against which we cannot fight. I had lost my career and my future; the least I could do was take their money and try to build a new one of each. I am neither a homosexual nor a pedophile. Nor am I a serial killer, for that matter."

I spread my hands and tilted my head to one side as an expression of apology. "Like I said, I had to ask."

"Detectives, I need to prepare for morning service. Will you catch the killer this time, or is this just another show to be abandoned in the next few days when you hit the same obstacles Epstein did?"

Dehan looked at me with raised eyebrows, perhaps wondering how I would answer. I looked the reverend square in the eye and assured him, "Oh, we'll catch him, you can be very sure of that, Reverend."

He didn't seem real impressed. He stood up and asked us, "Is there anything else?"

Neither of us answered immediately. We watched him a moment and Dehan said, "No, that's about it for now."

And we left.

Scan the QR code below to purchase FALLEN ANGELS.
Or go to: righthouse.com/fallen-angels

Printed in Dunstable, United Kingdom